SHADES
AND
SHADOWS

<u>BOOK YOUR PLACE ON OUR WEBSITE</u> <u>AND MAKE THE</u> <u>READING CONNECTION!</u>

We've created a customized website just for our very special readers, where you can get the inside scoop on everything that's going on with Zebra, Pinnacle and Kensington books.

When you come online, you'll have the exciting opportunity to:

- View covers of upcoming books

- Read sample chapters

- Learn about our future publishing schedule (listed by publication month *and author*)

- Find out when your favorite authors will be visiting a city near you

- Search for and order backlist books from our online catalog

- Check out author bios and background information

- Send e-mail to your favorite authors

- Meet the Kensington staff online

- Join us in weekly chats with authors, readers and other guests

- Get writing guidelines

- AND MUCH MORE!

Visit our website at
http://www.kensingtonbooks.com

SHADES AND SHADOWS

Sophia Shaw

Kensington Publishing Corp.

http://www.kensingtonbooks.com

ACKNOWLEDGMENTS

To my mom, Iris Thomas—You have always encouraged me to be strong and independent, and to strive to be more than I am. Good luck with the completion of your PhD. I am so proud of your accomplishments.

To Aisha Wickham—What would I have done without your editing skills? Thank you for taking on the task and for helping me to be a better writer.

To my sister, Natasha Jackson—You are the one person I knew I could call, day or night, for words of inspiration. I know you will accomplish all your goals.

To my husband, Jonathan Shaw—Thank you for your never-ending support. I love your intelligence and honesty and I am inspired by your commitment and drive. Together, we can accomplish anything.

Chapter 1

Jade Winters awoke with a start. Her alarm clock was vibrating with an annoying ring. Blinking rapidly, she reached over to the bedside table and turned off the alarm. She was shocked to see how late she had slept. Usually, she was up at eight o'clock sharp, yet it was already after nine. She must have hit the snooze button repeatedly in her sleep.

Slowly, Jade flipped up her comforter, swung her legs off the bed and scratched her head, mentally noting that it was time for a visit to the hair salon.

"Damn!" she exclaimed, remembering that she had no time to spare for her usual hair ritual. Just thinking about it made her want to curl back up under the covers. "Well, I guess it's a ponytail today," she mumbled.

After forcing herself to get out of bed, she quickly showered, brushed her teeth, and completed her facial routine. While standing in front of the bathroom mirror, she leaned close to inspect her skin. Facing her was the reflection of a naturally beautiful black woman. By any society's standard, Jade was stunning. Her oval face held large almond-shaped eyes accented by defined brows with a perfect arch. A cute nose topped a generously full mouth. However, Jade did not see these features in her mirror, nor did she notice the smooth softness of her milk chocolate complexion. She was too busy looking for signs of the blemishes that occasionally popped up. It was disgusting, she thought, to still get pimples at twenty-nine years old.

Remembering the time, Jade quickly combed her thick, shoulder-length hair into a ponytail, then ran into the bedroom and dragged on her sports bra and Lycra pants. It was late April, so the weather in Chicago was still chilly, especially in the morning. Quickly, she also pulled on one of her Adidas shell suits. Checking her watch again, she stuffed additional clothing and other necessary items into her knapsack and ran out the door.

While fumbling with her house keys, Jade wiggled her sock-covered toes and realized that she had forgotten to put on her running shoes. Shaking her head at her absentmindedness, she ran back in and grabbed them, then tugged them on while she waited for the elevator. Within a couple of minutes, Jade was pulling out of the underground garage. It was a ten-minute drive into the downtown core of Chicago, and Jade was able to unlock the front doors to her dance school before 10:30. She still had a good thirty minutes before her first class.

After preparing the studio, Jade went into her office to wait for her students to arrive. For two years, she had been the owner and principal dance instructor at Winters School of Dance. Along with the pride and fulfillment that her career gave her, Jade always felt a sense of wonder. Ten years ago, when she started dancing again for the first time since her early teens, it had been for exercise and to get out of the house. She had never thought she was very good, never really analyzed her abilities. For her, especially at first, dancing was therapeutic. During the worst times of her marriage, she was able to escape the pain and disappointment through music and movement. After she had left her husband, Peter, Jade had used dancing to help rebuild her sense of self. The strength and control required to dance replaced the strength and control that she lost in her marriage. While dancing, she found she could rely solely on her own abilities to accomplish anything.

When there was an opening for a new instructor, Jade approached then owner Mrs. Stoica and asked to be considered for the position. By the time Jade graduated from college five years ago, she was teaching most of the classes in the small studio. The routine lasted until Mrs. Stoica slipped on the ice and broke her hip. At sixty-seven years old, the former Russian ballerina felt it was time to pack it in and move to a warmer climate. Since Jade was practically running everything, the generous older woman made it easy for her to get a bank loan and take over the lease. Jade's life changed dramatically. Though the studio was too small to make her rich, it had a consistent number of students, allowing Jade to live more than comfortably.

Realizing that some of the students for the eleven o'clock jazz class were entering the studio, Jade took off her shell suit, stretched, and left the office to begin her day's work.

In the northern end of the city, Noel Merson was leaning against the front door of his sister's home, waiting impatiently for his twelve-year-old niece to finish fussing with her dance clothes. He loved Laura with all his heart, but God, she could be a pain.

"Laura, if you don't hurry up, you're going to be late."

"Okay, I'm ready," Laura finally informed him as she came flying down the stairs and ran right out the front door. She practically shoved Noel out of her way.

"Come on Uncle Noel, class starts in twenty minutes!" She was already sitting in his Jeep as though Noel had been the one holding them up.

"Nicki," he yelled to his older sister, "I'll bring her back after her class at about one o'clock, okay? 'Bye!"

Without waiting for a response, he closed the front door, ran down the front path, and jumped into the Jeep parked at the curb. In seconds, they were off.

"Laura, I hope you know how to get there," Noel stated as he turned off the residential road and onto one of Chicago's main streets.

"Don't worry, Uncle Noel. We'll be there in ten minutes flat," she responded emphatically. "And I'll show you the way."

Noel shook his head at her patronizing tone. He knew roughly where the dance studio was located. According to the address his sister had given him, it appeared to be only a few blocks from his office building. However, Laura liked to be in control, so Noel kept quiet and let her direct him.

He was used to Laura's bossiness, so when she ran out of the Jeep complaining that his slow driving had almost made her late, it did not faze him. His only response was to tell her that he needed to grab something off of his desk at work, and that he'd be back in an hour to pick her up. As Noel drove away, he smiled to himself. Laura could be frustrating at times, but he had to admire her spirit. Even so, she didn't inspire him to have children of his own any time soon.

His smiled faded as his thoughts turned to the past. There was a time when kids were something that he wanted very much. He hadn't felt that way in years. Without the perfect woman, Noel did not have any yearning for a family.

The problem was that he had thought of Sandra Mc-Callum as the perfect woman. At thirty years old, Noel had thought he was ready for the responsibility of a family. Sandra, with her model's body and manicured beauty, had appeared to be the woman to commit to. After eighteen months together, Noel had been ready to pop the question. He had even spent several Saturdays searching for the perfect ring. Unfortunately, she had not felt the same way. That fact was made painfully obvious when he decided to surprise her at her apartment one evening after returning home early from a business trip . . . and found her mouth at work between someone else's legs. Needless to say, the relationship ended abruptly, along with Noel's ideals on beautiful women and everlasting love.

So, for the next three years, he played "the game": he dated, hung out with the guys, had a lot of meaningless sex, and went back to his big empty house alone each night. He also stopped wanting or looking for a relationship. If Noel was honest with himself, he would admit that Sandra was nowhere near as perfect as he had first thought. Her faults went much deeper than her promiscuity. Love, or what he had thought was love, had blinded him to her self-indulgent and egocentric nature. He was not going to let it happen again.

When Noel left his office at Momentum Advertising about twenty minutes later, he decided to head straight back to the dance studio. He pulled out of the tall State Street office building and drove four blocks

north. He would be just in time to catch the end of
Laura's lesson. For months now, he had been forced
to listen to her go on and on about how "amazing"
the classes were. When he ran up the front steps to
the studio after parking in the lot across the street, he
was sure he was going to be bored out of his mind.
How exciting could it be to watch a bunch of unco-
ordinated kids?

At the top of the stairs, he opened the door on the
landing and went into the waiting area. Across from
the main door there was another set of doors that
opened to the dance studio. The waiting room was
lined with backless couches, some occupied by parents and students waiting for the next class. On the
left side of the room were two doors that led to separate dressing rooms, showers, and bathrooms. On the
right side of the studio was another door designated
as the management office.

Noel took in his surroundings with a quick sweep of
his head, then walked across the room and opened
one of the studio doors. There were other spectators
leaning against the front wall watching the class, so he
joined them.

"Okay everyone, let's take it again! Five . . . six . . .
five, six, seven, eight! And one, kick, step, and turn.
Pirouette . . . pirouette . . . jump and slide," the instructor coached to the beat of the music.

The class was facing a mirrored wall along the
longer side of the large rectangular room. Noel's attention was immediately drawn to Laura as she
performed the dance routine. She was doing well as
the whole class moved in almost perfect unison. The
routine they performed was very funky and energetic
to match the popular R&B song that they moved to.

The students ranged in age from preteen to older teenager, and it was obvious they had all been dancing for a while.

Again and again, the dancers went through the routine, stopping from time to time as the instructor gave some students individual help.

"That's a wrap! Let's begin the cool down. Legs in second position, arms high, let's breathe. And bend, and up . . ."

The students were guided through the stretches after they spread out in front of the mirrors. Instead of coaching from the side of the room, the dance teacher was positioned in front of the class doing the exercises as well. As she moved rhythmically with one heel tapping to the music, Noel's eyes were drawn to her.

The first thought that came to his mind was *Damn, she is sexy!* He watched her effortlessly stand on one leg while gracefully unfolding the other to the side, foot pointed to complete a perfect arch. As his eyes traveled along her extended leg, he admired the finely toned muscles that were clearly visible through her tight stretchy pants. Her firmly held abdomen was equally as impressive. His eyes then followed the elegant line of her lightly defined back and took in the beautiful curve of her slender neck. He could not help but visualize running his tongue over the peaks of her breasts, clearly outlined through the thin spandex fabric of her sports bra.

Wow! Noel quickly looked around to make sure that he had not actually spoken aloud. No one was staring at him, so his attention was drawn back to her as the class began to applaud.

"You guys did great. On Wednesday, we'll start a new routine. See ya later," she responded to the many farewells from the dancers as they made their way to the dressing rooms and showers.

The room was then empty except for Noel and Jade.

Noel tried to look casual as he watched her from the corner of his eyes.

Jade knew she was being watched but did not pay much attention. People watched her dance classes all the time. The next class was a beginner ballet class, and she walked over to one of the *barres* that extended from the mirrored wall and began to practice the routine for the next session. In the mirror, she could see that the man was covertly studying her movements.

He appeared to be about six feet tall but far from thin. His corded muscles were very evident through his light cotton sweater. *Not bad,* she thought to herself. Suddenly, their eyes met in the mirror and Jade froze.

"Uncle Noel? There you are. I thought you would be in the waiting room," Laura said breathlessly as she barged through the studio doors.

"Oh, I was just looking around. Are you ready?" Noel asked as he reluctantly took his eyes away from the stunning woman.

"Yeah. Remember, you promised me ice cream, so let's go," she commanded, grabbing his hand insistently. "'Bye, Jade. See ya Wednesday!"

"'Bye, Laura," Jade replied.

Chapter 2

As Noel drove downtown the following Saturday with his niece chattering away beside him, he wondered to himself how he had become her personal chauffeur. He did not mind the chore, although it was starting to feel like a regular routine. While searching for a parking space near the studio, Noel pondered the sense of anticipation he felt. His palms were slightly damp, and his heart was beating a little faster than usual.

Noel refused to acknowledge that he was anxious to see Laura's dance instructor again. Granted, she was a memorable sight. In fact, pictures of her swaying body had floated through his mind, and vaguely in his dreams, all week. Though he could not recall her face very clearly, he knew she was beautiful. Not the type of made-up, sophisticated beauty who usually caught his eye, but a captivating, earthy type—completely sensual and natural. *Jade.* Noel felt the name suited her perfectly.

Laura ran up the stairs to the studio and Noel followed her slowly, once again wiping his palms on his jeans. *Damn,* he thought, *I'm acting like a teenager!*

Jade was already in the studio when the students began to file in. She was practicing an addition to the routine they had started on Wednesday, and her focus was completely devoted to counting the music and mapping the steps. By the time she was satisfied with the combination, almost everyone was ready and spaced evenly apart on the dance floor.

"Okay, everyone, let's begin the warm-up," she stated as she restarted the CD in the stereo system. "We'll start with isolations. And one, two, three, four," Jade counted, snapping her fingers to emphasize the musical beats.

"Keep your backs straight, tummies tucked in, and butts tight. . . ." Continuously, she coached the class through the standard routine of stretches and strength exercises. After about twenty minutes, everyone was warmed up and ready to dance.

"Okay, let's go through the section you guys learned last class; then we'll add on to it. Watch me; then we'll do it together."

Jade changed the music to a more funky selection. She took her spot in the front of the class and began a short series of steps that the class was to imitate. While the students watched with intent interest, Noel was looking in from outside the studio door with his mouth open.

Finally, he admitted to himself that he had been looking forward to watching this woman dance again. But it wasn't only her dancing that captured his attention. There was something about the way her body moved that turned him on. The way her hips rotated and the look of damp cotton clinging to her full breasts made him hot.

He had been watching through the glass from the beginning of the class and could not seem to take his eyes off her. It was as though she was dancing just for him, even though she probably didn't even know he was there. Her actions were not deliberately enticing, and the students in the class were all dancing the same way. As Noel snapped his mouth shut to prevent himself from drooling, he acknowledged that some of the best strippers he had ever watched had not affected him the way this woman was.

While the students applauded their instructor at the end of the class, Noel stepped through the doors of the studio before he could stop himself. He moved to the side of the room as the others rushed out the door. Laura, whose existence he had forgotten up to that point, waved to him before she also left the room.

Like the week before, the room was empty except for Noel and Jade.

Noel was nervous; he had not thought very far in advance. All he knew was that he wanted to meet her. How to do that without looking like an idiot was the question. At that moment, Jade was bent over the stereo system organizing the CDs. She did not appear to be aware of his presence. Slowly, he walked toward her crouched figure. When she heard footsteps approaching her, she looked over her shoulder to find a pair of brown Timberland boots planted almost directly behind her.

She stood up quickly with a look of surprise on her face. "Oh! I didn't realize anyone was here. Can I help you?" she asked breathlessly. Immediately, she recognized the man from last week, and then was held almost spellbound by his eyes: they were a stunning, translucent hazel that seemed to glow brightly against his golden skin. Any woman would die for his thick black lashes, yet they made this man look incredibly masculine. A sharply edged goatee complemented the four inches of glossy black curls that hung from his head. Jade knew she was staring, but as there was a God, she couldn't help herself!

Noel did not notice, since he was in a similar situation. Her mouth hypnotized him. Her lips were lush and full, untouched by lipstick, and they begged to be kissed. As he blinked to clear his thoughts, he tried to formulate an answer to her question. But his mind was blank.

Though it felt like minutes, the silent pause between them lasted only seconds. When Noel opened his mouth to introduce himself at last, Laura interrupted his attempt as she rushed through the doors. "I'm ready, Uncle Noel. Are you coming?" Like a breeze, she was gone.

Jade could see the resemblance right away. Though Laura's skin was several shades darker and her eyes were brown, her features were equally as defined as his. Her hair, although pulled into a chignon, had the same unprocessed wavy curls.

"Bloody hell! I should be getting paid for this," he muttered to himself, irritated by Laura's interruption. He did not realize how loud he had spoken until he noticed the amused smile on Jade's face. He smiled back in response.

"I'm Laura's uncle, Noel Merson," he stated offering his hand. "I just wanted you to know that I was impressed by your class," he finished, as Jade placed her hand in his.

"Thank you. Do you like dance?" Jade asked.

"Actually, I've never really watched it before. To be honest, I thought it was all about twirling around in tutus," he responded with a wry smile.

Jade laughed lightly in response. "I think you're referring to ballet. Jazz is a little more fun."

"Well, in either case, Laura loves your class. It's all she talks about. And trust me, that's often."

Jade continued to smile, then lightly tugged at her hand. Noel then realized that he was still holding it. She had a lovely smile.

"Well, Mr. Merson . . ." she began.

"Noel, please."

"Noel. I'm glad you enjoyed watching the class." Jade turned back toward the stereo system as the children for her next class began to collect in the room. "A ballet class is about to start if you would like to stay." She gave a mischievous glance over her shoulder.

"Ah . . . no! Thanks for the offer, but I think I'll take a raincheck. Good-bye, Mrs. . . . ?" he explored.

"Winters. *Ms.* Jade Winters. It was nice to meet you. 'Bye," Jade responded, again with a quick look over her shoulder.

Noel nodded, then turned around and walked away. Another quick glance over her shoulder confirmed what Jade had instinctively known would be true: Noel Merson had a very sexy ass!

Chapter 3

Despite Jade's lack of concentration, the hour-long ballet class went by quickly. She had no plans for the rest of the afternoon, so she began to do some much-needed administrative work. With the summer coming, she would have to organize several short-term courses during the weekdays in addition to the classes already running. For most of the year the school held classes on the weekends and in the early evenings during the week. There were also a couple of stretch classes during the day designed for older women and housewives. This schedule allowed Jade a lot of free time but only during the day. Most evenings, she did not get home until at least 7:30. Since she did not exactly live a wild life, it worked out fine for her. She could barely remember the last time an evening meant more than reading a good book or watching TV.

On Saturdays Jade usually did her socializing either with her brother, Jerome, or with friends. However, she did not have any specific plans for that afternoon. Her intention was to spend the next couple of hours paying some bills over the Internet and straightening her paperwork. As she turned on the computer, the phone rang.

"Winters School of Dance, how can I help you?" she answered.

"Hey Jade, it's Trish," the caller stated.

"Hey, Trish. How's it going?"

"I'm still alive. So, what's up? I haven't talked to you in so long," Trish said.

"I know, but I've spoken to your answering machine several times," Jade said with a laugh.

Enthusiastically, the friends quickly caught up on the recent events of their lives. It turned out to be Jade listening to the events of Trish's life, but that was the norm.

"What are you doing later?" Trish asked fifteen minutes into the conversation.

"Nothing, really. Why? What's up?"

"I just thought you might want to come over, that's all. Ian and I are going to rent a couple of movies and order some pizza."

"That sounds fun. I'll call you before I come over, okay?"

"Okay. Talk to you later."

"'Bye," Jade replied, then hung up the phone. Her bookkeeping could wait until tomorrow.

She decided that if she was going over to Trish's, then she would not bother to go home first. Instead, she took a quick shower in the private dressing room next to her office to refresh herself. After applying scented bath oil to her wet body, she toweled off, leaving her skin silky-soft and well moisturized. She pulled out a fresh black thong underwear and matching underwire lace bra from her gym bag and slipped them on.

While standing in front of the door mirror, she released her hair from the ponytail and combed it back

into a soft, wavy fall. Then she applied her makeup.
Jade didn't wear much, only a light face powder to
prevent shine, mascara, eyeliner, and mocha lip liner
softened with clear lip gloss. She learned a long time
ago never to go out without looking your best,
because if you did, you were certain to run into someone you knew.

Then she pulled on a pair of loose, washed-out blue
jeans and a fitted black T-shirt. With critical eyes, she
looked at her reflection in the mirror. Each of her
parts looked okay, but she felt that the total package
would never be enough for a man to die over. She
could almost hear Peter's voice filled with mockery
and scorn, but she pushed it away after a fleeting moment. Considering that she had not spoken to him for
more than four years, he should not be in her
thoughts. She was just grateful that the memories
rarely surfaced anymore, though it was still too often
for her liking.

Dismissing those depressing thoughts from her
mind, she pulled on her black leather boots. After
bundling her dance clothes and runners into her
knapsack, she stepped out of the private changing
room and back into her office. One more quick check
in the mirror next to her office door and she was satisfied. As she was about to turn off the lights in the
office, she paused, thinking she had heard footsteps
in the studio waiting room. She stood still and listened.

"Hello?" she heard a man's voice call out. Suddenly,
Noel Merson filled the doorframe of her office. She
revised her earlier assessment; he was closer to 6'2".

"Hi," Jade responded, slightly breathless from the

surprise of his sudden appearance. "Did you forget something?"

"No, but I did come back for something," Noel stated mischievously.

Jade took a step back, very much aware that the rest of the studio was empty.

"Well, whatever it is, you're lucky you caught me. I was just about to leave." With that statement, Jade turned off the lights and closed the office door behind her. Her right shoulder brushed his chest before he stepped out of her way.

"Well, aren't you curious?" Noel asked with the devilish grin still on his lips.

"About what?" she asked, trying to be nonchalant but unable to deny the pull of his charm. Their bodies were still very close, and she was very aware that they were alone in the building.

"About what I came back for."

"Oh . . . yeah. What is it?"

"My raincheck."

"Your raincheck," Jade repeated, slightly confused. "You came back to watch a ballet class?"

"Well, actually, I was hoping to trade that invitation in for something a little bit more enjoyable. Like, say . . . lunch?"

Jade could not tell if he was being serious. "Lunch," she repeated as she glanced at her watch. It was past 2:30.

"Okay, a late lunch. That's if you haven't already eaten." He seemed serious.

"No . . . no, I haven't." She was still trying to understand the conversation.

He suddenly smiled, "Well, then let's go!" He lightly

touched her arm to propel her toward the front door. By then, Jade had already turned off the main lights.

"Wait, I forgot my jacket," she explained as she ran back into her office, then came out wearing the jacket of her shell suit. Her confusion was clear on her face as she walked back to Noel.

"Let me get this straight: you're asking me out to lunch?" She still could not believe this was happening.

"Do you like Italian?" he asked as he guided her down the stairs and out to the street.

"Italian is fine," Jade responded, surprising herself by accepting the situation.

"Great! There's a little bistro nearby that has great pasta."

"Really? Where? I don't think I've ever noticed it," she said as she quickly locked the main entrance door on the street level. "Let me just drop my bag in my car. Is the restaurant within walking distance?"

"On a nice day, but we'll take my car."

Jade shrugged in response. The whole situation was very strange to her. She did not understand why exactly he wanted to go to lunch, but before all else she was a curious person. If Mr. Noel Merson turned out to be a gorgeous psychopathic murderer, then her curiosity would kill her. Either that or she could trip and break her neck while staring at him.

She broke out of her reverie as they reached her car.

"Nice car," Noel stated appreciatively as he took in her sporty silver Volkswagen Jetta. "It suits you perfectly."

"Thanks. I've only had it for a few months, but it's great to drive," she responded with a proud smile.

"One of the best feelings is driving a new car. You

don't have to worry about it falling apart, then having to cough up the money to fix it."

"I know what you mean," she agreed, slamming the trunk door after putting her bag inside.

"I'm parked right over there." Noel indicated a parking lot across the street. Jade followed him toward an aged black Jeep Laredo with a removable hard top.

"Nice car," she said, imitating his earlier compliment. "It suits you perfectly."

"Thanks. I've had it for years and it drives like crap."

They laughed at his tone. Then their eyes met and the laughter faded. Awkward silence followed.

Noel opened the passenger door for Jade, then walked around to the driver's side and climbed in.

"About the only thing that works properly in this thing is the heater. It'll be on in a few seconds," he informed her after starting the engine.

"That's okay, I'm not cold."

After another awkward pause, Noel cleared his throat, and then broke the silence. "So, how long have you been dancing?"

"I actually started when I was about ten but stopped in high school. When I was in college, I took a few dance electives and they renewed my interest."

"Which college did you go to?" he asked, giving her a quick glance.

"University of Chicago."

"A Chi Town girl."

"You know it!" Jade said with a proud smile. "What about you?"

"What school did I go to? The University of the West Indies."

"Oh." She could not think of anything else to say. Jade had no clue what school that was, and she was too self-conscious to ask questions.

Suddenly, the reality of the situation hit her. She was in a car with a man—an extremely gorgeous man—she had briefly met just hours before. Was she nuts?

"Well, this is it," he said as they turned into a parking lot several blocks west of the studio.

Noel escorted her into the small, casual restaurant with a light touch on her waist. While she looked around, he requested a table for two.

"Smoking or nonsmoking?" the young Italian hostess asked.

Jade and Noel looked at each other.

"Non," they both said at the same time as their eyes remained locked. They both smiled.

"Have you decided what to order?" Noel asked once they were seated and looking over the menu.

"I think I'll try the salmon. How about you?" Jade asked politely.

"I'm not really that hungry, but I'll have the lasagna with a Caesar salad to start. And maybe I'll try some of the bruschetta as well."

"That's all? I suppose it's a good thing you're not hungry," Jade teased.

Noel laughed softly.

After they gave their orders, they were silent for a couple of minutes. Jade's nervousness increased. This was a mistake. Why on earth had she agreed to this lunch? She was just setting herself up for disappointment. Give it an hour, tops, and he was going to reveal himself to be an arrogant idiot. They all did sooner or later.

Jade's thoughts ran in circles as she casually pretended to be looking around the restaurant. When her gaze returned to the man in front of her, the ability to think evaporated. He was looking at her, and the look on his face could only be described as sexy. Her heart stopped beating, then began pounding again at twice the normal speed. Unconsciously, she licked her lips slowly, her eyes fastened on his full, well-shaped mouth. Noel gave her a devilish smile that showed off his sparkling straight teeth. Shallow dimples punctuated each cheek and emphasized the defined lines of his cheekbones.

"So, tell me more about your dancing," he requested.

Jade dragged her gaze away from his tempting mouth until her eyes met with his.

"Do you enjoy it?" He was still smiling.

"Very much," she responded breathlessly. "It's become my career. I haven't made any long-term plans for the studio, but for now, it's perfect."

Noel nodded in understanding, and the conversation took flight.

"So, Laura is your niece?" Jade asked. She did not want to talk about herself too much.

"Yup. She's my sister's daughter."

"Do you have any other brothers or sisters?"

"I also have a younger brother," Noel replied.

The waiter arrived with their drink order, Perrier water for her and iced tea for him.

"So you're the middle child," Jade noted. "Are you close to them?"

Noel took a long drink from his frosted glass before he replied. "We're all pretty close, but I don't get to see my brother too often. He lives with my mom and dad in Jamaica."

"Your parents are in Jamaica?" Jade's surprise was obvious as she put down her drink and leaned toward him. "Are you Jamaican?"

Noel nodded. "I was born there, then we moved to the States in 1973. About fifteen years ago, they moved back," he explained.

"They retired?"

"No, my father got a new job. He's a chemical engineer. My mom's a nurse. They both packed up and moved there," Noel explained.

"How old were you and your brother and sister then?" Jade asked. It was very hard to hide her curiosity.

"When they moved back? I was seventeen; my sister, Nicki, was nineteen; and I guess Alex was around fourteen." Noel paused as their waiter brought their meals and rearranged the items on the table. He nodded his thanks, then continued the story. "Alex started high school there, and I was able to register at the university in time for the fall semester. Nicki had already moved to Chicago, so she stayed in the States."

"The University of the West Indies," Jade said to herself as she started to eat her meal. "I guess it's in Jamaica?" she asked.

"Right outside of Kingston," he clarified.

"Wow, I would never have guessed. I mean, you don't have an accent or anything. I guess that's because you were so young when you moved here." Jade knew that she sounded slightly ignorant, so she rushed on. "So, you're not from Chicago?" Noel shook his head.

"No. I grew up in D.C. Nicki talked me into moving to Chicago when I finished my degree," Noel explained. "She told me that the Windy City had the most beautiful women." He was flirting with her openly for the first time, and the glint in his eyes raised her temperature several degrees.

"What did you take at the university?" Jade asked as she resisted the urge to fan herself. She wanted to know more about him, but she also wanted to hear his voice. It was smooth and deep and rhythmic. And sometimes she was teased by a glimpse of the dimples that punctuated his smile.

"Media and communications. What about you?" he returned.

"I took economics with a minor in dance."

"It appears that you made the right choice," he teased.

While they finished their meals, they continued to talk about school, then they moved on to favorite pastimes. They discussed most of the things people do when they want to fill in a blank page. Questions and answers were volleyed easily and honestly. But, there remained a sense of breathless expectation, a charge of sexual electricity. Both felt it and tried to ignore it without any success.

Soon, their waiter brought the check. As Noel picked it up and scanned it, Jade reached into her purse for her wallet.

"What's the damage?" she asked. Since there was still time for him to prove himself to be a jerk, she fully intended to pay her share.

Noel looked up from the bill, slightly surprised. "I'll take care of it," he informed her, placing a couple of twenties onto the table. "Are you ready?"

She nodded, and they made their way out of the restaurant. When they reached his Jeep, he unlocked the passenger door and let her in.

"Do you have any plans for the evening?" he asked casually as he drove back toward her car. Without thinking, Jade shook her head no.

"Well, I just picked up few new CDs this week. Why don't you come over and listen to them with me?" Even Noel had to admit he sounded pretty lame, but he was not ready for their time together to end.

Jade looked into his glowing eyes and knew she could not have heard right. She could not think of an answer.

"You could follow me in your car," he continued. "I live in the north end of the city. We can take Lake Shore and be there in twenty minutes."

When Jade still did not answer him, Noel reached out and lightly touched her hand resting in her lap. He cringed inside at the pleading quality that he detected in his voice.

"Come on, it'll be fun. What sort of music do you like? Not country, I hope!" he joked, trying to extract a response from her.

"What's wrong with country music? Garth is my favorite, and Shania rocks!"

Noel glanced at her, an incredulous expression on his face. "You're joking right?"

Unable to continue her jest, Jade began to laugh. "I like the regular stuff: R&B, hip-hop, jazz."

"Do you like reggae?" he asked.

"I like some of it. I have to admit that I can't understand some of the things they're saying, though."

"Well, I don't always understand it either, and I'm Jamaican," he said with a smile.

"Will you come over?" he asked again as he gave her hand a small squeeze. All sense of caution flew right out of her head as a shiver spread from her hand

straight to the center of her body. The whole afternoon had already taken on a surreal quality. It was as
though she was living someone else's life. So why not?

"All right," she heard herself say.

Chapter 4

On the way to his house, Noel frequently checked his rearview mirror to make sure that the silver Jetta was right behind him. He was not sure why he asked her to visit his house. Usually he preferred to go to the woman's place at the end of a date. It was much easier to leave someone than to convince the woman to go home without causing an emotional scene. But, the situation with Jade Winters was not usual. He had not met her at the usual bars or clubs, so the normal rules didn't apply.

It was still very early, and he was not ready for their time to end so soon. Noel chose not to analyze why.

Halfway though their meal, he had realized that he was having a good time. He found her very interesting. She was smart, articulate, and funny. She also had an innocence and lack of conceit that were very rare in beautiful women. Most of the women he dated with a pretty face and a sexy body knew how to use both to their advantage. They certainly would not have offered to pay for the first meal. Actually, they rarely paid for any meal, but that was just another cost of playing "the game." Jade, however, appeared very natural and sincere. Even her laugh lacked that artificial quality other women often displayed.

Yet, without the obvious display of sexuality he was used to, Noel had still been unable to take his eyes off her. He pictured her licking her lips while her eyes clung to his mouth, and he felt himself harden. Remembering the line of her jaw, the curve of her neck, and the voluptuous swell of her breast almost brought him to full length. Noel shifted in his jeans to ease his discomfort and once again checked in the mirror.

As he pulled into his circular driveway, he tried to remember the state in which he had left the house. A cleaning lady came by twice a week, so he knew it wasn't dirty. He just hoped there weren't any T-shirts or socks on the living room floor.

Noel lived in a gray stone manor in the northeast area of Chicago. The 5,000 square foot house sat on a half-acre rectangular lot and backed onto a lush lakefront park. Four white columns framed the front entrance and enhanced the traditional, symmetrical lines of the home. Matching bay windows sat on either side of the columns, and large double doors with full-length, smoked-glass inserts hung inside.

As Jade drove into the interlocking stone driveway behind Noel's Jeep, she took a moment to appreciate the elegant beauty of his home. She parked her car in the driveway while Noel drove up to the two-car garage attached to the left wall of the house. He stopped beside a black Audi TT sport coupe.

They met on the walkway and went together up to the front doors. Noel unlocked the doors, pushed open one with a twist of his wrist, and flamboyantly indicated for her to enter first. She smiled at his majestic antics as she stepped over the threshold and into the spacious foyer.

Slate tiles the color of wet Caribbean sand spread

invitingly into the center hall of the house. They ended where dark polished hardwood flooring began at the edge of the family room. Numerous uncovered windows at the rear of the house provided an unbelievable view of the woods, beach, and lake behind his property. Instinctively, Jade bent over and began to remove her boots.

"Would you like something to drink?" Noel asked after he took her jacket and hung it in the closet next to the front door. He kicked off his own boots and left them near the door.

Jade pulled her eyes away from the décor to focus on him as he walked toward the end of the hall. "What do you have?" she inquired.

"Let's see . . . wine, beer, and some orange juice. Do you like white wine?"

"Sure, as long as it's not too dry." As Jade followed Noel, she walked past a large powder room, a sitting room, a dining room, and a cluttered office behind French doors. She also passed the circular wooden stairs that led to the upper floor. She caught up to him in the open-concept kitchen. She was not sure what she had been expecting of his place, but it wasn't this spacious, sophisticated house. Jade was also surprised by how relaxed she felt in the unfamiliar setting.

"This bottle should be okay; it's a leftover from Christmas. You don't mind if I add ice, do you?" Noel asked, as he pulled a bottle of white Masi out of the back of the pantry. The bottle was covered with four month's worth of fine dust. Noel took two wine goblets from a beveled-glass cupboard and dispensed ice from the inside of a Sub-Zero built-in refrigerator. After fishing around for a corkscrew, he popped the cork and filled their glasses. They were both silent as he handed her a drink then led the way to the casual family room.

A contemporary sky blue leather sofa was flanked by two matching armchairs and faced a media center of light maple and glass. Jade's eyes were then drawn to the colorful African oil painting that was mounted above the fireplace at the end of the room. While obviously expensively decorated, the room was inviting and very masculine. From what she had seen so far, it also had the most furniture in the house, except for the office. Absently, Jade wondered if Noel had decorated the room himself or had had someone do it for him.

"What do you think?" Noel asked, indicating with a tilt of his head the painting over the fireplace. It depicted three African warriors at three stages of manhood.

"It's stunning! I like the colors. They're so rich and vibrant."

"I'm not usually into art, but when I saw it, I knew that I wanted it to hang in this room. My friend who owns the gallery I got it from tells me it's a fantastic investment, but I just bought it because it spoke to something inside me," Noel analyzed, then seemed embarrassed when he caught Jade looking at him.

"That's pretty deep," she teased.

"Hardly. I've just had plenty of time to sit and stare at the wall, that's all," Noel said.

"I find that very hard to believe." Her eyes were inadvertently drawn to the outline of his pecs visible through his sweater.

"What?"

"That you spend a lot of time alone staring into space."

"Then you would be surprised," Noel stated softly,

almost under his breath. He then bent down in front of the media center and popped open a glass door. "Let's get this party started! What do you want to hear first?" he asked, glancing over his shoulder with a smile.

Jade decided to test him to see if he had really picked up some new music. "Do you have the new one by Mary J. Blige?" she requested.

"I tried to pick it up a couple of months ago, but it was sold out. How about Maxwell, or would you prefer Janet?"

"I haven't heard the new Janet one yet, except for that one song they're playing all over the radio," she responded, trying to hide how pleased she was that their tastes ran in the same direction.

Noel popped in three new CDs and grabbed the remote off the top of the unit. He then sat down on the couch and patted the seat beside him, indicating for Jade to join him. As she sat down, he laid out two silver coasters on the square glass coffee table. The room then filled with a funky beat and the smooth, sexy voice of Miss Jackson.

As they listened to the music, they talked and drank their wine. They discussed the CDs, gossiped about different artists, and laughed about some of the lyrics. Jade was surprised at how easily they communicated and how much they had in common.

She was not sure what she expected, but it was not this. It was very rare that she could meet a stranger, particularly a man, and feel so comfortable and at ease.

The first CD finished, and the sounds of Maxwell filled the room.

"Can I be honest with you?" she asked, not expecting an answer. "I was pretty sure that you were going to turn out to be a pig, or an ass, or something. But, I've had a really good time so far."

"Why would you expect me to be an ass?" Noel asked, pretending to be more offended than he really was.

"I don't know. That's usually what happens when a stranger asks me out. And the better looking he is, the bigger ass he is." Jade wondered if the wine had gone to her head, because she wasn't sure that her last sentence made any sense.

"So, you find me good looking."

Jade just smiled and shook her head at his lack of humility. He certainly did not need another woman to tell him how beautiful he was.

"What other preconceptions do you have about me?" Noel asked.

"None, really. I only met you this morning," she said.

"Well, you must have had some ideas since then," he coaxed.

"Okay, okay. I'll be honest: I have been thinking that this whole thing is sort of strange."

"What thing?"

"This," she explained, indicating the space between them.

"You mean us?" he asked.

She nodded to confirm his assessment. "I don't know why exactly, it just is. Why don't you tell me what you think 'this' is?" Jade inquired, suddenly feeling bold.

"It's a man and a woman enjoying each other's company and listening to music."

"And what else?"

"What else could it be?" he responded, refusing to acknowledge her point.

"I don't know. It's just that I don't usually do this sort of thing. And I know that sounds very cliché, but it's true." At his raised eyebrows, she elaborated. "I don't date very much, and I definitely do not go to a man's house within hours of meeting him."

"Well, if it makes you feel any better," Noel replied in a serious tone, "I didn't think that you did."

Their eyes met and held until Jade looked away to hide the heat rising in her body.

"So," she breathed. "Let me hear some more of that new music you bought."

Kindly, he let her change the subject. "I have lots of Latin music. Do you ever listen to it?" he asked, getting up from beside her.

"You mean, like Ricky Martin?"

"Well, I didn't really mean that. His stuff is more like Latin pop. I mean the real stuff, like salsa and merengue," he clarified, as he shuffled through the large collection of CDs that filled the shelving unit of the entertainment center.

"Not really," she said, leaning forward.

"Well, then. Along with my musical tastes, you'll be surprised to know that I can also dance, even though I didn't know the difference between jazz and ballet," he informed her with a teasing smile.

"Really?" she said, playing his game and exaggerating her intrigue.

"Yeah. I can teach you how to merengue. That is, if you don't already know how."

The music was fast, rhythmic, and pulsating. Noel moved away and indicated for her to join him as he walked to the open area by the rear windows. He held his arms out in a waltz position and Jade stepped into them.

"Now, follow my lead. You should be a natural at this," he instructed. They began to move in the simple steps of the traditional Latin dance.

"Obviously, you've done this before." He looked disappointed that she was able to follow his lead so easily.

"It kind of reminds me of ballroom dancing except with a bit more hip action and attitude. And better music."

"Well, then I'll just have to make it a little more challenging for you."

Suddenly, he pulled her close to him, so close that their bodies were fused from chest to thigh. His right hand pressed into the center of her back. The music suddenly felt louder, more throbbing. Jade became very conscious of her hand in his, her arm over his shoulder, and the tickle of his hair on her skin. Then they began to move and her whole body began to tingle.

With the gentle press of his hand, Noel urged her hips to rotate and sway with his while their legs moved to the steps. Their eyes were locked on each other, and they danced intimately and sensually for what seemed like hours. Each was held in a web of heat.

Their stare was broken when Noel's hand slid lower to cup her buttocks and completely fuse their loins together. His eyes slid, hypnotically, to her moist lips. Jade closed her eyes and swallowed. She could feel every inch of him, every inch of his aroused penis, and it made her weak. She opened her eyes to look once again into his. They had turned a deep, dark green.

"Jade," he breathed as they both stopped dancing. Her lids lowered in consent.

Noel bent his neck and his mouth brushed hers with a feather-soft touch. Then he withdrew, his lips hovering close to hers. Again, Jade licked her lips, slowly, unconsciously, and it was Noel's undoing. His lips ravished hers with uncontrolled passion. He invaded her mouth with his tongue, thoroughly tasting her incredible sweetness. It was more than a kiss; it was an arousing intimacy that increased the heat of their bodies.

"Touch me," he said softly, urgently. Jade looked up into his eyes and her breathing stopped. As though in a trance, she slid her right hand down his solid chest and over his rippling stomach. As she skimmed over his belt, she watched Noel close his eyes. He swallowed in anticipation as he slid his arms up her back to caress her shoulders. Continuing to watch his face, she reached lower and ran one finger along his penis from tip to base, lightly, slowly. His flesh felt hot, even through his jeans, and as hard as steel.

Noel moaned softly, his eyes still closed, jaws clenched. Still fascinated by his facial expression of desire, Jade flattened her hand and ran it firmly back up his rigid penis to the vulnerable tip. She felt amazing power as he shuddered. This had to be part of what women craved from sex, she realized for the first time: the ability to make the strongest man weak with want for them. It was a liberating realization for a woman who had never really felt anything during sex other than obligation.

Their eyes met again as they both were trying to understand what was happening and why it was happening so uncontrollably fast. While Noel continued to stare into her beautiful chocolate eyes, he slowly slid her T-shirt up her body until it was bunched at the top of her chest. He looked down at the tempting flesh that was revealed. Cupping her breasts in his large, masculine hands, he gently rubbed their sensitive tips with his thumbs through her bra.

Their fates were sealed and there was no turning back for either of them.

Soon, her T-shirt joined her jeans on the living room floor, leaving her vulnerable in her bra and panties. Years ago, this position would have resulted in her feeling the urgent need to cover herself and hide a lumpy body, but not now. Instead, intense arousal left her breathing heavily, her breasts rising and falling rhythmically. There was still some shyness, and to hide it she fixed her eyes on his wide chest.

Jade felt Noel's hand reach over and gently nudge her chin up so that she would again look him in the eye. He was smiling, a gentle soft smile that made her heart race even faster. Unconsciously, she leaned toward him and placed her hand on his chest.

In a daze, Jade let Noel take one of her hands and lead her upstairs to his bedroom. She barely took in her surroundings, too concerned about what was going to happen between them. Within a minute, they were standing beside his king-sized bed and he was taking off his shirt. Common sense invaded her clouded mind.

"I'm not using anything," she blurted out. "I mean, I'm not on the pill or anything," she clarified.

"That's okay, I have condoms," he said.

Jade was not surprised. He looked like the type who was always prepared.

"Come here." His shirt was now on the floor and his pants were undone.

Jade was unsure of what would come next but very certain that she wanted to experience it. When she stepped into his arms and leaned against his muscular body, the sensual kisses and caresses began all over again. The feelings were intensified by the texture of skin against skin.

Noel did not even break the kisses as he removed her bra. After the garment hit the floor, he pulled away to admire the luscious, firm fullness of her naked breasts. Jade felt limp as his fingers tenderly fondled her flesh, creating intense pleasure. After several minutes, he turned her around and gently laid her across his bed, giving him full access to her body. Then his lips replaced his hands. She shuddered as his tongue trailed erotically over her nipples, and she groaned softly as he continued to lick, stroke, and tease her.

Soon, they were both breathing heavily, and Noel moved his attention lower, across her taut, flat stomach to remove her panties. Playfully, he ran his fingers in small circles up her inner thigh. Jade could do nothing but sigh, groan, and toss her head in frustration. Finally, his fingers reached her sexual core.

"You're so wet for me," he whispered in her ear as he moved to lie beside her on the bed. Jade's only response was to whimper at his assault on her senses. She could not think, only feel. She was unable to do anything except cling to Noel's shoulders as he tormented her body with his arousing touch and teasing mouth. Then he began to stroke that sensitive nub. Jade moaned softly, sure that she was going to go over the edge. Again and again, he played with her most erotic points until she knew that she had to have all of him or die of frustration.

"Please," she begged softly, reaching down his body, wanting to feel the fullness of his hot penis. "Now!"

Noel knew what she needed, and he was ready to give it to her. As quickly as he could, he shed the rest of his clothes, then pulled a condom out of the wallet in his jeans. Effortlessly, he slid it on and reached for Jade before she could miss his touch. While kissing her eyes and forehead, he positioned their bodies comfortably on the mattress. Then he gently eased her legs apart and began to slide into her slick, hot center. They both groaned loudly.

"You're so tight," he gasped as he gently buried more of his penis into her body.

"Oh, God!" he gasped again as Jade flexed her hips, unable to remain passive any longer. She was hanging on the edge of an abyss, and his fullness was almost too much, too frustrating to withstand.

"Please," she begged again, wanting to feel him stroke her and take her over the cliff. Despite his restraining hand on her hip, she flexed upward, filling herself completely with his thick flesh. Noel groaned through clenched teeth, and Jade could only wrap her arms around his neck and gasp soundlessly.

"God, I can't wait," he whispered harshly. "Wrap your legs around me . . . oh, yes!" he exclaimed, as she followed his instructions mindlessly. With his weight rested on his elbows, he clenched his hands in her hair and began to move. Slowly, he withdrew and reentered her body, over and over again until neither of them could control their moans of pleasure. Unable to keep still, Jade joined the dance to match his rhythmic thrusts with equal intensity. Wanting to give him as much pleasure as he was giving her, she gently bit the side of his neck, then bathed it with her tongue. Noel shuddered, his pace increasing. Jade bit him again a little harder.

"Oh, sweetheart!" he whispered urgently. He grabbed one side of her hips and his strokes became faster and deeper, and more urgent.

"Yeah!" Jade urged, not recognizing the pleasure-filled voice as her own. "Oh, yeah! Don't stop . . . oh!"

He was unbelievably deep.

The pleasure was too much, too overwhelming. Noel groaned, his body shuddering uncontrollably as he buried himself in her tight warmth with a final thrust. He groaned again, and Jade could feel his throbbing fullness inside her as he reached the ultimate peak.

Chapter 5

When the haze around her brain faded and the beat of her heart slowed, the first thing that Jade noticed was that the room was very bright. Not only was she in bed with a man she had met only that day, but she had not even asked him to turn off the lights! The next thing that she noticed was the weight of a masculine leg draped across her thighs and the touch of an equally masculine hand stroking her naked breast.

Once the sensual fog was completely lifted from her brain, reality seemed overly sharp. Quickly, she looked at the man who lay naked next to her, and his eyes, mercifully, were closed. She held her breath as his hand stopped moving and lay limp on her chest. He had fallen asleep!

She knew that she should use this opportunity to get up and get out of the situation, but she could not stop watching his face. He was truly gorgeous. Even asleep, he was the type of man that women drool over. With his golden complexion and his thick cloud of curly jet-black hair, he had the exotic look of a black man of mixed racial heritage.

A slow appraisal of his body came next. Jade quickly glanced back at his face to make sure he had not wakened to find her ogling his body. And what a body!

Her inventory of his naked torso and legs confirmed what she had felt during their lovemaking: Noel was very well put together! His chest was thick and well defined, his stomach washboard firm. His arms and legs were muscular and well cut, obviously from regular exercise. He was too perfect for his own good. And probably too perfect to be real.

Her fear that he would wake up and catch her staring finally made Jade stop her appraisal. Gently, she removed his hand and leg, and as soon as the coast was clear, slid off the bed. One more quick glance confirmed that Noel was still asleep; then she was out of the room and down the stairs. Almost in a panic, she pulled on her discarded clothing and boots, grabbed her purse and coat, and ran out of the front door.

Jade drove back to her apartment in a daze. By the time she let herself into her place, she felt really stupid. She had run from Noel's house as though demons were after her. The only explanation for her irrational behavior was that she could not picture herself confronting him again. What would she say? How was she supposed to act? It had been so long since she had been intimate with a man that it felt very strange. She never had casual sex and certainly not a one-night stand!

She knew of plenty of women who did this sort of thing all the time, and she had never judged them. If two people want each other and no one will get hurt, then why not? It was just that she had never needed, wanted, or felt that kind of uncontrollable lust. Not until tonight, anyway. There was no other explanation for her behavior, and it was hard to accept that her body had such raw sexual cravings. Not to mention the fact that she could experience and enjoy such pleasure from a virtual stranger.

Still confused by the day's events, Jade slowly showered, and changed into shorts and an oversized T-shirt. The phone rang.

"Hello?" she answered.

"Jade? I thought you were coming over?" Trish demanded. "What happened?"

"Oh, Trish, I'm sorry. I forgot all about it," Jade responded contritely. "Something came up."

"Well?"

"Well, what?"

"Well, what came up?" Trish asked impatiently.

Jade paused, not sure how to verbalize the details of the past few hours. "Nothing really," she began, "I just went out with a friend."

"Who?"

"Uh . . . someone I just met." Jade knew this was going to be difficult.

"You mean a guy?" Trish asked incredulously. "Like out on a date?"

"Well . . . sort of."

"What do you mean 'sort of'?"

This was definitely going to be difficult. "You know, Trish, I'm so tired. I'll come over tomorrow after I finish at the gym and tell you all about it."

"Wait, you can't just leave me hanging like that, Jade. It's inhuman!" Trish begged.

"I promise I'll tell you everything tomorrow. 'Bye," she said sweetly before hanging up. Jade was too tired and too unbalanced to explain anything to anyone. All she wanted to do was to go to sleep and forget the whole thing had happened.

After fifteen minutes of twisting and turning, Jade

knew sleep was not even close to coming. Frustrated, she sat up and propped her pillows against the headboard as a cushion. Try as she might, images of Noel Merson doing the most amazing things to her body would not go away. Since her first sexual encounter at seventeen years old, she had never felt so aroused. Sex had always felt okay, even mildly pleasurable, but never like it had tonight. She had just assumed that she was not a sexy person, and it was not important to her.

Tonight was new. Just thinking about Noel was doing delicious things to her insides. Maybe this was what happened when you didn't have sex for four years, Jade thought to herself. Considering her final encounters with her husband, Peter, she was surprised that she could ever want to have sex again, much less enjoy it to the degree that she had tonight.

Peter had betrayed her physically and emotionally in the worst way, and it had taken years for her to stop feeling used and degraded. She still had dreams about those horrible nights and sometimes still felt the emotional scars left behind by their marriage.

Perhaps that was why she had lost control tonight: Noel had made her feel attractive. It was not anything that he said, it was just the way he looked at her and spoke to her. And touched her. He had shown her nothing but respect.

Feeling relieved that she had analyzed the reason for her out-of-character behavior, Jade lay back down and effortlessly drifted to sleep.

At the same time, Noel awoke from his deep slumber. Still not fully alert, he could only focus on his incredible thirst. The events of the evening came back to him as he opened his eyes and realized that he was naked on top of the sheets. Quickly, he looked beside him expecting to find Jade also taking a nap, but the bed was empty. Assuming that she was in the bathroom, he got up and walked across the room, unconcerned by his naked state.

"Jade?" he inquired, as he knocked on the door of the master bathroom. When there was no response, he tried the door to see if it was locked. It was not, so he swung it open. "Jade?" he called again.

The room was dark and empty.

She must be in one of the other bedrooms, he told himself, and went to check. She was not in them either. Puzzled, he went back to his bedroom and pulled on a toweling robe. While tying the belt, he noticed her bra and panties on the floor by the edge of the bed. Either Jade was still there, somewhere, or she had left them behind. Even more perplexed, Noel went downstairs to the front door. Glancing outside, it was obvious that Jade's car was gone.

Feeling incredibly disappointed, Noel stared blankly out the window. Why would she leave without saying good-bye? he pondered. Maybe she was insulted that he fell asleep? Now that he thought about it, dozing off after sex probably wasn't the most graceful or considerate thing to do.

Suddenly, he was aware of how large and empty his house really was.

After drinking a couple of glasses of water, Noel went back upstairs for a long, hot shower. Other than refreshing him, it did not make him feel any better. He felt frustrated and almost unsatisfied. It was not that their lovemaking had not been good—it had been amazing—but he was sorry that the evening had ended. Furthermore, it had ended without his knowledge.

Why would she leave like that? He was not insecure about his sexual abilities or physical attraction, but he would have liked to find out how she felt. More to the point, he would have liked to make love to her again more slowly and thoroughly, allowing her to obtain a release as amazing as his had been.

Still caught up in his thoughts, he walked over to the bed and unconsciously picked up her discarded undergarments. They were made of delicate satin and lace—the type of underwear that was made for a man's touch. Noel sat down lazily on the bed, with a sigh. He really wished she had not left.

The next day, Jade stopped by Trish's house as promised.

"Hello?" Jade yelled, peeking around the front door. "Trish?"

"I'm in the kitchen," she heard Trish yell back. "Just a sec."

Jade let herself in and made her way to the kitchen at the back of the house.

"Hey. What's up?"

"Ian decided he was going to make breakfast for us, and this is the result," Trish explained, indicating with her gloved hands the dirty dishes, pans, and countertops.

"Was it good?" Jade asked.

"It was until I saw the kitchen. Now there's only a bad aftertaste," Trish analyzed. "Don't suppose you want to help?"

"Actually . . . no! But I don't mind watching."

"Your generosity is overwhelming."

"Where is Ian, anyway?" Ian was Trish's live-in boyfriend, and they had been going out for the past three years.

"Out playing football."

"Oh," Jade acknowledged.

"Okay, enough of the small talk, I want to hear the juice," Trish stated excitedly. "Who, what, where? And I can guess why."

Jade knew this was coming, and after a long night, she needed someone to talk to. She sat down at the kitchen table.

"His name is Noel Merson, and I met him at the studio," she started but was cut off.

"He's not one of your students, is he? I can't see you with a wimp running around in tights!"

"Not all male dancers are wimps, Trish, and he isn't," Jade lectured. "His niece takes jazz classes."

"Is he cute? How old is he?" Not giving Jade a chance to respond, Trish continued, "I can't believe you went out with someone, on a date."

"It's not that incredible," Jade said defensively.

"Yes it is. For years you've been avoiding men like a disease. Do you know how many I've tried to set you up with? Then you calmly inform me that you've been out on a date? Damn right it's incredible."

"Okay, it's a little strange, but it just happened. I didn't even know it was happening until it was over," she tried to explain.

"Well, what does he look like?"

"He's tall, over six feet, and sort of big. Very cut actually, like the kind of guy who spends a lot of time playing sports."

"Go on," Trish prompted.

"Trish, he's beautiful, not just cute, but the kind of guy that women dream about, the kind of guy who usually turns out to be too good to be true. He must be mixed or something because his eyes are halfway between brown and green, and his hair has the softest, fattest curls. And he has the sexy goatee thing going on."

By then, Trish had stopped cleaning and was leaning against the countertop.

"He's actually a nice guy, too. None of the attitude or arrogance that most good-looking guys have. You know, like a woman should feel privileged to be in their presence."

Trish nodded in understanding.

"What did you guys do?" Trish asked.

So Jade decided to begin at the beginning. "He took me out for lunch at this really nice Italian restaurant near the studio."

"Did he pay?"

"Yeah, he did. I even offered to pay my half, but he insisted," Jade explained.

"He sounds really nice. Then what happened?"

"He invited me back to his house."

"Excuse me?" Trish was suddenly sitting at the kitchen table beside Jade.

"We went back to his house."

"And . . . ?"

"And . . . we listened to some music, drank some wine . . . and then had sex." The last admission came out whisper-quiet.

"Uh, can you repeat that last part? I'm sure I heard you wrong."

"All right! We had sex. He made love to me and it was great!" Jade said defensively.

Trish started laughing.

"What's so funny?"

"Jade, you kill me. You have finally joined the land of the living," she said, still smiling. "How was it?"

"It was nice," Jade responded, still a little embarrassed by her behavior.

"Nice?" Trish prompted.

"Okay, it was absolutely amazing!" she blurted, wanting to discuss her confused emotions. "I have never felt that much excitement before. All I could think about was how much I wanted him. It was frightening but wonderful."

"You know what it is, don't you? It's called 'withdrawal,' and you've just had a major dose of medicine," she joked.

"It's not funny!" Jade said giggling.

"Seriously though, Jade, I'm not even surprised when I really think about it. You wanted a man. You've just had all those lustful urges built up for so long that you finally exploded," she analyzed, a big grin on her face.

"No. It's more than that. I haven't thought about sex for a long time, and intellectually, I didn't want a man intimately ever again. But it's like my body just took over."

"Well, I still think it's a good thing. Now you can begin living normally instead of like a half-dead person."

"Trish, this is going to sound weird, but I've never had the big 'O.' In fact, I don't even know if it really exists."

"Trust me, it exists," Trish said. "You said last night was amazing, but it didn't happen?" she continued, confused.

"Well, before, like with Peter, sex was okay but hardly anything to dream about. Noel made me feel explosive. Kind of like I was building up to something, but I'm not sure what," Jade explained, as she got up and began to pace with nervous energy. "I just felt that I was so close to what could only be an orgasm. Is that possible?"

"Why not? I read somewhere that women have to learn how to have one, while it comes naturally to men. Maybe you're starting to learn."

"Yeah, well it's pretty pathetic that I'm learning when I'm almost thirty."

"Are you going to see him again?"

"I don't know," Jade answered, nervously chewing on her bottom lip.

"Why not? You two seemed to have already started something."

"Well, we really didn't discuss what would happen next," Jade explained. "I don't even have a phone number for him."

"So? Just get it from his niece."

"I don't know. I just feel a little weird," Jade said with a sigh as she dropped back into the chair, her face resting on a palm propped up by her elbow. "It might be that he got what he wanted and is no longer interested. Plus, I'm not sure what I want. I don't need a casual sex partner, and I'm not ready for another relationship, so I don't see the point. And I know I didn't wake up yesterday and decide a man was the answer to all my problems."

"Then don't analyze it, just go with the flow, you know?" Trish suggested.

Without answering, Jade got up to see what was in

the refrigerator. "So, what's up with you?" she asked Trish.

"Same as usual: nothing! I need a life," Trish answered as she also left the table to resume cleaning. "There doesn't seem to be a point to it all. You get up, go to work, come home, then go to sleep."

Jade leaned against the counter beside her, chomping on an apple.

"Jade, I'm thinking about having a baby," Trish stated.

"Seriously?"

"I don't know. I'm so bored with life."

"Is everything okay with Ian?"

"Yeah, but the excitement seems to be gone, you know? It's like we're stuck in this monotonous routine and nothing's happening."

"Well, break the routine."

"Yeah, well, I've tried but—" Trish's words were cut off as the front door opened. "I'll tell you about it later," she finished in a whisper.

Ian Phillips strolled into the kitchen, 6'4" tall but with the grace of a dancer. His height made a striking contrast to Trish's 5'3" frame, yet they somehow fit perfectly. Jade watched in silence as he bent down and kissed Trish on the back of her neck. He did not even look awkward bending that low. Relaxed with his show of affection, he pulled Trish to lean her back against his stomach and casually draped his arms around her shoulders. How could Trish complain about being bored with a man who treated her so well?

"What's up, Jade?" he asked between nibbles on Trish's ear.

Jade did not bother to answer.

"Stop it, Ian!" Trish protested ineffectively.

"I brought a movie with me, but you two look like you could use a little privacy," Jade said, no longer embarrassed by Ian's playfulness.

"What movie?" he asked, still biting on Trish's ear between nudges from her elbow.

"That new karate movie," Jade replied.

Finally, Trish nudged him away.

"Cool, we were looking for it yesterday, but they were all out." Ian responded as he walked into the living room. "Where's the disc?"

Jade and Trish just looked at each other and shook their heads. There were two prerequisites for any movie that interested Ian: violence and sex. Like most men, he was not too keen on the "sentimental bullshit" that the girls sometimes rented. But Jade knew that it was just a front, ever since she had witnessed him laughing his head off a few years ago during *Beauty and the Beast*. When she had pointed it out to him, he responded that since it was a cartoon, it didn't count.

The threesome spent the rest of the afternoon watching movies and TV. It was almost like the ritual they followed on most Saturdays, except for the last few months. Things had come up every week either for Jade or Ian and Trish, so this time together was long overdue. They always had fun, and Jade never felt like a third wheel with them. She had developed a brother/sister relationship with Ian over the past three years, and he was as good a friend as Trish was. Plus, she never overstayed her welcome.

Since Jade was still a little drained from the night before, she left a little earlier than usual and was home by early evening. The first thing she did was to check her voice mail. There was only one message and it was from her brother. At thirty-one, Jerome was two years older than she. For weeks now, he had been bothering her to work with him on expanding his portfolio. He was a photographer and wanted to use her as a subject for a new series of photos. He was putting on the pressure and trying every trick in the book to convince her to do the work.

It was not that she did not want to do it, but Jerome could be so irritating when he wanted something. He always acted as though anything he asked for, any sort of favor, was owed to him. His attitude just bothered her! She already knew that she would agree to help him, but she just wanted him to sweat a little first.

However, that was not the real reason that Jade did not return Jerome's call right away. When she first heard his voice, for a second she had thought that it was Noel; then she had felt a tremendous sense of disappointment when she realized it was not. Logically, she should have known that Noel did not have her home number, nor was she listed in the directory. Her own rapidly beating heart both surprised and bothered her.

Irritated and frustrated with the whole situation, she spent the rest of the evening doing mindless, necessary chores. When midnight finally rolled around, Jade forced her body into a dreamless sleep.

Chapter 6

On Tuesday afternoon, Noel was sitting in his corner office on the twenty-third floor having a conference call with one of his clients. His desk faced a wall of windows providing a view of the Chicago cityscape and the coast of Lake Michigan.

"We have several boards prepared for the presentation. You were pretty open on the direction you wanted to go with the campaign, so I've put together a couple of very interesting concepts and themes," Noel explained to the CEO and VPs on the other end of the telephone line. He paused to hear their response. "Tomorrow morning is fine. Let's say 11:30? Perfect, I'll see you then. 'Bye."

Noel hung up the phone just as someone tapped on the door to his office. His best friend, Kyle Williams, popped his head into the room. Noel was the owner and Chief Executive Officer of Momentum Advertising, and Kyle was his Chief Financial Officer. The agency was eight years old and currently had fifty employees. Noel and Kyle were living the reality of a dream that Noel had put down on paper in his midtwenties after working for two years in an advertising sweatshop.

"You got a minute?" Kyle asked.

"Sure, let me just finish this," Noel responded, quickly keying in some ideas into his laptop before they flew out of his head. "Done!" he said when he was satisfied.

By then Kyle was lounging in the black leather couch placed near the door. "What are you doing Friday night?" he asked.

"Nothing, why?"

"Monica is throwing a dinner party for her newest clients. Do you want to come along? There will be quite a few beautiful ladies there," he added as enticement. He was always trying to set Noel up.

"Yeah, that sounds fun," Noel responded.

"I don't know about fun, but at least with you there it won't be unbearable."

"Is it okay if I bring someone?" Noel asked.

"Sure, but you only have three days to find a date. Do you think you can do it?" Kyle teased.

"Don't worry, I'm sure I can handle it. Actually, I have someone in mind."

"Anyone I know?"

"No. We just met, actually."

"Well, bring her along. As long as she doesn't mind obnoxious artsy types she'll be fine."

"Actually, she is one of those artsy types; she's a dancer," Noel explained.

"Really? What type?"

"What do you mean what type?"

"What type of dancer? You know: tap, ballet, jazz . . ." Kyle clarified.

"She probably does all of them. She's a dance teacher."

"Oh," Kyle said. "Well then, she'll fit right in."

There was a pause as Kyle watched Noel gaze at some spot over Kyle's shoulder.

"Well," Kyle said to pull Noel back to reality, "she must be very flexible." A mischievous smile was plastered on his face.

"What?" Noel asked, realizing that he hadn't heard what Kyle had said. He became even more curious when he noticed the grin that widened on his friend's face.

"Nothing," Kyle responded, sounding too innocent. He stood up and walked to the office door. "I'll e-mail you the details. See ya later."

Noel just nodded absently as Kyle left his office. Once again, his mind wandered. It had been three days since his date with Jade, and he wasn't sure what to do. He did know that he wanted to see her again. And again and again. He couldn't seem to stop thinking about her and remembering the silky feel of her skin.

It was so frustrating. Since he didn't have her home phone number, his only option was to call her at the studio. He hadn't been able to reach her on Sunday or Monday, and he wasn't comfortable leaving a message on the answering machine.

Pensively, he stared at the phone. Part of him didn't want to call her because he was afraid that their evening had not had the same lasting effect on her. He didn't want to find out that she had left his house so abruptly because their time together had not been good for her. If he wasn't so annoyed by the whole thing, he would acknowledge the irony of being worried about whether a woman wanted to see him again. God sure had flipped the script on him.

After checking his watch, Noel quickly dialed the

telephone number to the dance studio. Impatiently, he stood up and walked over to the wall of windows. His wireless headset allowed him to pace back and forth as his disappointment grew with each unanswered ring.

"Winters School of Dance," a breathless voice announced into the phone after the sixth ring.

Noel was momentarily speechless with surprise.

"Hello?" the girl responded to the silence.

"Hello, can I speak to Jade Winters, please?" he rushed to say.

"She's in a class. Do you wanna leave a message?" she asked.

Noel checked his watch again. It was 4:45 and he would not be leaving the office for another forty-five minutes. "Do you know what time the class finishes?"

"Uh, I think it goes 'til five o'clock, but then there's an advanced jazz class right after."

"Oh." Noel's disappointment prevented him from saying much else.

"Do you wanna leave a message?" the girl repeated, sounding slightly impatient.

"Uh, no . . . thanks," he said before he hung up.

Noel continued to stare out onto the busy city streets while he tapped his fingers on the tinted glass. He had hoped that by speaking to Jade he could get a sense of where things stood. Now he was not sure what to do. After a few minutes, he shook his head and walked out of his office to speak to his executive assistant.

"Sarah, I've confirmed a meeting with Babylon Fashions for 11:30 tomorrow morning. There will be about six of us, so book the boardroom and arrange for lunch."

"Sure, Noel," Sarah replied. She was a petite Korean girl with blue-black hair cut in a sharp bob. "Coffee and soda to start?"

"Yeah," he confirmed. "Let Latonya and Pawan know. And tell them we'll meet in my office at nine o'clock."

Noel spent several more minutes getting updates from Sarah before he returned to his desk. At ten minutes to six, he began to pack his briefcase, and arrange notes and diagrams for his morning meeting. As he left the office and headed for the parking lot, he admitted to himself that he wasn't going home until he had seen Jade again. Coming to this decision immediately made him feel lighter, and after dropping his things in his car, he headed up State Street with a determined stride.

He could hear the music before he opened the door to the school, and it was pulsing through him by the time he reached the top step. The waiting room was empty, so he headed to the studio to watch through the window. He didn't want her to know he was there yet.

The volume of the music made it impossible for Jade to shout instructions. In any case, instructions were not necessary. They were all moving in perfect unison. Their quick, effortless strides, leaps, and kicks were flowing and full of energy; their bodies at one with the vibrating rhythm. Noel could see why this was an advanced class.

He continued to watch the students and deliberately avoided the cause of his anticipation. However, once the routine came to a climactic finish, Jade stepped forward to lead them through a series of stretches. She had on a purple racer-back sports bra and black thigh-length tights. Noel could not look away. The stretching of sleek muscle and the flexing of satin-smooth skin mesmerized him. His hands clenched as his eyes followed the swells and curves of her body. He knew that if he closed his eyes, he and Jade would be alone again in his bed, naked.

Abruptly, he turned away from the door just as the music stopped and the students enthusiastically applauded. The only visible evidence of Noel's struggle was in the gentle flaring of his nose.

As the sweating, flushed bodies rushed toward the dressing rooms, Noel tried to appear interested in one of the many posters on the wall. With his back to the studio he attempted to be casual, as though he were not waiting for anyone. After a few minutes, the talking and laughter quieted, and he was alone except for a couple of quick dressers who headed out the main doors. He glanced over his shoulder and figured that Jade must still be in the studio, because he was sure that she had not passed him. Impatiently, he read the same poster for the tenth time, not comprehending the images on it.

Ten minutes later, Jade still hadn't come out, and Noel's nervous tension worsened. He also realized that he was not as inconspicuous as he thought. As the trickle of bodies leaving the dressing room grew to a small flow, so did the number of inquiring glances in his direction. Unable to wait any longer or to pretend interest in the same poster anymore, he swung around and walked over to the studio doors. After pausing for a calming breath, he pushed into the room. He could not believe how nervous he was. It was pathetic!

Jade had been going through a series of routines

and exercises for tomorrow's classes. Unfortunately, her concentration was so poor that by the time Noel opened the door, she was at the limit of her patience.

"What the hell is the bloody problem?" she swore to herself.

"I didn't realize there was one," Noel answered.

Startled, Jade turned around to face him.

"Hi," he said as he walked toward her. She observed that he had obviously just come from work, since he was dressed in a dark gray tailored suit.

"Hi," she responded. Turning away, she grabbed a towel off of the *barre* and hastily dried the wetness off her chest and neck. Even after three days of wondering if or when she would see him again, she still wasn't prepared for his sudden appearance. She would have preferred some advance notice.

Nervously, she glanced at him through the mirror as he stood behind her. Their eyes met and clung until Jade looked away suddenly.

"I didn't expect to see you today," she said while quickly gathering her things.

"I hope you don't mind, but work ran late and I was just passing by so . . ." he paused, then sighed. "Well, that's not entirely true. Actually, I called and one of the students told me you would be here, so I stayed late to catch you," he amended.

She reached for one of the studio doors, but he beat her to it and then held it open as they exited. He did the same with her office door. The silence between them filled the room as Jade dropped her things on one of the two chairs in front of her desk. She did not know what to say, how to act. He seemed to be waiting for her to speak as he casually looked out the window.

"So," she finally said. "What's up?"

"Nothing really. What's up with you?"

She shrugged slightly. "Nothing really." She refused to mention that she had been waiting anxiously for him to contact her or that she could have killed herself for running out of his house like a child. Desperate for something to do, she reached behind the office door and grabbed her shell suit off the hook. After kicking off her dance slippers, she quickly pulled the pants and jacket over her dance clothes, then bent down to slip into her running shoes.

When was he going to let her know why he was there? As she straightened up from tying her laces, he was directly in front of her, so close that the arousing scent of his cologne surrounded her. Lightly, he touched her chin, tilting her head up until their eyes met.

"I owe you an apology," he stated with sincerity.

Jade looked down at his chest and swallowed nervously. He tilted her head up again.

"My only defense is that I had such a good time and I was so satisfied that I became completely relaxed."

As a teasing smile played on his lips, Jade suddenly realized that Noel was apologizing for falling asleep after they made love. Before she could stop herself, she started to giggle. It turned into a full-blown laugh when she saw the look on his face.

"Sorry!" she apologized, trying to cover her smile.

"That's not very nice," he responded seriously. "Do you have any idea what a blow it is to a man's ego to have to apologize for his actions in bed?"

Jade started to laugh even harder.

"If you don't stop, I'm going to develop a complex."

"I'm sorry," she said again with a hand over her mouth.

"That's better. Now, back to my apology. I can only assure you that that sort of thing doesn't happen to me often, since I'm not usually so completely satisfied."

Jade started to laugh again.

"You're not going to make this any easier for me, are you?" he said, still pretending to be offended by her laughter.

"It's just that I was so embarrassed about the way I left that I had no idea what I would say to you if I ever saw you again."

The smile that had begun to form on Noel's lips faded away.

"If you ever saw me again?" he repeated, frowning. "Of course you would see me again. Unless you didn't want to," he added when she looked away.

"It's not a matter of that. I know it sounds like a line, but I don't usually do this sort of thing and I'm not . . . oh, I don't know," she started to explain. "I guess I just don't know the rules."

"The rules," he repeated, trying to understand what she meant. "What rules?" Suddenly he was afraid he knew exactly what she meant.

Jade tried to hide how uncomfortable she felt about the conversation. She sighed, trying to find the appropriate words.

"To be honest with you, I don't know how to respond to this casual sort of thing. I mean, I wasn't sure what comes next," she answered, staring at his polished leather loafers. She didn't want to see the look on his face.

"What makes you think it's casual?" he asked.

The question brought her head up with a quick snap.

"What else can it be?" Jade walked over to the window behind her desk at the rear of the office. She stared out into the alley with her back to him. "I hardly know you."

"I admit things went a little fast, but we're both adults."

She could hear his footsteps approaching her.

"And I certainly didn't intend for Saturday to be a one-night stand," he assured her.

"I don't mean to sound old-fashioned," Jade told him as she turned around to face him, "but sometimes I find myself in situations that could have been avoided if I had been clear about things at the beginning. Do you know what I mean?"

Noel nodded.

"Therefore, I think it's best that I explain up front that I'm not looking for a casual bed-buddy."

"What *are* you looking for?" Noel asked, a gentle smile on his face.

"To be honest with you, I don't really know. I didn't realize I was looking for anything," she responded thoughtfully.

"Well," he said as he leaned toward her, resting his weight on the arm that was propped against the window behind her, "now that I know that I'm not invited to be your . . . what was it?" he asked snapping his fingers.

"Bed-buddy," she supplied.

"That's it . . . your bed-buddy, I guess I can't expect a quickie on the desk?" He whispered the last part of his question directly into her ear, his lips brushing her sensitive skin.

"I don't think so," she responded, slightly breathless yet trying to match his playful attitude.

"Damn," he swore, pretending to be upset, "then I better get something else for compensation."

Jade looked into his sparkling hazel eyes not inches from her own. Her breath caught as his gaze dropped to her lips. Her mouth suddenly felt dry, so she lightly licked her top lip, her tongue slowly skimming the surface. She was certain that she heard Noel groan softly before his mouth descended onto hers.

Chapter 7

"Explain to me why you don't have a boyfriend?" Noel asked as he sat across from her in her dining room. After a very passionate kiss in her office, they had decided to get something to eat. Since she was underdressed for most restaurants, she invited him back to her apartment for a quick pasta dinner.

"There's really no reason," she answered. "I just haven't been going out enough to meet anyone."

"Why not?" he inquired between forkfuls of food.

"I don't know . . . I guess I just haven't wanted to look."

She leaned back to watch him finish his second helping of fettuccini.

"I would have thought you would be out every weekend dancing up a storm."

"When I was younger, I had a lot of friends who did the dance club scene, but I never really got into it. I mean, it's okay, but they're such pick-up spots," she explained with a grimace of distaste.

"True, but people also go just to dance and have a good time. And some people want to be picked up."

"True."

With a satisfied sigh, Noel finished the last noodle and put down his fork.

"If I hadn't watched you make this meal, I would think that you were trying to impress me by presenting a restaurant meal as homemade," he teased.

"I'll take that as a compliment," she responded as she began to clear the table.

Noel followed her into the kitchen carrying his plate, then helped her load the dishwasher.

"Thanks," she told him as he put the last plate into the cleaning tray. When he straightened up, they were standing quite close, facing each other. Again, Jade found herself distracted by his wonderful smell and the inviting curve of his lips. Realizing that her stare had caused an embarrassingly long pause, she quickly glanced up at his eyes only to find them locked on her lips with equal intensity.

"Um . . ." she stuttered as she glanced away from Noel and toward her bedroom. "I really need to get in the shower. Do you mind . . . ?" She was about to suggest that they cut the evening short, admitting to herself that she was a little embarrassed and overwhelmed by her hunger for him, but Noel cut her off.

"I don't mind at all. Take your time," he said as he walked away from her and went into the living room. Obviously, he wasn't ready to go. He took off his tie and undid the top three buttons of his crisp white shirt. Silver cufflinks adorned his wrists. "I'll just watch some television, if that's all right."

"Yeah, sure," Jade responded, after he had already turned on the TV and flipped to a popular local station. Her anxiety grew as he sat on her couch and casually hooked an ankle over a knee. After taking a calming breath, she made her way to the bathroom.

Jade was determined not to let him see how nervous she was, so she took a little longer than usual, allowing the hot water and scented soap to relax her. Twenty minutes later, she emerged wearing a fitted white T-shirt with baby blue soccer shorts. Refusing to get all dolled up, she reapplied only the lightest coat of mascara and added a touch of lip balm to her freshly scrubbed face. She pulled her hair into a loose ponytail at the top of her head. Maybe her boring, plain appearance would send him on his way. On the other hand, it wasn't like he had ever seen her looking glamorous.

She took a deep breath, then joined him on the couch.

"What are you watching?" There was a commercial on.

"Just a sitcom." She jumped as she felt him play with the fall of her hair. He then put his arm around her shoulders and slid himself close enough to press a kiss at her temple.

"Mmmm, you smell sweet enough to eat."

Jade could only manage a quick smile as she desperately tried to slow her quickening heartbeat. By the end of the show, Noel had her snuggled so close that her head rested on the pads of his chest, and she was surrounded by the strength of his arms. The steady beat of his heart meshed with the pulse at her temple. Their silence made it easy for her to accept her position and relax.

"This is a very nice apartment. How long have you lived here?" Noel asked during a commercial.

"Thank you, I bought it just over a year ago."

"Where did you live before that? With your parents?" Jade knew he was fishing for information. She wasn't sure how much she was ready to tell.

"Not far from here. My mom lives in Florida now, but I've been on my own since college."

"Well, you couldn't have finished that long ago."

"If you're trying to find out how old I am, you'll have to do better than that."

"All right, but I was just being subtle about it. At thirty-three, I might be a little too old for you, since I'd guess you're about twenty-two, twenty-three at the most."

"Flattery will get you everywhere, but I'm an old woman of twenty-nine."

"That old?" Noel said, laughing. Jade slapped him on the shoulder. "You're very successful for your age, I mean, with your own business. Maybe that also explains the lack of spouse."

"Lots of women are single at my age," Jade replied. She was starting to feel uncomfortable with the direction the conversation was taking.

"True, but not women like you," he stated as he lightly traced the curve of her ear.

"What's that suppose to mean?" she asked, slipping from the circle of his arms to confront him face-to-face.

"Fishing for compliments, are we? I'm just teasing," he added after seeing the defensive expression on her face. "I only meant that you're the type of woman most men wouldn't let get away."

His eyes were once again on her lips. Jade looked over his shoulder to avoid his stare.

"You don't know me very well. Anyway, some men don't think anything is worth keeping, especially if it means working to keep it." She tried very hard to keep any trace of bitterness out of her voice.

"The smart ones do," he responded softly.

"I don't think it's a good idea for us to start a discussion about ex's, do you?" She still avoided his eyes.

"You're right. I'd much rather talk about you. Tell me about your family. You didn't say much about them on Saturday," he asked, sensing her discomfort.

They spent the next hour or so talking and exchanging sibling stories, and before they knew it, it was almost midnight. After a slight lull in the conversation, Noel picked up one of her hands and gently began to massage her palm.

"I'd like to ask you something," he began. Jade kept her eyes fixed on their joined hands. "I've been invited to a party on Friday, and I was wondering if you'd like to come with me?"

Her gaze flew up to meet his. She didn't know what to say.

"I'm not sure that's a good idea, I mean—" she began to refuse.

But he cut her off. "I would really like to take you with me . . . as my date for the evening." Sensing her hesitation, Noel leaned down and brushed his lips against hers. "Say yes," he tried to persuade her.

"What sort of party is it?"

"A friend is hosting it at her art gallery. Knowing her, it'll be something very elegant with food and a little dancing. She has one of these a couple of times a year," Noel described while teasingly brushing her bottom lip with the pad of his thumb.

"All right." Again, she was breathless from his nearness.

Jade was slowly realizing that Noel was the type of person who liked to touch. Whether it was softly brushing her shoulders or playing with her fingers while they talked, he had not let go of her since she had sat down beside him. She had to admit it was nice even though it did funny things to her lower stomach. She tried to ignore the sexual tension his caresses created, since he seemed to be unaware of what his hands were doing. As it got later, her anxiety had grown.

"Well, now that that is settled, I better get going." With that, he took one of her hands in his, stood up, and pulled her with him to the front hallway. "What time does your last class finish on Friday?"

"At 5:30," she answered, watching him shrug into his suit jacket.

"Okay. I'll call you tomorrow and let you know what time I'll pick you up."

Jade nodded faintly.

"Well," he said as he took her hand again and walked the last few steps to the front door. With a tug, he pulled her directly in front of him. "I had a nice evening. Thank you for inviting me over."

Jade did not have time to respond before his mouth came down on hers in a light, brushing kiss that lasted mere seconds. Noel lifted his head and let go of her hand as he reached behind himself for the door handle. He opened the door a crack.

"I'll talk to you tomorrow."

Jade nodded, still without speaking, then reached up to play with a button on his shirt. Now that he was leaving, she wanted to touch him, to keep him with her. When her knuckles brushed the light dust of hair on his chest, his hand came up to still hers. She could hear his labored breathing.

"I have to go," Noel said urgently and so softly that she barely heard him. His other hand reached up to clasp the back of her head and he kissed her with unleashed intensity. Jade gave herself to the embrace and allowed her arms to fall around his neck. Both of his arms moved lower to the arch of her back. She wanted more.

Without considering the consequences, she slid her hands down his chest inside his jacket, lightly brushing his flat nipples through the expensive cotton. When he groaned lightly, she brushed them again.

Noel responded by deepening the kiss, his tongue teasing and thrusting against hers. His hands slid lower to cup her bottom, bringing their bodies into full contact. His lips trailed away from her mouth to slide erotically down to bite and nibble her neck. He rhythmically rubbed her hips against the hot, bold thrust of his obvious arousal.

As Noel tried to lean their bodies against the door and deepen their touch, it closed with a loud thud. The sound brought them both crashing to reality. Neither of them moved except for the rise and fall of their chests as they tried to slow their heart rates. The only sound for several seconds was their deep breathing.

Noel slid his hands up her back and wrapped his arms around her in a deep hug. "I have to go," he repeated softly in her ear before he kissed her lobe.

Jade nodded as she stepped out of his arms and wrapped hers around her waist. Their eyes met and held for a second before Noel opened the door and closed it softly behind him as he left.

Slowly, Noel made his way down the hallway and stopped to wait for the elevator. As he licked his lips, he could still taste her. He could not stop himself from glancing back at her door, wishing he did not have to leave. When the elevator doors opened, he was still deep in thought until he sensed a movement at the other end of the hallway to his left. He paused. When he finally stepped into the elevator, he could have sworn that the exit door had opened and closed. It was as though someone had been watching the hall. But no one came out from the staircase. Strange, he thought. The elevator doors closed and his thoughts returned to Jade.

Chapter 8

Jade was running out of time. She was expecting Noel at eight o'clock and only had another twenty minutes to get ready. All she had left to do was her makeup and hair.

The last three days had been really hectic. A quick glance through her closet had revealed that there was nothing suitable for her to wear to a gallery function. In fact, Jade could not remember the last time she had gone to a party like the one tonight. She had been out a few times over the last couple of years, but this time it was different. She wanted to make an impression; she wanted to look and feel beautiful and sexy. At other functions over the years, she had wanted only to look suitable, maybe even invisible, since there wasn't anyone she wanted to impress.

There were other things that would be unusual for her. She would be among strangers and on the arm of a very attractive man. She was going to meet his friends and she was going to look her best.

In addition to a new dress and shoes, Jade even had to update her makeup. Trish had forced her to visit the M·A·C Cosmetics counter for a makeover. As she nervously blotted her new glossy dark red lipstick, she had to admit that the overall effect in the mirror was impressive. It was a big difference from sweat clothes and a ponytail, and she liked what she saw.

For a May evening, the night air was still very cool. Jade was going to have to wear a coat. She slipped on her new sling-back black shoes and was just tying the belt on her leather jacket when Noel knocked on the door. According to her watch, he was almost five minutes early. She was standing in the foyer, but Jade waited for a second knock before answering. She needed those extra seconds to take a few deep breaths.

"Hi," she said, swinging the door open for him to enter.

Noel responded with a quick peck on her lips. "These are for you," he said as he presented her with a bouquet of one dozen cream roses mixed with white baby's breath.

"Oh, they're beautiful! Thank you," she gushed before she sniffed the warm fragrance they exuded. "I'll put them in water."

Noel followed her into the kitchen and took down her glass vase from the highest cupboard for her as she took out a pair of scissors. "Are you ready?" he asked.

"Yeah, I just need to grab my purse."

"I'll do this," he said, gently taking the scissors out of her hand.

"Thanks, I'll just be a second."

She was back in under two minutes, carrying a small black purse. "Ready."

Noel had just finished putting the arrangement of flowers on her coffee table.

"Great," he said as he walked toward her. "Kyle told me to be there by 8:30, so we're right on time."

While they made their way through the lobby of her building, Noel told Jade a little about Kyle and his girl-friend, Monica. She owned a gallery in the core of the city near the Sears Tower. She featured new artists in all mediums but primarily African Americans. Monica had these parties once or twice a year to celebrate the success of recent shows and to introduce upcoming artists. There would be 100 to 150 people socializing and dancing.

Within twenty minutes, Noel was pulling the Audi TT into a spot behind the renovated storefront location.

"Are you okay?" he asked her when he opened the passenger door and watched as she hesitated to leave the car.

"I know it sounds silly, but I have to tell you that I'm really nervous." She looked up at him, still biting her lip.

"Trust me, you have nothing to worry about. Come on." He took her hand to help her out of the vehicle and closed the door behind her.

A muscle-bound guy dressed in black opened the door to the Monica Brown Gallery. Once they were inside, he helped Jade out of her coat. Meanwhile, Noel walked into the main room to join one of his employees who had called out to him. Jade thanked the bouncer for his help, then turned around to face the gallery.

Already, the party was filled with about seventy people of all different types. There were several people by themselves, casually looking at the numerous pieces of art. Others were gathered in small groups talking and laughing, or lounging in the assortment of couches and chairs. Everyone was dressed in expensive attire and seemed friendly and sociable. It was definitely a group of artists and art enthusiasts. She began to relax just a little.

Noel was barely listening to John Granger as he went on about a traffic incident that happened on his way to the party. Noel was too occupied watching Jade as she took in her surroundings. She looked stunning. His eyes followed her as she began to look at some of the sketches that lined the wall closest to the door. Her back faced him. She wore a slim-fitting, knee-length black dress with thin spaghetti straps and a low back. Her long, toned legs were wrapped in silky-sheer black nylons, and a side slit in her dress showed her right thigh.

Noel casually ran a hand through his hair, suddenly grateful that he was wearing a sweater that ended just below his hips. It easily hid his body's reaction to the naked skin at the base of Jade's back.

Noel realized that this was the first time he had seen her in something other than casual or dance clothes. Their previous meetings had always been spontaneous, and he had been attracted to her natural, sensual beauty. But this was different. Tonight, she was just plain sexy. There was also an elegant and unapproachable quality to her, as though she was unaware of the effect she had on men.

Jade turned toward the rest of the gallery, obviously searching for Noel among the unfamiliar faces. When she spotted him, Noel's heart jumped at the smile that spread across her face. As he watched her walk across the small room to join him, the sway of her hips made him want to confirm the length of his sweater. Her hair bounced with each step and created a glossy frame around her face. There was no doubt that she would have captivated him regardless of where they had met.

"Well, what have we here?" Noel heard John say under his breath.

A quick glance told him that John was also watching Jade's approach and was also enjoying the view. As she stopped beside him, Noel could not decide which emotion he felt more: immense pride or intense irritation. Irritation won out when he noticed that John's gaze never went higher than the soft, full swells of Jade's breasts.

After a quick introduction, Noel made their departure with the excuse that they were going to get drinks. As they walked away, he could practically feel the heat of John's eyes on Jade's departing back, and wondered if anyone around the office would notice if, come Monday, John was sporting a brand new busted lip.

"Sorry about that." He felt obliged to apologize for his worker's crude behavior.

"For what?" Jade questioned as they approached the bar at the back of the gallery.

Noel ordered white wine for her and a Heineken beer for himself.

"John can be a little obnoxious at times," he explained, slightly puzzled that John's ogling hadn't been obvious to her. He knew that many beautiful women kept a mental record of the number of men that gave them the eye.

"Really?" she questioned.

John had practically stripped her naked with his eyes. How could she not have noticed? Kyle saved Noel from further speculation and discussion.

"You made it," Kyle said as he came up behind them. "And you did find a date after all."

"Very funny," Noel replied as he handed Jade her wine and picked up his beer.

When Jade turned to face Kyle, she found a slender, dark man with perfect dreadlocks that fell below his shoulders. Noel made the introductions.

"The dancer, I presume," Kyle stated with a knowing raise of his eyebrows.

Jade decided to play a trick on him. "Dancer? I'm not a dancer! Noel, who's this dancer chick he's talking about?" she demanded, pretending anger as she turned to Noel, carefully hiding a wink.

"Oh, uh . . ." Kyle stuttered in an attempted at damage control. "No, uh . . . he, uh . . ."

"Relax, Kyle," Noel said, feeling sorry for him while Jade struggled to keep a straight face. "She's only kidding."

Both Jade and Noel started laughing at the look of confusion, then incredible relief that passed over Kyle's face.

"Well, that will teach me to make assumptions," Kyle said as he wiped imaginary sweat off his brow. "Did you guys just arrive?"

"Not long ago," Noel answered.

"Well, come," he urged as he started to walk the perimeter of the room. "Let's introduce Jade to everyone."

The next hour or so was spent in meeting different artists, acquaintances, and coworkers. After about thirty minutes, Jade stopped pretending to remember anyone's name.

At the buffet table Kyle introduced his girlfriend. Monica Brown was a very petite woman with a rich, dark complexion and natural hair shaved almost to the scalp. She was elegantly dressed in a white linen pantsuit. Even in her three-inch heels, she was perhaps 5'2". Jade thought that Monica was stunning. Immediately, she was drawn to Monica's confidence and style. As the owner of the gallery, it was clear that she knew almost everyone and easily kept conversation flowing. When Monica saw Noel, she grabbed both his hands and kissed both his cheeks in a welcome.

"Kyle mentioned that you're a dancer," she said to Jade after they were introduced.

"I'm more of a dance teacher, really," Jade clarified.

"I've always loved watching dance performances. There's something so graceful about movement."

"It's true," Jade agreed. "When I'm dancing, it's like gravity doesn't exist. It's a wonderful feeling, and it's just as wonderful to watch." Jade was surprised by her own outburst. She rarely expressed how passionate she felt about dance, or how powerful it made her feel. Both women easily went into a discussion about their respective art fields and the impact of modern culture on art appreciation.

"Does your studio ever put on any performances for the public?" Monica asked.

"Usually, no. But a lot of the kids lose their motivation unless they're working toward something. I've been looking into spaces that we can rent for an open house. I figure that the kids could show their stuff to their friends and families, and I can also do some advertising to get others to take classes," Jade explained.

"That's a wonderful idea." Monica urged. "Let me know what happens. I would love to put up some posters or leave flyers around the gallery for you."

"Great!" Jade responded. She was suddenly very excited about the project. Until now, it had only been a faint idea.

"If you'll excuse me, I see someone I've been waiting to have a word with all night. Get my number from Noel, and we'll keep in touch." With a quick squeeze of Jade's hand, Monica headed toward the front of the gallery.

Left by herself while Noel spoke with some friends nearby, Jade decided to take a quick trip to the bathroom. It was empty except for one woman fixing her lipstick. Jade took a few minutes to check the fit of her dress and to make sure her makeup was still in place. She was still quite nervous about how she was dressed. It was strange to reveal so much of her body outside of the dance studio. The dress was a far cry from her usual conservative outfits. She knew that she looked okay, maybe even great, but she was a little bothered that Noel hardly seemed to notice. Or, maybe he thought her dress was too skimpy and overdone?

Life was so weird, Jade thought to herself. It felt like just yesterday that she would look at women in magazines wearing tight, size-six dresses and think that her life would be perfect if only she looked like that. Back then, she had wasted so many hours thinking that if she were different, slimmer, Peter would love her more. She should have spent the time understanding that it was Peter who needed to change, not her. More precisely, she should have understood that he would never change and that she was better off without him.

Unfortunately, she did not see things clearly until months after his abuse had gone from verbal to physical and she had hit the lowest point of her life. The irony was that she finally left him not long after she bought her first pair of size-eight jeans! Tonight was the first time since then that Jade wanted to reveal the body that she had dreamed of having for most of her adult life, and had worked so hard to get.

With a deep breath to revive her confidence, Jade started back to find Noel. A few steps outside of the bathroom, she was approached from behind.

"Jade, is that you?"

When she swung around, she found her brother, Jerome, looking at her as though she had two heads. "What are you doing here?" he asked.

"Great way to greet the sister you haven't seen in weeks." With that statement, she pulled him into a hug. The last time they had seen each other was at the traditional family Easter dinner.

"Well?" he questioned as he pulled away from her, his arms still around her waist.

"Well, what?" she countered, playing dumb. Her arms remained on his wide shoulders.

"Well, what are you doing here? I mean, it's great to see you, but . . . damn, Sis, I hardly recognized you." He looked meaningfully at her legs. "So the butterfly has finally left the cocoon. You look great!"

"Well, I'm about to shock you even more; I'm here on a date." The last part of her statement was said in an exaggerated whisper, one hand cupping her mouth. At Jerome's raised brows, Jade giggled. "He knows the owner of the gallery and asked me to come with him. How about you?" she asked.

By that point they were standing beside each other, her arm around his waist and his still around hers. Jade was so glad to see him. It was as though she had been given a lifeline to grab onto and prevent herself from drowning. Okay, that was a bit dramatic, she acknowledged to herself, but having Jerome there made her feel less out of place, less like she had to hang on to Noel's arm the whole night.

"I came with Garfield," Jerome said. "His paintings were exhibited here a couple of months ago. Plus, I wanted to check out some of the photographs. You know, scope out the competition."

"Oh, I see," she said with conspirator's nod. "So, when do you want to start working on the photos?" Since she had finally agreed to pose for him, they had not made any specific plans.

"Jade, you're not going to believe this. I was only going to do the shots to boost up my portfolio; you know how much I've wanted to move away from commercial work. But a friend of mine told me about a musician looking for a new album cover. His name is Carlos Rodriguez and he plays Latin guitar. So, I'm going to present him with some ideas next month. Isn't that great?"

"Wow, sounds like a great idea." Jade was suddenly distracted by Noel, who was clearly searching for her in the crowd. When he finally did spot her, he seemed strangely agitated, looking over but sort of acting like he wasn't.

"That's where you come in," Jerome elaborated. "I thought a Spanish dancer, or something like that, would be perfect."

"But there's one problem, Jerome: I'm not Spanish."

"I know, silly," he responded, playfully punching her arm. "But, with a wig, the right costume, and my amazing creative abilities, you'd be great!"

Jerome went on to suggest some specific ideas. While Jade listened and occasionally contributed to the plans, she was very much aware of Noel's movements. What she was not aware of was that Noel was finding it very difficult to concentrate on anything that anyone around him was saying. From the moment when the well-dressed guy had approached Jade, he had been itching to find out who he was and how well they knew each other. However, his pride prevented him from going over to them or from asking anyone about the guy. It did not help that they seemed to be having a very interesting and lengthy conversation that entailed a lot of casual physical contact. At that particular moment, Jade was laughing, one of her hands carelessly resting on the guy's shoulder. And it also did not help that the stranger was tall, dark, and somewhat handsome.

"I'm told that competition is a good thing," Kyle said as he came up behind Noel.

For the past five minutes, Noel had been standing by himself at the edge of the room, unaware that the people he had been speaking with had moved on. The focus of his attention was obvious to Kyle even though Noel was doing a good job of not staring. Noel's mood became evident when he failed to laugh at Kyle's attempt at humor or to even acknowledge Kyle's presence.

"Do you know the guy?" Kyle continued, trying another approach.

"I was about to ask you the same thing," Noel responded after taking a long swallow of his beer. It was still the same bottle from earlier in the evening.

"Can't say I do. But I think he came with one of Monica's artists," said Kyle. "C'mon, man, you can't stand here all night trying to think of ways to kill the guy. Go over there and stake your claim."

"Kyle, give me a break. He's probably just some old friend or something. I might be feeling like a jealous ass, but I refuse to act like one," he responded as he turned his back to Jade to put his empty beer bottle on the counter behind him.

"Does this sort of thing happen often?" Kyle asked.

"I have no idea. We haven't been going out that long."

"Well, she's quite an eyeful. You kinda have to expect that she hasn't been sitting at home alone until she met you," Kyle said.

Noel had turned around again, still trying not to look perturbed, with one hand in his pocket. "Tell me about it. She didn't look like this when I met her. I guess I wasn't prepared to have to fight men off her arm. I don't think I'm up to it, to tell you the truth. I can't believe I even give a damn."

"Man, you've got it bad. Are you sure you know what you're getting into? She is definitely not your usual catch." Noel gave him only a dirty look in response.

Even though he was trying to tease Noel, Kyle was half-serious. There was more bothering Noel than just normal jealousy. Kyle could read Noel like a book because they had been friends for a long time: eleven years to be exact. They had shared some really good times together and some pretty bad ones. One of the worst was the Sandra episode, or episodes. There was certainly more to the story than the final act that had changed Noel forever. Sandra had been a very stunning woman. She knew it and needed everyone to know it also. Flirting with every man and making enemies of their girlfriends and wives was as natural as breathing for her. Even Kyle's woman at the time had had a run-in with her.

Now that Kyle thought back on it, he did not believe that Noel had ever really loved Sandra. Noel obviously enjoyed looking at her and thrilled at having her by his side, but she had no depth. She was only a pretty showpiece and that was all she ever wanted to be. Once Sandra's ugly side appeared, any feelings that Noel had had for her disappeared. He had even confided to Kyle after it had ended that he felt sorry for her because all she had was her appearance, and she had to be reassured about it constantly. Nevertheless, the whole thing had left Noel disillusioned and cold.

Kyle glanced over to Jade as she casually swept her hair behind her ear. Yeah, he knew exactly why Noel was agitated: he didn't want history to repeat itself.

Chapter 9

"So, where's this date of yours?" Jerome asked Jade after they confirmed plans to start shooting photos the following weekend.

"His name is Noel Merson. I don't know if I want to introduce you to him, you might scare him off," Jade responded.

"That was kind of the point," Jerome said as he flexed a thick biceps muscle.

"Anyway," she rolled her eyes. "See those two guys talking by the wall beside the drawing of the lion?" She watched as Jerome discreetly searched for the two men. "Noel's the lighter one with the goatee."

Garfield, Jerome's long-time friend from art college, interrupted her.

"There you are, man. You've got to meet this chick. I think she's the model for one of the nudes in the back." He paused as he noticed Jade for the first time. "Hey, Jade. How ya doing?"

"Okay, how are you?"

"Fine, just fine."

"So, where's this chick?" Jerome asked, pulling Garfield's attention from Jade's chest. He knew that Jade had never liked Garfield.

"Oh, yeah," Garfield remembered as he slapped

Jerome on the back. "She's near the front. Come on, we have to get going soon anyway."

"Jade, I'll see you before I leave," Jerome promised.

She nodded as she watched them walk away; then she made her way across the room to join Noel and Kyle. She stopped beside them to inspect the enormous and intricate sketch of a lion.

"Isn't it wonderful?" she said to announce her arrival. "From across the room, it's amazing. And I can't believe the amount of detail involved." The artist was somehow able to create an image of both control and power using black ink. When Jade glanced up to see Noel's reaction to her observation, she noticed that he was not really paying attention.

"Are you having a good time?" he asked glancing down at her with a blank expression on his face.

"Actually, I am. You'll never guess who's here."

"Really?" Noel stated indifferently.

At that moment, Jerome came up behind her, slipping a hand around her waist.

"I'm going in a few minutes. I'll call you during the week to confirm for Sunday," Jerome said, obviously in a rush.

"Okay," she responded, suddenly anxious about having her brother meet Noel. Jerome could be overbearing when his protective instincts were aroused. She was so busy watching Jerome that she missed the look that passed between Noel and Kyle. "Well, before you run off, let me introduce you."

"Noel, this is my brother, Jerome. Jerome, this is Noel Merson."

"Oh," was all that Noel said, as he looked back and forth between Jade and her brother, feeling like an idiot. He had to admit that they looked a lot alike.

"By the way," Kyle interrupted with a silly grin on his face, "I'm Kyle."

Jerome didn't appear to notice any tension as he shook hands with each of them. "Nice to meet you," he added politely.

"Nice to meet you, man," Noel responded. Again there was an uncomfortable pause.

"Well, I gotta go," Jerome stated as he reached over to hug Jade. "I'll call you." He nodded to Noel and Kyle before he walked away.

Jade noticed that both guys now seemed to be in a much better mood than when she had first joined them. For the rest of the evening, she and Noel talked and socialized and stayed close to each other's side. By midnight, he was pulling into the parking lot of her building.

"Thank you for inviting me out tonight. I had a lot of fun," Jade told him when he shut off the engine.

"Well, it was certainly interesting," he responded.

Jade nodded in agreement then looked at her hands clasped nervously in her lap. "It was pretty weird to see my brother there."

"Why?" Noel asked.

"I don't know. We don't really go out a lot together or anything. He always invites me out, but I never take him up on it," Jade tried to explain without saying too much. Now was not the time to let him know that she has lived like a nun for years.

"Well, he seems pretty cool," Noel said as he unbuckled his seatbelt and turned to face her.

"Yeah, he is," she answered with a smile while looking into his eyes.

She sat still as he trailed a finger from her ear down the side of her neck. His hand came to rest on the upper swell of her breast revealed through the opening of her coat. Their eyes unlocked only when his dropped to her lips to watch her lightly remoisten them with the tip of her tongue. Jade's eyes closed in anticipation of the touch of his lips on hers.

Breathlessly, she waited while Noel opened her coat even further and rhythmically brushed her exposed flesh with the pad of his thumb. But the kiss never came. When she slowly opened her eyes, it was to find his gaze fastened on the twin peaks of her aroused nipples as they pressed through the light material of her dress.

"Did I mention that you look beautiful tonight?" Noel asked. Jade only shook her head. She was throbbing and he had not even kissed her yet. "I think I better walk you upstairs now." With that announcement, he regretfully closed her coat to cover her skin and all signs of her arousal.

As they got into the elevator, Noel pulled her up against him as he relaxed on the rear wall. Jade found herself intimately pressed against his body, both her legs between his.

"What are your plans for the weekend?" he asked.

She was still a little off balance by their interaction in the car, and feeling his hard erection pressed on her lower stomach was not helping. Noel obviously wanted her to know that he was as stimulated as she was.

"Um, I have a couple of classes tomorrow, then nothing much," she replied.

"Well, we could go see a movie or something if you're up to it," he suggested.

The elevator door opened.

"Sure," she responded with a smile. They made their way to her door, their fingers lightly entwined.

"Okay, then. Call me at home before noon and we'll arrange to meet," suggested Noel.

Jade had already entered the apartment and switched on the light. When she turned to face him, Noel was not behind her as she expected, but was still leaning against the doorframe.

"Okay," she agreed. It was obvious that he was not planning to stay. Disappointment rushed through her so strongly that she turned away from him in case it was visible on her face. She then occupied herself by taking off her coat and hanging it in the closet.

"Okay," she repeated. "I'll call you before my first class." The smile she gave him was overly bright, her voice a little too loud to her ears. As she walked back to meet him at the door, Noel reached down and kissed her quickly but thoroughly.

"Good night," he said before he left.

Jade kicked off her shoes and began removing her dress as she headed for the bedroom. She didn't understand Noel at all. It was as though last Saturday had never happened. He was deliberately putting some distance between them when it came to sex. Now that her body had cooled down a little, Jade acknowledged to herself that a part of her was relieved. But why had he stopped?

As she slipped into a T-shirt and climbed into her bed, she was distracted by an unusual odor lingering in her room. Jade sniffed with disbelief. It smelled like stale masculine sweat. With a mental shrug, she dismissed it as something that must have blown in from outside. Then she drifted off to sleep.

The next day, Noel picked up Jade at her apartment late in the afternoon and drove her to a seafood restaurant on Lake Shore Drive in downtown Chicago. The plan was for them to eat an early dinner, then drive out to the suburbs to catch a movie.

The hostess guided them to a table at the front of the restaurant, where they could look out onto the street and watch the pedestrians and traffic go by. Once they were seated, Noel placed an order for a bottle of Ontario Chardonnay.

"What do you think?" he asked as he watched her take her first sip. "I know you don't like dry wine, but this one is very fruity."

"Mmm, it's very nice," Jade replied. "I'm impressed. Are you a wine connoisseur or something?" she teased as she took another sip from her glass.

Noel smiled back. "Not really. I used to work for a company that had this winery as a client. We were sent a couple of cases of their products to try, and I thought it was great stuff. I still order it when it's on the menu. And that's pretty much the extent of my knowledge of wine," Noel explained.

"What company did you work for?" she asked. Jade still did not know what he did for a living.

"A large advertising agency here in Chicago. It was my first job after finishing school."

"Wow, advertising. That must have been pretty exciting," Jade replied.

"It was my dream job. I remember when I saw the ad in the paper, I was so excited. It was your typical mailroom/gopher position, but I knew it was my in. I was going to do my time, lay low, until I could show them what I could do." Noel shook his head at the memory. "Two months after I started, they had an opening for four junior associates and that was it."

"You got the job?" It was more of a statement than a question.

"Yup, but it wasn't what I thought it was going to be."

"What do you mean?" Jade asked as she nibbled on the sweet, spicy cornbread that had been placed on their table.

"Looking back, I was so idealistic," he recollected. He paused to sample a morsel of cornbread that Jade offered from her slice. "Ummm. That's nice."

"So, what happened?" Jade prompted.

"Well, basically, I went from mailroom errand boy to office errand boy. My boss was this arrogant, fast talker who was the new golden boy of the firm. He had landed this multimillion dollar client and just wanted extra bodies around to make him feel more important."

Their waitress came by and took their orders; then Noel continued his story. "It wasn't horrible, it just wasn't what I had expected, you know?"

"In what way?"

Noel took another chunk of cornbread from Jade as he thought about an answer. Deep frown lines appeared between his silky eyebrows. "I guess I had envisioned working with high-profile clients, pitching sexy and original campaigns, directing photo shoots. There is that side to the business but not when you're at the bottom of the ladder."

Jade only nodded in understanding and waited for him to tell the rest of the story. She loved looking at him while he talked about his work and his past. His facial expressions were animated and passionate. She also loved the sound of his voice: smooth and deep.

She was surprised that she was able to retain any details of the information he shared with her.

"At the time, I was so frustrated and impatient with my place in the company. I loved the work and I worked hard. But I felt like they were taking my creativity and making me work twelve-hour days, and someone else was getting the credit and the financial rewards. Like I said, I was very idealistic—and maybe a little arrogant. At first, I didn't understand about paying dues to learn the business. Later, I just realized that I didn't like playing by other people's rules and struggling within someone else's hierarchy." Noel smiled slightly, then took a sip of his wine.

"You sound like a misunderstood rebel," Jade teased.

Noel laughed lightly as he topped up their wineglasses. "No, I'm not a rebel. Just very driven and stubborn when I know what I want." That statement was made while he looked into her eyes with a penetration that pierced her soul. Both were aware that the topic of discussion has shifted. After several seconds, Jade was the first to look away. She took a long swallow of the crisp wine, then regretted it as she noticed a soft warmth radiating from the base of her stomach.

When she glanced back to Noel, his eyes were still fixed on her. "What is it that you want?" she forced herself to ask.

"Everything."

The temperature of Jade's body went up a couple of degrees and it wasn't from the wine.

Their waitress chose that moment to place oversized plates in front of them. Noel immediately put his attention on his lobster, which had been steamed

with ginger and garlic, then chopped into large
chunks. Jade went to work on her mussels sautéed in
a spicy tomato sauce.

Both were content to eat without conversation, but
their eyes continued to flirt and entice with each encounter.

"How was your food?" Noel asked while the remains
of their meal was being cleared away.

"Very good," Jade replied politely. "But the lobster
was phenomenal! I've never had it cooked that way."
Noel had urged her to try some from his plate.

"I know," he agreed. "Would you like some desert
or coffee?"

"No, thanks."

"You're sure?" he asked as he signaled their waitress
for the bill. "So, what movie do you want to see?"

"I don't know. What do you want to see?"

"Anything's fine. But I have one request: please, no
chick flicks!"

"Not you, too," Jade complained with exaggerated
exasperation.

"What?" Noel asked as he shrugged his shoulders
attempting to look innocent.

"You men! You're all so afraid that your masculinity
will be damaged if you're exposed to the smallest
amount of sentimentality."

"That's not true," Noel denied. "I'm very in touch
with my feminine side. I just don't want to watch a
two-hour movie about it."

"Whatever. You're just like my friend Ian. You want
to give the impression of this macho exterior, but
you're probably a closet Oprah fan."

"Come on now, let's not let this get out of control.

You might say something that you can't take back,"
Noel advised as he counted out the cash for their tab.

"You are, aren't you?" Jade accused when she recognized the guilty gleam in his eyes. "You're an Oprah
fan! Dr. Phil, too?"

"I don't know what you're talking about. And if you
dare to repeat these outrageous allegations, only you
will be responsible for the outcome."

Jade's response was to let out the burst of laughter
she had been trying to suppress. Noel gave her a look
of disgust as she continued to show obvious pleasure
in his discomfort.

"Fine, no chick flick. How about a comedy?" she re-
lented.

"Now comedy I can do."

As they left the restaurant, they compared what they
knew about the new film releases. They discovered
that their tastes were very similar and easily agreed on
the movie they would see.

The drive to the theater was filled with teasing questions and easy banter. They compared likes and
dislikes, starting with books, then with theater, and
ending with outdoor activities. Jade revealed that she
found guilty pleasure in crime/suspense and fluffy ro-
mance novels, while Noel admitted that he rarely read
anything other than the *Chicago Tribune* or the *Wall
Street Journal.* Noel had seen only two theater produc-
tions: "Chicago" and "The Lion King," while Jade
went often, mostly to smaller independent shows. He
played basketball in the summer and football in the
fall, and she didn't play any sports all. They ended up
sharing a good laugh about how little they had in
common.

By the time Noel drove into the parking lot outside

of the theater, there was a comfortable feeling of companionship between them. Noel took her hand when they left the car and held it throughout the movie. His touch was sensual and warm, even slightly erotic. At first, Jade felt uncomfortable about the constant arousal his caressing fingers evoked in her. She could barely focus on their whispered conversation. Then halfway through the movie, as they laughed and shared jokes, she began to relax and accept the unavoidable sexual chemistry between them.

Jade wasn't sure what she expected would happen at the end of the evening. She tried very hard to maintain a casual mood and not think about how much she wanted to feel the strength of his naked body against hers. Or how vulnerable it made her feel to want him so much.

Like the night before, Noel walked her to her door. And, like the night before, he left her with a brief but heated kiss. Jade was left more confused and conflicted than ever about his motives and her feelings.

Chapter 10

During the next three weeks, Jade and Noel fell into a comfortable routine. Friday and Saturday evenings were spent going to restaurants, to the movies, or relaxing at each other's homes. Throughout the week, they spoke frequently on the phone. Though they didn't discuss or define their budding relationship, it was clear that things were leading toward a mutual understanding.

At the end of May, Noel went to Toronto for two weeks to supervise the launch of a major campaign. Usually, he enjoyed the opportunity to travel for work. There were worse things than exploring the sites and women of a new city, all covered by a generous expense account. This trip was very different. Instead of checking out the local bars and clubs, Noel looked forward to returning to his hotel room and talking to Jade. On the weekend, he found himself wishing that she were beside him to explore the beautiful city and enjoy the multicultural food.

When he returned to Chicago, it was with the realization that he was ready for a commitment with Jade.

On Sunday afternoon Noel and Kyle were at an outside basketball court sitting on the bleachers, waiting for their turn to play. The hot sun made everyone sweat from the slightest movement. Noel had reclined on the old wooden seat so that he was almost lying down, legs spread wide. He chose that moment to check his home voice mail messages using his cell phone.

"Hey Noel, it's me. I hope you're okay. I thought I would give you a call; I haven't heard from you in a while. Give me a call, and maybe we can get together soon. 'Bye."

Noel pressed the erase button. Though she had not left her name, Noel easily recognized the artificial sultry voice of Helen, a waitress who worked at a nightclub downtown. It was Helen's third message in the last few weeks. He was surprised that she still kept calling even though he had not once called her back. In fact, they had not been together for almost two months. She was very energetic and slightly empty-headed, but she had a very sexy body that had kept him interested for a few evenings. He had been honest with her from the beginning and told her that there couldn't be anything serious between them. It might take her longer than most, but eventually she would understand and move on.

Noel had discovered many years ago that some women could not be casual about dating. No matter how much he tried to be brutally clear about his intentions or lack thereof, some women always freaked out when it ended. It had taken him a long time not to feel as though he had somehow misled them. Now, he understood that if they chose to believe that they could change his mind and make him want to marry them, that was their problem.

The second voice mail message was from Debbie, a flight attendant he used to get together with casually whenever she was in town. Until recently. Noel erased that message as well, swearing under his breath.

"Was that her again?" Kyle asked as he plopped down beside Noel. Noel knew Kyle was referring to Debbie, since they had spoken of her briefly on their way to the court.

"Yeah. I don't get it. She seemed okay when I told her that I wouldn't be seeing her anymore," Noel responded. "The last time I went to her house was the day after Monica's party. We didn't do anything, but I could tell she had been expecting us to have sex. Actually, we hadn't ever really done anything but have sex. Anyway, I told her that I had met someone, so we couldn't continue getting together."

Noel shook his head, wondering how he had gotten himself in his current situation.

"What did she say?" Kyle asked. He had a towel draped over his head to block out the late afternoon sun.

"She said it was too bad, and I should call her if things didn't work out."

"Does Jade know anything about her?"

"No. I mean, it wasn't like Debbie and I were anything more than casual partners. She was only in town a couple of times a month. And she was very vocal about wanting to stay unattached. But now she's acting like I broke her heart or something," Noel explained. "She just keeps calling and asking if we can get together and that sort of thing."

"Well, from the way she's been calling you, it sounds like her competitive instincts are in overdrive."

"I guess," Noel said shaking his head.

"What are you going to do?"

"I don't know, man. Maybe I shouldn't have told

her about Jade. Plus, after that first night, Jade and I haven't slept together. Partly because I didn't want her to think that I was sleeping with other people at the same time, you know?"

They both stopped the conversation to watch a heated interaction on the court. As usual, the players were disagreeing on a foul call.

"I can't keep putting things off, though. With Jade, I mean. I don't think my body will let me 'cause I swear I'm about to explode," Noel continued.

"I can't even understand why you're letting Debbie get in the way of you and Jade, anyway," Kyle said, his eyes glued to the court. The current game was about to end, and their team would be up next to play the winners. "If you're not sleeping with Debbie, then what's the problem? You're not, are you?"

"No, not since I met Jade," Noel answered. He didn't want to go into detail and explain that he felt that Jade was not ready to resume a sexual thing. It was not anything she said, just the way she reacted to their intimacies. This thing with Debbie was really just an excuse, and Noel knew it.

"I guess I just wanted to completely end things with Debbie," Noel continued. "I mean, things were good with her, really hot sometimes, but that's it. With Jade, they're just different. I didn't have to think too hard about who I want to be with."

"Why do you have to choose at all? See them both. You said it yourself, Debbie's only in town occasionally, and it wasn't like you guys had a commitment," Kyle said with a sly grin.

"Yeah, I can really see Jade going along with that plan," Noel said sarcastically.

"Well, that's why I suggested it to you. I'm trying to live out my fantasies through you."

"And I go through hell while you stay happily in love."

"What? So you're saying you want to be in love?" Kyle pounced on the opportunity to understand Noel's motives. "Is that what I'm hearing?"

Noel dodged the question. "Anyway," Noel continued, "I'm going to ask Jade to stay over next weekend. You know, to take things to the next level."

"Finally," Kyle exclaimed. "I've never known you to wait this long for a woman since college. Usually, you're knocking boots faster than it takes to get a woman's number."

"Well, it's not like we haven't being doing stuff. But, you know, she's kind of different. Plus, I just got back two days ago," Noel responded.

"Yeah, whatever." Kyle dismissed the explanation with a wave of his hand. "It's more like it's been so long that you've forgotten what to do with the sweet dark meat. That's what's holding you up."

Noel slapped him on the head for the insult as they got up with the three other guys on their team. The current game ended and they prepared for the switch.

"Anyway," Noel continued, "I'm going to need the whole weekend to get over this dry spell. If something doesn't happen soon, you'll be visiting me in the hospital when I'm getting the swelling in my balls surgically reduced!"

On Wednesday evening of that week, Jade stopped by the lobby of her building on her way upstairs.

"Hi, Stuart," Jade said as she approached the

concierge of her building. "Is there a package for me?"

Jerome was to have dropped off the proofs from their photo shoot. They had done the pictures a few weeks earlier and she was anxious to see the results.

"Hello Jade," he answered with a warm smile. "You're looking pretty, as always."

Stuart was always so nice to her. It was as though he was always looking out to make sure that nothing ever went wrong in her life. He always did more than was required. He was a plain-looking man in his midthirties, bald with unattractive oversized plastic glasses. Jade felt sorry for him.

"Let's see," Stuart said, "here we go. Looks like it was dropped off this morning."

"Oh, great! Thanks a lot, Stuart. I'll see you later." She turned to leave.

"Have a good evening. And remember that the third elevator will be out of service tomorrow morning," he added.

"Okay," she responded.

As she turned the corner to go to the elevators, she overheard Stuart speak out in an angry voice.

"What are you looking at?"

Jade didn't hear anyone reply. Then again, she hadn't even seen anyone else in the front lobby.

"I'm watching you! Don't think I don't know what's going on in your mind. One slip up, just one, and you're out of here!"

Who was he talking to, Jade wondered.

"And don't let me catch you anywhere near her apartment!"

Jade had paused to listen to the yelling, but she still

did not hear a response. Stuart was sweet, but sometimes he acted a little strange and overprotective.

As she entered her suite, the phone was ringing. She ran to grab it but heard it click into voice mail. The call display on the kitchen phone told her that it was Trish, so she quickly called her back.

"Hello? Hello!"

"Trish, it's Jade."

"I was just leaving you a message," Trish said with a laugh.

"Sorry, I just came in," Jade explained. "What's up?"

"I'm about to leave so I wanted to see if you needed anything." She was coming over to Jade's apartment to watch movies.

"Nope, I got the latest Morris Chestnut movie right here," Jade explained as she picked up the DVD jacket to admire his fine form. "We'll order Chinese when you get here."

"Okay, I'll be there in about twenty minutes," Trish predicted before she hung up the phone.

Ian was playing in a basketball tournament and wouldn't be home until late. Trish and Jade had decided to spend the evening together. However, Jade suspected that Trish was just depressed and didn't want to be alone. For the past couple of months, she had not been acting like herself. She kept mentioning that she wanted to change her life. Sometimes it was leaving her job as a nurse, other times it was leaving Ian. Most recently, it was that she wanted to get pregnant. Under normal circumstances, Jade would be thrilled that Trish was ready to have a baby, but not when in the next breath she was ready to end her long-term relationship.

Maybe Trish was bored. She was bored with the monotony of her life and wanted to create a crisis. Jade only hoped that she did not do anything too drastic and unfixable.

By the time Jade stripped off her dance clothes and took a cool shower, Trish was already knocking on the door. By 7:30, they were watching the movie and had disposable wooden chopsticks digging into chicken soo-guy, shrimp fried rice and seven-vegetable stir-fry.

"That brother is sooo fine!" Trish said when she finished her meal and put her plate aside on the coffee table. She was referring to the enticing image of Morris.

"It's those lips. Look at the way he licks them. Damn, I'd have his kids any day!" Jade added while munching on a fortune cookie.

"Forget the lips, look at those arms!" Trish observed.

"Good point. The whole package is so yummy," Jade stated; then they both broke into giggles like teenagers.

When the movie ended, Trish flipped through the cable channels while Jade began to clear up the dishes and food containers.

"So, where's Noel tonight?" asked Trish.

"Ummm . . . I'm not sure. I'm not seeing him until Friday."

"When am I going to meet him?"

"Soon, I hope. But you better behave yourself or you're dead," Jade threatened.

"How are things going?"

"Well, they're okay. I really like him."

"Do you guys spend a lot of time together?"

"Just once or twice a week. He was away for a couple of weeks on a business trip. But we talk a lot."

"Sounds like things are working out well."

"I don't know. I mean, there aren't any labels or expectations or anything."

"Is that good or bad?" Trish asked. They were both reclined on the couch watching the latest reality dating show.

"I don't know. I'm kind of used to being on my own, you know? Not depending on anyone. Part of me wants to give him everything, and the other part wants to put a hold on the whole thing. I mean, I don't want to have to start all over again when it ends."

"You don't think it will last?" Trish asked, her surprise evident in her voice.

"Come on, it's only been a few weeks. How could I possibly expect that either of us is thinking in terms of a serious commitment? Even if we were, I stopped believing in forever a long time ago."

"There's a big gap between forever and a couple of months."

"Well, anyway, I think it's too soon to analyze anything," Jade stated, trying to end the interrogation. It did not work.

"I never knew you were so cynical, Jade," Trish mused, watching Jade's profile as though she was seeing her for the first time. "I guess it's been a long time since we've talked about Peter and everything."

"That's because there is nothing to talk about."

"Does Noel know about him?"

"No," Jade answered simply.

"Why not?"

"Come on, what difference could it possibly make except scare him off?" Jade responded.

"Well, everyone has a past. I mean, eventually you guys are going to talk about old relationships. Other than Peter, there isn't much for you to talk about," Trish reasoned.

"I'm sure that conversation will happen much later than sooner," Jade said. "We haven't even started having a sexual relationship yet."

"But I thought that's how things got started? You guys were steaming up the room on the first date, weren't you?" Trish was obviously trying to wrap her brain around this new information.

Trish and Jade had not discussed her relationship with Noel during the past few weeks. That was mostly because Jade did not want to acknowledge to anyone that he was becoming a regular part of her life.

"Yeah, and it began and ended that first night," Jade explained.

"But it's been weeks! He can't possibly be doing without it that long."

"I've been wondering the same thing myself. I mean, we've been intimate in other ways, but he always sort of puts a hold on actual sex." Jade did not add that she often felt relieved that they had not gone any further.

"That's strange," Trish said. "Are you going to ask him about it?"

Jade suddenly put on a sly smile. "I don't think I'm going to have to. He's invited me over to his place for the weekend. No guy asks a woman to stay over just to have her sleep on the couch."

"After waiting so long, I don't think Noel plans to sleep at all!" Trish stated with her own sly grin. "Are you nervous?"

"Why would I be?" Jade asked, suddenly doing a detailed inspection of her nails.

"Jade, this is Trish you're talking to. We both know

that Peter was the last man you were with, and it wasn't a pretty memory. So there's got to be a part of you that's a little scared of spending a whole weekend with a guy."

There was a long pause.

"It's been four years, Jade. You look different and you're much more mature, but there are a lot of things about you that are still very much the same. I know you."

Jade still did not respond.

"I know this isn't going to help, but not all men are like Peter."

"I know that," Jade finally said.

"Do you really? Is that why you've gone on a grand total of six dates in all that time? Isn't there a small part of you that thinks Noel might treat you the way that Peter did?"

"What's your point, Trish?" Jade asked without answering the question.

"I don't really have a point," she responded. "I'm just a little worried about you. I don't think you're as together as you pretend to be, that's all."

"Well, don't worry about me, okay? I'm fine," Jade said as she patted Trish's knee in a patronizing fashion. "I just don't want to be angry and bitter and scared."

"Well, be careful anyway," Trish advised.

Jade only smiled. A few minutes later, Trish was putting on her coat.

"Are you going to stop over on Sunday?" Trish asked. They had continued the routine from the spring.

"I don't know, I'll call you on Saturday from Noel's."

Trish opened the door and stepped into the hall-way. "Yeah, sure. As soon as a woman finds a man, she dumps her friends," Trish teased while shaking her head in disgust.

"Anyway!" Jade responded as she playfully pushed Trish's shoulder.

"Well, have fun."

"I will," Jade assured her with a giggle.

Chapter 11

When Friday evening finally rolled around, Noel found himself in a dilemma. It was almost four o'clock in the afternoon, and he was going to have to make a phone call that he had been putting off for over a week. With a sigh, he dialed his sister's phone number from his office phone. Laura picked up the line.

"Hi, Munchkin."

"Uncle Noel, you can't call me that anymore. I've grown up, you know," Laura scolded.

"I know you have, sweetheart, but it's a habit," Noel explained.

"Well, you're gonna have to come up with another name, okay?"

"Okay." He would have to remember that, or she was going to ball him out every time he spoke to her.

"You're coming tomorrow, right?" Laura asked.

"Of course I am. You would kill me if I missed your birthday dinner."

"That's true. I'll get Mom for you."

Nicki was throwing a small family dinner for Laura's thirteenth birthday on Saturday evening. After that, Laura was going to have a few of her girlfriends over for a pajama party. Noel just wanted to let Nicki know that he would be bringing a friend for dinner.

"Hi Noel. You'd better not be calling to cancel," his sister warned.

"Never! I'll be there at exactly seven o'clock," Noel promised.

"Good, because Laura's driving me crazy with her excitement. If anything went wrong, you'd think she would commit suicide."

"Well, I guess turning thirteen is a big deal for her. She's having all the popular girls in the school sleep over at her house on a Saturday night. She was so excited when she told me that almost everyone she invited said they would come," Noel explained.

"I know. I just hope she doesn't get disappointed," Nicki added.

Laura always acted strong and confident, but only those close to her knew how vulnerable she really was. Noel remembered several occasions when she would go off to cry privately over some small criticism or embarrassment she had experienced, usually from her mother. She always hid her hurt from everyone. It was as though she was not allowed to feel pain and was ashamed to let anyone know that she did. That was why Noel was never really bothered by her attempts to be controlling and bossy. He knew it was often a defense mechanism.

"You're still bringing the cake, right?" Nicki asked.

"Yeah, sure. I ordered this great ice cream cake with a ballet dancer on it."

"Oh, she's going to love that!"

"Is it okay if I bring someone with me for dinner?" Noel asked as he prepared himself for an interrogation.

"What do you mean?"

"I mean, I'd like to bring a friend along . . . a female friend," he added before the question could be asked.

"A girlfriend?"

"I didn't say that, but she's someone I've been seeing."

"Sure, that's not a problem," she replied. Noel could not believe he was getting off so easy. "I'll see you both tomorrow," Nicki said before saying goodbye.

Noel sat there staring at the phone for several seconds. Now he was not sure he had made the right move. Jade was to meet him at his office in about an hour. They were going to a nearby jazz bar and bistro before they went to his house. Somehow, he was going to have to convince her to go with him to meet his family for this dinner tomorrow night.

He was not sure if it was a good or a bad thing that she probably already knew his sister from the studio. But he really had no choice, since he could not abandon her on Saturday night while she was staying with him for the weekend. And it was obvious that he could not miss his niece's thirteenth birthday dinner.

With a sigh, Noel resigned himself to telling Jade the plan as soon as possible. There was no way for him to predict her reaction. Other than the gallery party and the chance meeting with Jerome, they had not interacted with friends or family. He had suggested the weekend because he wanted to get closer to Jade, and not only sexually. For a reason he could not explain, he just wanted to spend more quality time with her.

However, the weekend was turning into a bigger transitional event than he had expected. Jade's reaction to this dinner would indicate to him how close she was willing to get. Never mind that he still did not know or understand his own needs or expectations.

At ten minutes to five o'clock, the receptionist called to inform him that Jade had arrived. When he walked to the reception area, he found her looking around at the décor. Noel was very proud of his office's image, and he took a couple of seconds to watch her reaction.

She looked sexy and casual in snug jeans and a halter top.

The offices of Momentum Advertising took up more than half of the twenty-third floor of the building. The reception area sat in the middle of the space, dividing the art and sales departments from the accounting, technical, and executive offices. Light maple hardwood floors ran throughout as did stainless steel and mahogany surfaces. Oil and watercolor paintings hung on the walls gallery-style.

Jade didn't notice Noel until she sat down in one of the four chairs upholstered in dark gray linen. She stood up again and stepped into the hug he offered. The smell of his aftershave filled her nose and made her sigh with contentment.

"Hi," Noel said as they moved apart.

"Hi," Jade replied with a smile. "So you're still in advertising." With a tilt of her head, Jade referred to the name of the firm in deep cobalt blue on the glass entrance doors of the company.

Noel only smiled, revealing the edges of even white teeth. "When I couldn't get ahead in someone else's company, I started my own. Would you like a tour?" he asked.

"Sure," she said.

"You can leave your bag here if you'd like," he suggested when she reached toward her large overnight bag.

Noel spent the next twenty minutes showing her around the office. He introduced her to the few employees still around at the end of a Friday afternoon. His office was the last stop on the tour. Jade glanced at the bronze plaque beside the door that showed his title. Once they were in the room, she could not resist walking over to the windows and looked down at the street.

"What a perfect view," she stated.

"I know. It's the reason I leased this space."

When she turned around, Noel pulled her into his arms and placed his lips over hers. The kiss was sweet and simple.

"I've missed you this last week," he added as he kissed her again, this time a small brotherly peck on the forehead. They had not seen each other since the previous Friday, the day after he got back from Toronto.

"I've missed you, too," she responded simply.

"Come on, let's head out so that we can get a good table at Evans's." He picked up his briefcase, took her hand, and led her out toward the reception area.

"Where's the bathroom?" Jade asked when they reached the spot where she had left her luggage.

"The women's is to the left of the reception desk," Noel replied.

"Thanks. I won't be long," she promised.

Once she was in the ladies room, she peered at herself in the mirror. She was nervous. Within a few hours, she would be at Noel's house and she would be there for the whole weekend. Earlier in the week, Noel had suggested that she leave her car at home and said that he would drop her off at home on Monday morning. So she had taken a cab to work and to his office, and was now committed to the weekend.

She knew that she wanted Noel sexually and wanted to spend this time with him. But she was still nervous. Her conversation with Trish was still fresh in her mind. What if she was not ready for all this? What if she froze and then started to scream in panic? Her fear was not unrealistic, since she occasionally still had nightmares. The really vivid ones made her wake up with the overwhelming urge to scream in terror.

Jade wiped off her damp palms on her jeans, then took a deep breath. It was going to be okay. Noel was going to make her feel as wonderful as he did the first time they had made love, and before she was able to think too much about what she was doing and the possible consequences.

Before she left the bathroom, she moistened her lips with lip gloss and ran her hands through her hair.

"Ready," she announced as she rejoined him. Noel picked up her bag and they made their way to the underground parking. He opened the passenger door of the Jeep for her.

Once he stood directly in front of her, his eyes were stuck on her glistening lips. A soft sigh escaped their lush fullness. He cupped her face between his strong hands and brought her mouth up to meet his. This kiss was the direct opposite of the chaste kiss he gave her when she first arrived. It was hot and deep, and it lasted forever.

"Are you sure you wouldn't rather skip dinner and go straight for the dessert?" Noel asked, while his tongue in her ear demonstrated exactly how he wanted to spend the next couple of hours.

Jade looked into his eyes but all she could do was nod. Noel brushed his thumb over her bottom lip. He closed his eyes as her tongue slipped out to wet his skin.

"Then we'd better leave now, before it's too late."

Three hours later, they walked through the doors of Noel's house holding hands.

"I know it's a little overwhelming, but I can't get out of it," Noel was explaining.

"Well, I could always do something else, then meet you back here," Jade suggested. They took off their shoes and headed into the family room. She sat down on the couch while Noel headed into the kitchen.

"If you would prefer that, then that's fine. But I think it's a good idea for you to come with me. Like you said, you do know them, and Laura never stops talking about your classes," Noel explained as he poured her a glass of wine and grabbed a beer for himself.

"The thing is that I didn't tell them who I was bringing, so it'll kind of be a surprise."

"Oh yeah, that's going to be a nice surprise," Jade stated sarcastically. "I can't wait to see the look on their faces."

"I think they're going to love having you there."

"We'll see," she responded to his optimism.

"Does that mean you'll come?"

"Should I bring a gift?"

"Actually, I haven't picked one up yet, so we can get one together," Noel suggested. He was smiling to himself as he picked up the drinks. Carefully, he brought them into the living room and placed them on the coffee table. Jade was watching the news.

"Thanks," she said as she picked up her glass.

"Thanks for coming with me tomorrow. I know it was a little unexpected." She only smiled in response. "What time will you be back from the studio?"

"I finish at about 2:30, so I'll be here by three," she estimated. He had offered her the use of his Audi to go to the studio.

"Okay, then we'll make a trip to the mall when you get back," said Noel.

Jade nodded, then took another sip of her wine. They lapsed into silence and became engrossed in the daily news on a local television station.

During a commercial break, Jade picked up her empty glass and his beer bottle, and went into the kitchen to put them away while Noel took her bag upstairs to his bedroom. It was the first act to emphasize the fact that she was going to be staying the night. As he put her things next to his closet, he wondered if Jade was ready for it. He also wondered if she would tell him if she was not. He was better off assuming that her agreement to be here meant that everything would be fine.

Though Noel was very anxious about being with her again, he was not sure what he would do if she pulled away or froze up again. Should he stop and discuss it, or just move a little slower and ignore the signs? For certain, he could not brush it off again by saying he had to leave or that he was tired. Those excuses just were not going to work this time.

Jade had not realized that he had returned downstairs until his hands circled her waist.

"I have something to ask you," he began, "and I want you to be totally honest."

"Okay," Jade agreed, holding her breath.

"Are you ready for this?" he asked as he pressed a light kiss on her temple.

Jade turned off the tap.

"Because if you're not, we can wait a little longer. I won't pretend that it will be easy because I want this very much; I want *you* very much. But I don't want you to think that your being here this weekend forces you to do anything that you don't want to do."

Silence followed his declaration. When she did not respond, Noel turned her around to face him.

"Be honest with me, okay?" he urged. "I stopped all those times because I could feel your hesitation. You would freeze on me like you were about to do something you were afraid of."

Jade still did not say anything, but her surprised glance at Noel's face told him that she had not realized that that was the reason things had not progressed further than passionate kisses and heavy petting.

He sighed. "Trust me, I didn't stop because I wanted to. Do you want to talk about it? Is it something I did that first night?"

He was referring to their first date almost six weeks ago. In response, Jade could barely shake her head no. She was reeling over the fact that Trish was right. A part of herself had been dreading being intimate with Noel again, even while her body craved his touch. And he knew it!

But she was not ready to discuss her confused and irrational feelings. She certainly was not ready to discuss the shadows of her past. All she wanted to do right now was to forget her fears and give into her body's demands for this man. If things got out of control, she would just have to trust that he would stop.

After all, she reasoned, that was exactly what he had been doing until now. She certainly could not keep avoiding the situation.

She was forced to respond to his many questions when Noel tilted her face up, making her look into his eyes. When she saw the uncertainty reflected in their depth, she made her final decision. Again, she shook her head to let him know that it had nothing to do with their first night together. Lightly, she ran her hands up his chest.

"No, let's not talk. I want to make up for lost time," she reassured him. There was no turning back. Jade ran her hands up the back of his neck, then pulled his lips down to meet hers while she entwined her fingers into his soft hair.

Noel was immobile for several seconds, but he eventually gave in to the kiss. It was as though they were both finally released from constraint and were free to express their desires. It was explosive. Their tongues and lips were entwined in a fierce dance as they exchanged wet heat.

Jade was light-headed with passion. She could feel the arousal emanating from his body, and realized that Noel was feeling those things for her. He had always felt them, but had stayed in control because he did not want to rush her. Now she wanted to push him, to make him lose that control.

While teasing his lips with the tip of her tongue, she trailed her fingers down his hard stomach and began to unzip his jeans. Noel sucked in his breath harshly, then grabbed her shoulders.

"Please tell me you're sure," he begged as he tried to slow his breathing, his forehead resting on hers. "I need to know before we go any further."

Jade slipped her hand inside his briefs and allowed the sensitive tip of his penis to spring free. It was enough of an answer for Noel. He groaned loudly, and suddenly Jade found herself sitting on top of the center island as Noel quickly dispensed of his shirt. She was too busy watching the flex and folds of his lean muscles to get very far with her own clothes. After Noel threw his shirt across the room, he unbuttoned her jeans and slipped them over her hips as she balanced herself on her arms. The sturdy cloth fell to the floor with a soft thud, but neither of them heard it. Noel was too busy trying to slow down, while Jade was thinking of how to speed him up.

Her hips were at the edge of the counter, so she let her hands slide back allowing him full access to her body. As he ran his large hand over her thighs, she let them open, silently inviting him to touch her. But Noel did not accept the invitation. He was determined to go slowly and enjoy every minute. He was afraid that if he did what his body was throbbing to do, he would be done in about thirty seconds. And Jade would still not be any closer to relaxing with him. He needed to know that she wanted this, the way he wanted it. So he was going to take his time, even if it killed him.

"Your skin is so soft," he said as he slid his hands up her inner thighs. Jade closed her eyes in anticipation of his touch at the center of her being. She inhaled sharply as he teased the flesh at the edge of her panties. But he did not explore there any further. Instead, he began to unbutton her shirt and let it fall open.

When he teased her sensitive nipples with his fingers, she opened her eyes again. She watched, nearly forgetting to breathe, as he cupped the fullness of her breasts through the sheer lacy material of her bra. There she was in a brightly lit kitchen, almost naked on a counter. She found it incredibly erotic and did not want it to come to an end.

When his soft lips swept over the exposed swell of her skin, she groaned deeply.

"You like that?" he asked, excitement making his voice quiet and deep.

"Yeah," she answered as he caught her eye. Slowly, she sat upright, then undid the front closure of her bra. She brushed the lace aside, exposing her fullness to him. "Yeah," she whispered again, begging him to touch her.

Noel stepped into the junction of her legs, bringing their bodies together in a teasing touch. She watched, languidly, as he brushed her skin with his tongue. She bit her bottom lip hard, trying to hold back the lusty groan that swelled up in her throat. But she could not hold it back when he caught a swollen bud gently between his teeth.

"Oh, that feels good," she squealed softly. "God, yes. Don't stop," she begged softly as he gave equally thorough attention to the twin globe.

Soon Jade wanted more. There was a tension building inside her and she needed Noel to release it. Gently, she pulled his hair until his lips left her breast and settled on her mouth. With the heat of her tongue, she tried to tell him what she wanted. When that didn't work, she reached down and gripped the base of his solid erection through the cotton of his briefs. She could not have said it any louder.

As her panties, shirt and bra joined the rest of the clothes on the floor, Noel still tried to hold on to his control by holding on to his jeans. And if Jade did not stop running her silky hands up and down his throbbing flesh, he knew he was going to embarrass himself.

"Let me touch you," he whispered harshly as he gently pushed her naked body back so that she rested on her elbows. "I want this to be for you."

Noel knew exactly where to touch and stroke her delicate flesh. He watched her taut body respond to his attention, heard her deep uncontrollable groans, and it made him feel invincible. He wanted to keep touching her swollen pink center and feel her slick wetness until she went over the edge.

"Oh, God! Stop, I can't . . . Oh, God, Noel!" she sobbed as he pressed a long finger deep into her trembling flesh. She shuddered as he withdrew then thrust into her again. Her back arched in passion, her eyes closed tightly.

"Relax," he urged. "Just let it happen, sweetheart."

He could feel her reaching her peak, but she would not let it happen.

"Noel, I can't take it!" she pleaded as her hips began to rotate uncontrollably. They were both damp with sweat.

"Just trust me." Noel was breathing heavily, fighting the overwhelming urge to thrust himself into her hot body.

"Trust me," he begged again as he added a second finger to his deep rapid thrusts. "That's it," he groaned. Her hips moved faster as he began to rub her swollen nub in deep circles.

He knew her moment was approaching, and he wanted to be inside her feeling her muscles convulsing around him when it happened.

"Wrap your legs around me," he instructed in a rough voice as he picked her up at the hips and carried her to the kitchen table.

"God, Noel, don't stop," Jade begged.

"It's okay," he promised as he kissed her repeatedly before laying her back on the table. "It's okay. Just keep your legs around me."

He paused only for the moment it took to remove his wallet from his back pocket and take out a condom. He freed himself from his underwear and slipped on the protection. Then his hands were rubbing her flesh again while he slowly pressed into her with the tip of his shaft. Noel groaned deeply from the intensely erotic feel of her tight warmth around his sensitive flesh. He withdrew, then went a little deeper.

Jade was sobbing, her back arched as she finally began to throb in climax. Noel thrust himself into her center deep and fast. And then he lost control, holding her hips and plunging deep and hard over and over again.

"Yeah, yeah . . ." he breathed as he lifted her legs to drape them over his shoulders, allowing him to go even deeper.

"Oh, God, Jade . . . Yeah!" he panted, pulling her hips to meet his uncontrollable thrusts as they got faster. And then he made his final deep penetration as he climaxed violently. As the shudders racked his sweat-covered body, he threw back his head in a silent scream.

They both took several long minutes to recover their breathing and their awareness of time and space. Jade was lying with her arms outstretched, and eyes closed, savoring the feeling of her first real taste of true passion. Noel, with his softened body still meshed with hers, brought her legs down, and leaned over the table to press soft kisses on the damp skin of her stomach. He then lay for several seconds with his cheek resting on her heart, listening as the beats slowed to normal.

Chapter 12

Jade let the hot spray of water beat on her back and exhaled deeply. She stood still for several seconds, absorbing the heat and letting the pressure of the water relax her. She had about an hour to wash, blow-dry, and curl her hair, then get dressed. It was early Saturday evening, and Jade was not looking forward to this dinner at all.

So far, the weekend had been perfect. Being with Noel was like nothing she had ever experienced or even imagined. Last night, after their session in the kitchen, Noel had suggested they take a shower together. She had thought she was too spent to do anything but sleep. Instead, she found herself all hot and ready while soaping his broad shoulders and running her fingers through his curly wet locks. Needless to say, the shower was not about getting clean.

They had made slow, lazy love again after toweling each other off, then fell asleep naked. When Jade woke up the next morning, she was using his chest as a pillow, and he was holding her breast like an anchor. As she got dressed for the studio, Noel barely stirred. She left the house quietly after placing a light kiss on his forehead.

In the afternoon, they went to the mall and got

Laura a wonderful pair of dance shoes that she had recently begged her uncle for. Together, they shopped around for a couple of hours, laughing and having a relaxing time. Now, while Jade showered, Noel was picking up the birthday cake at a nearby ice cream parlor.

Jade stepped out of the shower and wrapped a towel around her body. As she blow-dried her hair, she thought about this new phase of their relationship. Should she ask him to talk about his commitment to her? Realistically, up until now, there had been no need to discuss the limits of their involvement, and she just let things develop of their own accord. But with the level of intimacy they had reached, she was not sure she could maintain that same detachment.

Noel made her feel sexy and alive, but at the same time, vulnerable and unsure of herself. Jade was very afraid of letting herself get in too deep but could not see how to stop it, short of ending the whole thing.

While she wound the last couple of loose curls with the curling iron, Jade heard Noel moving around in the bedroom. A few minutes later, he lightly tapped on the door to the master bathroom.

"Just like a woman to take over the bathroom," Noel said as she invited him in.

"I could use the other bathroom, if you like," she offered, not wanting to put him out.

"I'm just kidding," he said with a smile as he stripped down and stepped into the shower. "What do you want to do after dinner?" he shouted over the pounding of the water.

"I don't know. Speak to me when you get out. There's too much steam in here," she yelled back.

"If you can't take the heat . . ." he shouted back before he started singing a ballad that sounded vaguely like a Bob Marley song. Noel was not a particularly good singer, but he pronounced the words with the melodic slang of a native Jamaican. Jade smiled as she went into the bedroom to get dressed. It always caught her by surprise when Noel let his Caribbean accent come out.

He was still singing when he entered the bedroom with a white towel wrapped around his waist. "I have an idea," he said as he went over to his closet. "Why don't we go dancing?" He pulled a pair of pants and a shirt out of his closet and threw them on the bed.

"Where?" Jade asked as she straightened her clothes. She could not help tugging at the formfitted top that clung to the curves of her breast more than she liked.

"I don't know what's happening tonight, but I'll call around later. We'll go somewhere that's not too dressy."

"Okay," she said. "I'll be ready in about five minutes," she predicted as she headed back into the bathroom.

After getting dressed, Noel joined her. His hair was still damp, and Jade attention's was immediately drawn to his new haircut. Noel's shiny jet-black hair was so short that each shaft formed only a half-curl. She had seen the cut earlier while they were out, but it continued to catch her by surprise.

She paused from putting on her lipstick just to stare at his newly revealed profile. That soft, tingly feeling was returning to the base of her stomach again. When Noel asked her a question, she was pulled away from her appreciative inspection.

"Do you think I cut it too short?" He was looking at her in the mirror while her mouth still hung open.

"Not at all," she mumbled, licking her lips since they had suddenly become very dry. "Why?"

"Nicki has been telling me to cut it for months." He slowly ran his fingers over the spiky cap of hair. "She thought I was acting younger than my age. You know, trying to hold on to my youth." This was the first time she had ever seen Noel show any type of insecurity.

"Were you?" she asked.

"Who knows? But it's been over a year since I've had it this short." Again, he brushed a hand over the spiky ends. "What do you think? Did it look better longer?"

"You know, I never really liked men with longer hair. But it was you, or at least the only you that I knew, and I liked it. Your hair texture is so soft that it never looked messy or out of control. But, I think I can get used to his new 'mature' you."

"Really?" He was watching her put on her lipstick.

"Really." Their eyes met in the mirror, and Jade paused while applying deep brown lipliner. Noel pulled her hips back until her firm buttocks rubbed intimately against his obvious erection. "You find it sexy?"

A suggestive press of his hips accompanied the question. Jade gasped.

"Very," she said faintly.

Noel grinned. "Then I'll just have to keep it this short." He still had her pressed against him; their eyes were still locked in the mirror.

"We're going to be late," Jade stated finally, her voice sounding stifled.

Noel leaned down and kissed her neck, his tongue

lightly brushing her skin. She could have sworn she heard him promise "later" before he left her alone to finish her makeup.

They parked Noel's sports car in the driveway of his sister's home a few minutes before seven o'clock. It was a medium-sized, older brick house on a mature street. As Noel rang the doorbell, Jade admired the immaculate garden of flowers that lined the walkway. Nicki had obviously put a lot of time into their maintenance, or she had enough money to pay someone to do it. The door opened and Jade took a deep breath. Unconsciously, she rubbed her stomach as though she had a stomachache.

"Happy Birthday, Munch . . . I mean, sweetheart," Noel said as he reached down to hug Laura. Her eyes opened wide as she spotted Jade behind Noel.

"Jade, what are you doing here?" she asked in obvious surprise.

Noel answered before Jade could formulate a response.

"She's here with me," he told Laura as he slipped an arm around Jade's waist.

"Oh," Laura said simply as she took the gift that Jade extended to her. "Oh!" Finally, she understood what was implied. "Cool!" She was grinning from ear to ear.

"Mom!" she yelled as she ran back into the house. "Uncle Noel's here. And guess who's with him?"

Noel and Jade didn't get to hear Laura's question or Nicki's response from the kitchen.

"See, I told you they would be thrilled," Noel stated as he gave Jade a light hug to his side. She was not reassured. Though she had met Nicki only a couple of times at the studio, Jade had the impression that Nicki was snobbish. There was nothing specific that had happened, just a feeling that Nicki looked at Jade as though she was somewhere beneath her. However, the whole thing could just be Jade's imagination. In either case, tonight would be very revealing.

As to how Noel was going to explain their being here together, Jade didn't know what to expect. She just hoped he didn't fluff her off as a casual acquaintance. Even though they had yet to put a label on their relationship, she would be very upset if his family thought she was just the flavor of the month.

The man who approached them from the rear of the house interrupted her thoughts.

"Have you ever met Vince?" Noel asked. Jade shook her head. She assumed Vince was Nicki's husband.

"Hey, Noel. How are you doing?" Vince said as he approached them. His hand was extended.

"Good, good. How about you?" Noel responded as they shook hands. Vince looked to be in his mid-forties with a medium brown complexion, balding, and slightly portly. He reminded Jade of one of one of her college professors.

"Jade, this is Laura's father, Dr. Vince Thompson. Vince, this is Jade Winters," Noel said to introduce them. "If you're ever looking for a good ophthalmologist, Vince is your man."

"It's very nice to meet you," she said as she shook his hand. It all seemed so formal to her.

"Jade Winters. That sounds so familiar," he responded as he mentally scratched his head.

"I own the dance studio that Laura goes to," Jade supplied.

Vince snapped his fingers. "That's it! The unbeatable Jade. I hear Laura talk about you every single week. She's very impressed with you."

"I'm very impressed with her also. She's one of my favorite students," Jade said honestly.

"Well, she certainly loves to dance."

While Jade talked to Vince a little more, she pondered whether he was questioning her appearance at this obviously small family dinner. Did he realize that she was Noel's date? Vince did not give any indication that he found the situation odd or uncomfortable. Jade then wondered if Noel often brought other women over for dinner, other flavors of the month, perhaps.

As Jade explained to Vince her plans for the open house at the studio, Laura bounced into the foyer to say that dinner was ready and that Nicki wanted them to be seated at the table. As they walked into the formal dining room, Jade was surprised that there were no other family members present. Noel pulled out one of the expensive mahogany chairs for Jade, then sat beside her. Vince sat at the head of the table and Laura across from Jade. The spot across from Noel and beside Vince was reserved for Nicki, who was still absent.

"Uncle Noel, why didn't you tell me that you knew Jade? How did you guys meet?" asked a very curious Laura.

"We actually met at the studio," Noel offered as he casually rested his arm over the top of Jade's chair. "You remember, one of those days that I had dropped you at class?"

"But that was ages ago," Laura said, as though every week was an eternity. "And you guys have been dating ever since?"

Laura was oblivious to her father's warning looks to stop prying.

"Just about," was all Noel said in response. He did not seem at all bothered by Laura's interrogation.

"That's sooooo cool!"

"Laura, that's enough," Vince said very softly. It was clear that Laura was just getting warmed up.

Nicki broke the awkward pause that followed when she brought out a large dish of lasagna, a pleasant smile on her face. Seeing the family together, it become obvious that Laura got her nutmeg coloring from her father's side of the family. Nicki had the same creamy-toned skin as Noel and eyes that were almost completely green. Her hair bounced below her shoulders with a texture and weight of someone with mixed racial parentage.

"Nicki, you've met Jade Winters, right?" Noel asked as Nicki busied herself making sure that the dish was perfectly centered on the table.

"Of course. How are you?" she asked politely.

"I'm fine," Jade replied.

Even though the table was already set with napkins and utensils, it was obvious that Nicki had more items to bring from the kitchen.

"Let me help you," Jade offered as she pushed herself away from the table.

"No, that's all right," Nicki protested. "I'm almost done."

"I insist." Jade was already behind her and headed to the kitchen.

Jade rested her hip casually against the counter as she watched Nicki remove items from the refrigerator. Idly, she wondered to herself which of their frozen smiles looked more artificial.

"Noel mentioned he was bringing a guest. I wonder why he didn't mention it was you? I mean, he must know that I would know you from the studio," Nicki said to break the silence after a couple of minutes. Jade was not sure if Nicki was asking a question or just making a statement, but she felt it necessary to respond.

"He might have wanted to surprise you and Laura," she answered faintly. The look on Nicki's face told Jade that he had succeeded, although "surprise" was probably too positive a description.

"Have you two been friends long?" The overly polite smile was back, along with a glance that seemed to avoid eye contact. Jade interpreted the question to be: *Is it serious between you?*

"Not long." Meaning: *Ask your brother for more details.*

"Oh."

As Nicki lifted a large salad bowl, Jade reached for the dressings and condiments that were already on the counter.

"I'll help you with these," she offered as they headed back into the dining room. Once Jade placed the items on the table, she took her seat again.

"Mom, this looks great! I'm starving," Laura said as Nicki began to cut the lasagna.

"Thank you, sweetheart."

The next few moments were filled with the sounds of everyone passing around dishes overflowing with rolls and steamed vegetables. Nicki handed out large sections of baked pasta. When the activity died down, the only sounds heard were the silverware striking bone china and the ringing of Austrian crystal goblets.

At family dinners in the Winters's home, meals were never silent. Someone was always telling a story or making fun of someone else. Jade knew that not every family was as verbal or as energetic as hers, but it was at moments like this that she really missed them. Even Laura was unusually silent.

As Jade looked around at the others completely engrossed in eating, she caught Noel's eye. He paused, a forkful of pasta halfway to his mouth, and gave her an encouraging, teasing smile. Jade smiled back, then returned to her food. All of a sudden, the silence was not so bad, since it left her alone with her thoughts. Who would have thought that a haircut would make him look even sexier?

Chapter 13

The music was booming to a Latin beat. The dancers were moving in the intricate steps of the salsa filled with fast footwork and dizzying spins. It was a small club in downtown Chicago, and there was standing room only as spectators lined the edge of the dance floor and watched the display of skill. One dancer in particular stood out. Noel exuded tall grace as he effortlessly guided his partner through the moves he spontaneously choreographed. He seemed so at ease in this setting that he could almost be taken for a Spaniard.

After Laura's birthday dinner, Noel had suggested that Jade practice her Spanish dancing. A friend of his owned a club, and once a month they had a Latin night. After a quick call to confirm their plans, they left his sister's house very shortly after nine o'clock.

Oddly, Noel had suggested that they be on their way just after Nicki served the cake they had brought. Jade had been so relieved to be out of that awkward situation that she didn't notice the subtle friction between Nicki and her brother. She was certain that Noel's sister disapproved of her, though she wasn't sure why.

Before they arrived at the club, they had stopped at a popular dessert café for coffee. Jade had taken that opportunity to suggest they visit Trish and Ian the following afternoon before she headed home. She was pleasantly surprised that Noel thought it was a great idea. The way he agreed to the spontaneous plan was refreshing. There was no "We'll see" or "What are we going to do there?" or "What kind of people are they?" In other words, there were no questions, just an acceptance of what she wanted to do. It was also acceptance of the fact that they were extending the parameters of their relationship.

Jade would also have been relieved if she had known why Noel was pleased by the invitation to meet her close friends. To him it meant that she was on the same wavelength as he was when he invited her to Laura's dinner. As for Nicki's strange reaction to Jade, Noel labeled it as unimportant and put it out of his mind.

When the song finished, Noel twirled his partner for the last time, thanked her for the dance, then made his way back to Jade. She was waiting for him near the bar, a barely touched glass of Sangria still in her hand. While maneuvering his way through the crowd, Noel watched with amusement as some guy from the end of the bar repeatedly tried to catch Jade's eye. Noel stepped up his pace when it became obvious that the guy was no longer going to be subtle and as he started making his way to approach her. As smoothly as possible, Noel stepped up to stand beside Jade, avoiding an embarrassing situation.

"Did you miss me?" he whispered into her ear, causing her to jump. She smiled when she realized it was Noel and was oblivious to the nod of acknowledgment that Noel gave to her thwarted admirer. The look in Noel's eyes forced the guy to continue on his way, almost without pause.

"Are you having a good time?" he asked her.

"Very good. You weren't kidding when you said you could teach me to salsa," she responded. "When did you learn?"

"When I was younger," Noel answered simply. "Now it's your turn." He took the drink out of her hand and rested it on a table nearby. Then, he took both of her hands and pulled her to the edge of the dance floor.

"No, wait. I don't know what I'm doing," Jade protested over the beat of the music.

"Give me a break, Miss Dancer. I know you haven't forgotten my lesson already," he said as he pulled her close. "Just follow me and you can't go wrong."

They spent the next couple of hours having a great time. They made up their own moves until Jade was able to pick up the traditional steps, then switched partners several times with couples around them.

They also shared their first slow dance to a sad Latin ballad, their bodies sharing one heartbeat. Jade was too mesmerized to say anything. She knew a lot of men who could rip up the dance floor with the hottest club moves, but none held a candle to Noel. He was able to move his hips with a natural grace that she had not expected. He continued to surprise her.

They danced together for three more slow songs, then went to the bar to cool off before heading back to the dance floor. It was almost 2:30 in the morning when they left the club, and they were both starving.

"How about pizza?" Jade suggested. "Or Chinese?"

Noel had another idea. "Have you ever had West Indian food?" he asked.

"A couple of times," she responded. "Is that what you feel like?"

"Well, there's a place up here near Wrigley field

that's open all night." They were almost at his car, parked in an outdoor lot. He opened the door for her. "Do you want to go there?"

"Sure," Jade replied.

"Now, I'll warn you: Winstons's is for true West Indians looking for some authentic cooked food, not for Americans wanting to try some interesting 'Caribbean cuisine.' Are you sure you can take it?" Noel put it out there as a clear challenge.

"Don't you worry about me," she responded arrogantly. "I can handle myself just fine."

"All right. Don't say I didn't warn you."

"Whatever," Jade replied as they both laughed.

When they pulled into the small parking lot next to the restaurant, Noel asked her if she wanted to eat there or take the food with them. They decided that since they were only a few minutes from his house they would take their meals to go.

Though it was almost three o'clock in the morning, Winstons's was packed with late-night partygoers. The line for the cafeteria-style take-out counter extended out the door. The people waiting to be served represented every shade of West Indian from the dark of Africa to the red of India.

While they waited in line, Noel asked Jade how often she ate Jamaican food. With an embarrassed smile, she admitted that she had had jerk chicken once at a friend's house, and that was about it. Noel could not help laughing as they both remembered his earlier warning and her overconfident response.

When they finally got to the front of the line, Noel ordered a jerk chicken meal and a ginger beer for her, then oxtail and a rice-and-peas dish for himself. He also asked for a Kola Champagne pop. Though the names were different, the food looked and smelled a lot like the Southern food of her childhood. Jade could not wait to try it.

Once they were inside Noel's home and eating their late-night meal on the kitchen table, Noel brought up Laura's reaction to their birthday gift.

"Did you see the look on her face? She loved those dance shoes," he said.

"I knew she would," Jade agreed. "She'll feel so different next Saturday. It was so hard for me to not say something to her this afternoon."

"Was it weird?" Noel asked.

"Well, only a little weirder than it's been over the last few weeks. Usually it's been pretty easy to forget that you're her uncle, but not when I know I'm going to her house later in the day," Jade responded with a sarcastic smile.

"Do you know Nicki very well?" He was remembering his sister's cold behavior through dinner.

"She and I have only met a few times, like when she would drop off a check or something. Why?" Jade was curious to see if Noel was leading the discussion anywhere in particular.

"I was just curious." He had wondered if perhaps there was a reason why Nicki did not like Jade. It was the only conclusion he could come to to account for Nicki's reaction. Jade was looking at him expectantly. He knew better than to say anything more on the topic, so he changed it.

"So, tell me more about the open house you're planning."

Jade had sensed that Noel had been going somewhere with his questions but let him turn the conversation in another direction. She described the open house as something that would allow the students to show their families and friends what they were capable of. For those who were serious about a career as a dancer, it would be an opportunity for them to get used to performing. But there was so much to be done, like finding the right venue at the right price, advertising the event, and planning rehearsals. It was going to be a lot of work, but she was very excited about the project.

Jade continued to talk about her plans until Noel had finished his oxtail and she had eaten half of her chicken.

She yawned while he cleaned up the food containers and drink bottles.

"Are you tired?" he asked as he wrapped an arm around her shoulder and led her toward the stairs.

"Mmmm, a little. I can't believe how late it is."

"Well, let's take a quick shower, and I'll tuck you in," he said as he ushered her upstairs and into the bedroom.

He left her to undress and started the shower for them. When she joined him in the bathroom a couple of minutes later, naked, she helped him strip out of his clothes. Their movements were slow and lazy. As they shared the shower spray, their arousal began to build.

A series of quick pecks turned into a long, deep intimate dance, and within minutes they were both wide-awake. Noel ended their passionate kiss and turned Jade around so her lush behind was pressed against his arousal. His strong fingers teased her swollen nipples. Her soft moans filled the room.

The bathroom filled with steam as the hot water pounded Noel's back. But he was too overwhelmed by the heat of Jade's body to notice. Instinct replaced conscious thought. He gripped her hips and thrust into her core while she balanced her weight by pressing her palms against the shower walls. Together, they lost control while their moans echoed off the bathroom tiles.

Sunday was a beautiful day with a cloudless blue sky. June in Chicago was a funny month. The temperature could be as cool as 65 degrees or, like that day, a comfortable 82 degrees. Holding hands, Noel and Jade walked down State Street on their way to brunch. They were both wearing shorts and sandals, Jade in a fitted cotton T-shirt and Noel in a golf shirt. It was just after two o'clock in the afternoon, and they had woken up starving despite their heavy late-night meal. The plan was brunch, then shopping before heading over to Trish and Ian's to hang out.

The atmosphere between them was very relaxed and comfortable but for different reasons for each of them.

Noel avoided thinking about why it felt so good to wake up with a woman in his bed and just enjoyed the feeling. Six months ago, he would have laughed at the idea. Today, it felt so natural to be with Jade.

With any other woman, Noel would have been thinking about what he wanted to do after they had sex and had left the woman's house. Instead, spending time with Jade was what he wanted to do. Everything else had to be scheduled around it.

Jade, on the other hand, woke up feeling lighter. While she got dressed, she was able to recognize exactly why. All her apprehensions about dating again centered on her fear of getting intimate with someone. She had viewed it as opening herself up to being hurt and used. There was even a secret part of her that wondered if she could enjoy being close to a man again. Noel squashed those fears. She was a healthy woman who could satisfy a gorgeous, sexy man.

They spent brunch talking and laughing as Noel told her stories about some of his friends. They continued to laugh and exchange stories once they left the restaurant, meandering through the boutiques that lined the shopping district. They eventually entered a trendy clothing store. While Noel stopped to look at the leather jackets on the first floor, Jade made her way to the second floor to check out their women's sports clothes.

He was trying on a butter-soft black leather coat when he heard someone call his name. When he swung around, Debbie was walking toward him, her jet-black weaved hair bouncing around her shoulders.

"Hey there, Noel," she said as she casually reached her arms around his neck and pressed her cheek to his. He responded to her hug by reflex, then pulled away awkwardly. "How are you?"

"Good, Debbie. How are you?" he responded, trying to act natural.

"Good. I haven't heard from you in so long. Did you get my message from last week?" she asked, as she ran her fingers through her artificial hair, creating a sexy tousled look.

"Yeah, but I've been kind of busy," he answered, not really wanting to give an explanation.

"Well, I'm going to be here until Tuesday," she informed him with a smile and a bite of her lower lip.

Noel stepped back when it was clear that she intended to stay in his personal space.

If she noticed his discomfort, she didn't indicate it. "It would be nice to get together one night."

"Listen, Debbie," he said as he shrugged out of the leather coat and handed it to the store clerk hovering nearby, "I don't think that's a good idea." Damn, he hated these situations. It was almost as though she did not remember their conversation regarding Jade.

"Come on, Noel. What's the big deal? You know we'll have a good time." She was back in his personal space. "I like your hair, by the way." She ran her fingers through his cropped curls.

"Thanks." Obviously, approaching this straight on was not going to work. "Why don't I give you a call later and we'll talk about it?"

Debbie smiled widely then checked her watch. "I've got to run, but that sounds great," she responded, again tossing her hair. "'Bye, babe," she said, leaving an imprint of her red lipstick on his cheek and the scent of her perfume in her wake.

A couple of minutes after she left, Noel made his way to the upper floor of the store to find Jade. He caught up to her as she casually sifted through sweatshirts and suggested that they get going so that they could stop at the liquor store.

When they got into the Jeep parked several blocks away, Jade reached over and wiped the red smudge from his cheek. Suddenly, Noel realized how quiet she had been since they left the clothing store.

"An old girlfriend?" she asked, hoping that her voice came out steady and nonchalant.

"Not really," he responded wondering if she had seen anything.

"You guys seem quite close."

Well, that answered his question. "We went out a couple of times." Noel was hoping Jade would just drop it. He did not have anything to hide, but he did not feel like explaining everything right then.

"Are you guys still seeing each other? I mean, it's fine if you are. But I would rather know now. It's not like you and I—"

Noel cut her off. "Jade, I'm not seeing her anymore."

Frustration was evident in his voice and it rubbed her the wrong way. What right did he have to be upset with her? Was she just supposed to accept everything without question?

"Really? Let me guess: you guys are just friends, right?" She was getting angrier by the second and she was not exactly sure why. That comfortable feeling that she had been carrying with her all day was slipping away. The old familiar sensations of distrust and disappointment were rapidly replacing it.

"Don't you think you're overreacting?" Noel asked. "Her name is Debbie and I haven't seen her for weeks." He ended up sounding condescending and he knew it.

"Look. Let's not start playing games, Noel. I'm not an idiot, okay?" Jade knew she was replaying an old argument that had nothing to do with Noel. But how long did she convince herself that Peter really did have some female friends she did not know? God, she still felt like such a gullible fool. And she wasn't going to let it happen again. She was not going to blindly trust a man just because she was in love with him!

"Jade, there is nothing going on between Debbie and me." Maybe he should have chosen a phrase that was not so cliché, he thought. Even he had to admit that the whole thing looked pretty bad. Ironically, this was probably the first time in years that he really wasn't seeing anyone else on the side. Unfortunately, he was certain that Jade was not going to see the humor in the situation.

"The truth is that I've been trying to let her know that I can't see her anymore, but she's not hearing me. She's a flight attendant, and we used to get together when she was in town. It was never anything more than that." He tried to change both his tone and the direction of the discussion.

Jade did not respond. She was still upset, but it was not directed at Noel. She was upset that she was feeling the insecurity that came along with needing to trust someone. When did she arrive at this place again? Was she ready for it? How was she supposed to handle this? The one thing she knew was that she was not going to act like a jealous fool. Never again.

It was clear that she was starting to have feelings for Noel. Really strong feelings and it scared her. So she bit her tongue and stayed silent while he pulled the Jeep onto the street and headed toward the highway.

Noel reached over and took her hand. Jade let him, but neither felt the need to discuss it anymore. They did not talk again until they stopped at a liquor store to choose a bottle of wine. The discussion started out stilted and awkward, each trying to gauge the other's mood. In the end, they settled on a bottle of Canei—Trish's favorite wine—and a six-pack of Heineken. By the time Trish opened her door for them, the tension between Noel and Jade was barely detectable.

Jade made the introductions, then she and Trish

went to the kitchen with the alcohol, leaving the boys to get acquainted.

"Nice," was all that Trish said, but it was clear that they would have a lot to talk about later. Jade was dying to tell her all about the weekend but bit her tongue. There were too many small things she herself did not understand, and she was reluctant to listen to Trish's opinion or impression.

When the two girls entered the living room with drinks and snacks, Ian and Noel were going through the male-bonding ritual. Already, they were debating an upcoming middleweight boxing match, acting like they had known each other for years. Jade and Trish rolled their eyes in reaction.

The two couples spent the rest of the evening talking, laughing, and watching TV. The men continued to debate about a variety of sports, while the women communicated with a discrete language of facial expressions. To Jade's delight, it was clear that both her good friends approved of her developing relationship with Noel.

Chapter 14

Jade's Saturday afternoon was going by very quickly. It was almost two o'clock, and the 12:30 ballet class had finished about forty-five minutes before. She was in her office working on the show outline for the open house. Vince Thompson was the first parent she had spoken to about it. Ever since Laura's birthday two weeks before, she felt compelled to put her money where her mouth was. The date was set for the second weekend in September, and Jade was still searching for the right venue. She was reluctant to choose one until she figured out what the choreography would be like. Once she had the show outline put together, she could then choose a theater or hall with the right equipment, lighting, and performance space.

The purpose of the open house would be threefold: to give her students performance exposure; to show the parents the talent that their kids had developed; and to advertise the studio and the variety of classes that were available. The program had to accomplish all of those things as well as to entertain the audience. So far, she had settled on her beginner ballet class because they were so adorable, the intermediate and advanced jazz classes, and an all-level modern dance performance. But she needed something else.

Jade checked her watch again, very conscious of the passing time. She had a couple of hours before she needed to head home. Noel was going to meet her at her place at 6:30, and she wanted to stop at the grocery store on the way.

She was tapping her head with her pen when she heard the street-level front door bang closed. The studio had been empty for the past twenty minutes, but perhaps someone had forgotten something. After pausing for half a minute to see if she heard anything else, Jade stood up and walked toward her office door.

"Hello, can I help you?" Jade said loudly to announce where she was. But she was brought to a halt by the figure who suddenly blocked her office doorway. She inhaled her breath sharply, then was too frozen with shock to do anything but stare.

"Hello, Jade."

"Nicki, I don't think you should get involved."

"I'm not getting involved, Vince. I just think that I should talk to him. I don't want him to make the wrong decision over a woman again."

Ever since Laura's birthday, they had discussed this issue repeatedly. She would not be deterred from speaking her mind. It didn't help that Laura brought up Jade's name in almost every other sentence. Laura even mentioned how cool she thought it would be to have her as an aunt.

"I think Jade is quite nice," Vince said, realizing that his opinion mattered very little but feeling compelled to try to defuse the situation.

"Vince, that's not the point and you know it." Nicki was walking back and forth in their bedroom, her arms crossed defensively. "What could he possibly know about her? Granted, her studio seems to be doing well, but she's dancer for God's sake. Why would he want to get seriously involved with someone like that? I just don't understand what he's thinking!"

"Nicki, give me a break." Vince was losing his patience. Her stubborn attitude was starting to annoy him.

In about twenty minutes, Nicki was to leave the house and pick up Laura from the movie theater across the street from the dance studio. Several of the young girls had gone to see a matinee, which would end by three o'clock. "You know what I'm trying to say," she explained. "He owns a very successful company and could have any woman he wants. What could they have in common? I doubt if she even went to community college."

"Nicki, it's none of your business. That's all there is to it."

"He's my brother. How can it not be my business? What if he's serious about her? When was the last time you met any of his girlfriends? Think about it."

"So what?"

"So what? The last thing Noel needs is to marry someone beneath him."

"Nicki, it's not our business."

"Well, it's not okay with me." She was still pacing, too agitated to see the disappointment in Vince's eyes. "Noel is just not thinking clearly."

She picked up the portable phone that had been resting on her dressing table.

"What are you doing?" Vince asked, already knowing the answer.

"I'm calling Noel," Nicki stated simply. Vince

stalked out of the room, too exasperated to say anything more. She ignored him and dialed Noel's phone number.

Noel had spent the last few hours doing his laundry. While the final load was drying, he was comfortably relaxed on his couch, flipping through the television channels. The remnants of his omelet lunch rested on the coffee table beside him. The phone rang.

"Hello?" he answered.

"Hi, Noel," Nicki responded.

"Hey, Nicki. What's up?" They had not spoken for the past two weeks.

"Nothing. I just wanted to say 'hi.' How are you?"

"Okay. How about you? How are Laura and Vince?"

"Good. Everything is fine." They spent the next few minutes discussing the weather and how busy everyone was. "Laura still talks about her new dance shoes," Nicki added in the end.

"Well, Jade picked them out, so I'm sure they're the best."

That was enough for Nicki to bring up the point of her call. "So, uh, what's going on between you two?"

"Jade and me? What do you mean?" Noel asked trying not to sound too evasive.

"Well, are you serious about her? I mean, I can't remember the last girlfriend that you've introduced me to," Nicki stated. "Never mind the fact that you've cut your hair."

"What does cutting my hair have to do with anything?" Noel asked. He was starting to suspect that this was the real reason for her call.

"Noel, you refused to cut your hair for months. I always thought it looked childish and unprofessional, but you loved it. It was just such a shock to see you with it cut off on the same day that you bring her over to my house," Nicki analyzed. "Did she make you cut it?"

"What? Why would she do that?" Noel was obviously puzzled by Nicki's reasoning. "My hair has nothing to do with Jade."

"So are you saying that you're not serious about her?"

"I'm not saying anything at all about Jade and me, other than I really like her and we enjoy each other's company." Nicki was making him feel defensive and he did not like it. "What's this all about, anyway?"

"I'm just concerned, that's all. I mean, I just want you to be happy and to meet the right woman to settle down with," Nicki explained. She was starting to feel a little better about the whole thing. Maybe she had overreacted. "You can't spend the rest of your life just fooling around with these types of women."

"What types of women?" Noel asked not really understanding her point.

"You know what I'm talking about. I'm not saying you shouldn't have fun, but—"

Noel interrupted her. "No, I don't know what you're talking about." He was feeling uncomfortable, and it was evident in his voice. Jade was very different from the women he dated regularly, but Nicki could not really know that.

"Noel, you don't have to get so defensive. I know boys will be boys. I'm just saying that I'm sure you'll meet the right woman one day soon. That's all I want for you," Nicki finished.

Noel had heard her lecture about settling down

many times before, so it did not bother him. He was very bothered, however, by Nicki's suggestion that Jade was not the right "kind" of woman for him. He knew that he should leave it alone, but he could not stop himself from addressing it.

"Exactly what type of woman do you think Jade is?" His agitation was now very evident in his voice.

"Well, she's obviously very beautiful and talented. But . . ." She hesitated, clearly searching for the right words.

"But, what?" he demanded.

"Noel, she's a dancer."

"So?"

"Noel, don't be naive. I don't have anything against her personally," Nicki stated as though it should be obvious. "I'm sure she's very nice and interesting, but you're a very smart and successful professional. You need a woman to add to your success, not bring you down."

Noel was speechless for several seconds. "Nicki, I can't even believe what you're saying to me. You can't be serious."

"Look Noel, I can certainly appreciate your attraction to her. All I'm saying is that I know one day you'll realize that you need a woman that comes from a similar . . . educational level as you. That's all." She had paused to find the most appropriate words.

"Do you know Jade's background?" Noel had tried to resist the urge to debate this ridiculous point but failed. "What do you really know about her?"

"That's not the point, sweetheart."

"What *is* the point? That I can't be in any meaningful relationship with Jade because she's not a lawyer or from a wealthy family?" he summarized in an angry voice. He could not believe this discussion.

"Quite frankly, yes," Nicki admitted, trying to calm him down. "You know Mom and Dad didn't send you to private school so that you could wind up marrying some dim American hoochie."

"This is ridiculous, Nicki! You're talking like a snob."

"Noel, I just don't want you to get hurt, that's all."

"You know what, Nicki? I don't want to have this conversation anymore. I'll speak to you later." With that statement, Noel hung up the phone and tossed it aside angrily.

What the hell was going on? He shook his head, then stood up with nervous energy. Noel was used to her mothering him and being free with her opinions about his life and his lifestyle. But this was just too much. Could she really believe that Jade wasn't good enough for him because she wasn't obviously wealthy? He ran his hand through his short curls, then fell back onto the sofa.

During Laura's birthday dinner, Noel had sensed the tension in the air. Nicki had acted withdrawn, though he did not know why. At least not until now. He remembered that Laura had been the one to tell her mom that Jade was Noel's guest for the evening. He also remembered that Nicki had not come out of the kitchen to say hello until she started serving the meal. And for the rest of the evening, Nicki had been very quiet and overly polite.

While he and Nicki were alone in the kitchen during the cleanup, he had had the clear impression that she had resented the surprise.

"You could have told me who you were bringing," she had said with her back to him.

"Yeah, but I wanted to surprise you guys," Noel had responded teasingly.

"Noel, I don't think today was the right time for you to bring a new guest for dinner." It had been obvious that she was agitated. She kept cleaning the same spot on the counter over and over.

"What are you talking about? You were fine with it when I told you last night."

"Well, I'm just saying that tonight's a very big deal for Laura, and I don't think bringing Jade Winters was a good idea," Nicki responded vaguely.

"Why? Laura really enjoyed having Jade here." He was prevented from getting more clarification when Laura pranced into the room to ask if she could open her gifts.

That short discussion with Nicki had left a bad taste in his mouth, but Noel had just chalked it up to her usual meddling. However, it had bothered him enough to make him want to leave the dinner early. He and Jade had stayed to sing "Happy Birthday" and for the cake cutting but then made their excuses.

Noel continued to think back to that evening in order to analyze anything else that may have occurred. Could Jade have picked up on anything? The possibility made him even angrier. The idea that he may have unknowingly put her in an uncomfortable situation really bothered him. He just prayed that Jade had been oblivious to it.

Despite Nicki's accusation, Noel was not naive about his financial success. He knew a lot of people who treated him one way when he was your average black male, and a totally different way when they realized that he was the CEO of his own company. It had been that way for most of his life.

Back in Jamaica, the Merson family was well known for their vast business holdings in the St. Andrew and Manchester parishes of the island. Noel's great-grandparents had moved to the West Indies from Scotland around the turn of the twentieth century to grow coffee in the Jamaican Blue Mountains. They had one child, his grandfather, who expanded and diversified the family holdings. He married a black Jamaican woman and had three children.

Eventually, Noel's uncle and aunt took over the various manufacturing and produce operations while his father had gone to a university in England to become an engineer. Many of Noel's cousins currently work for the family businesses, and he had always known it was an option for him. But like his father, Noel felt the need to make his own mark in life and carve his own destiny.

There was validity to Nicki's statement that his parents would not be pleased if he married a woman who had nothing to offer and was after his money. Jade was clearly not one of those women, and he hated the fact that his sister had not taken the time to see that.

Noel was prevented from further thought on this subject when he noticed the time. In a half hour, he was to meet his friend Dave at the mall. Noel needed some new basketball shoes, while Dave just liked to shop. As he headed up the stairs to get dressed, Noel tried to shrug off his anger and agitation.

In the spare ten minutes he had, he washed up, then left the house wearing faded blue jeans and a white T-shirt. He stayed off the highway to avoid Saturday traffic and was able to make it to the mall with one minute to spare. Dave, however, was his typical fifteen minutes late. Noel spent the extra few minutes admiring some of the women's clothing in a nearby designer shop. When he spotted Dave strolling toward him, he was resisting the urge to purchase a very cool pair of jeans for Jade.

Noel watched with amusement as several young women nearby eyed Dave with appreciation. He was wearing black baggy overalls with a tight black tank top. His dark shiny skin rippled with muscles. There was no denying that women loved everything about him. He looked cool, strong, and dangerous.

There wasn't one female who could keep his attention for long though, and his attitude drove them all crazy. Dave's popularity and adventures with the opposite sex were legendary among their friends.

"Hey," Dave said as he approached Noel. His eyes were still on the pretty young things and they returned his flirtatious gaze.

"Hey," Noel responded.

"What's up?" Dave flashed the girls a dazzling smile and one of them actually giggled.

"Nothing much, man. What's up with you?"

"Nothing, nothing."

Slowly, they walked away from the girls and made their way toward the sports equipment shop. Soon they were both trying on a selection of ball shoes.

"So what's this I hear about you getting serious with a fine Nubian sister?" Dave asked out of the blue. He rarely pulled any punches.

"What's there to know?" Noel asked.

"So, it's true." Dave paused while tying up a pair of newly released Air Jordans. "You sure you know what you're doing?"

"Dave, man, what's the big deal?" Maybe it was the discussion earlier with Nicki, but Noel was not in the mood to be teased about anything to do with Jade.

"No big deal, I'm just looking out for you, man."

"Everything's cool."

"Listen, I'm just letting you know that sisters nowadays are on a different trip. They're not settling for anything less than a man that can pay their bills, if you know what I'm saying."

"Her name is Jade and it ain't like that. She has her own thing going on."

Dave was not deterred from giving his advice. "I'm just saying, man, that women today are only looking for one thing. Well maybe two things. They want a man to spend his cash and they want a man to go downtown, if you know what I'm saying." He shook his head in disgust.

"Well, I don't know about all that. Jade's cool. Like I said, she owns her own business. She's not looking for someone to take care of her car note and child-care bills," Noel replied sarcastically.

"If you say so, man," Dave said with a casual shrug.

"Why are you stressing me, man?" Noel asked, trying not to give Dave the satisfaction of seeing him get upset.

"Like I said, I'm just looking out for you, man. It's been a long time since you've been so wrapped up in a woman," he explained. "And if she's as beautiful as I've been told she is, she's probably trouble."

"I wouldn't worry about it, Dave. I've got it covered."

"If you say so, man," he responded, ignoring Noel's obvious sarcasm.

Noel was relieved when the girl behind the cash

register distracted Dave. She could not have been more than twenty-two years old, but he was not deterred from laying on the charm. His smooth talk got him a small discount on a new pair of ball shoes while Noel was forced to pay full price. The male cashier at the second register was obviously not impressed by Noel's smile.

The guys spent the next few hours looking at clothes and at Tower Records listening to tracks. By the time they were ready to part ways, it was after five o'clock, and Noel had to go back home and grab a quick shower before heading to Jade's place.

"We still on for Friday?" Dave asked. A group of guys were planning to go to a private party that happened on the first Friday of each month.

"Yeah, sure. I'll call you later in the week to confirm."

"Noel, man, this jam is the bomb. Last month, there were too many women for me to choose from. I guess I'll just have to pick up where I left off. I wouldn't want any of the ladies to feel left out, if you know what I mean." He was rubbing his chin with delight.

"Whatever, man." Noel said laughing at Dave's conceit as they both turned to head to their separate cars. "I'll catch up with you later."

Chapter 15

Jade could not seem to catch her breath. It was lodged somewhere between her lungs and her throat, and it was starting to hurt. She knew only seconds had ticked away, but it felt like a very long time without oxygen.

"How are you?" was all that Peter said, but hearing him speak again was enough to melt her from her frozen state.

"Hello, Peter," Jade said simply. "What are you doing here?"

"Just passing by."

"Really." They both knew he was lying. Peter never just 'passed by' anywhere. He would never do anything without a purpose or an expected gain. He was there for a reason. "How can I help you?"

"Come on, Jade. I haven't seen you in over four years. Is that all you can say?" He appeared relaxed, leaning with one shoulder propped against the side of her office doorway.

Peter was 5'11" but somehow he seemed much shorter than she remembered. He was quite fair in complexion, several shades lighter than Jade. He looked pretty much the same except a bit thinner in body and in hair.

"You're right Peter, it has been a few years. Why don't you just tell me why you're 'passing by' so I don't have to guess?" she replied, refusing to give in to the urge to step back and put some space between them.

Peter smiled at her sarcasm. He always enjoyed it when she got upset. Then he shrugged.

"The truth is, I've been thinking about you a lot lately, and I wondered how you're doing, that's all."

"Really. Now why would you do that?"

"I don't know. How are you?" Peter asked the question as he pushed his shoulder off of the doorframe and stepped toward her.

She could not resist the reflex to take a step back, but hid it by turning away from him and walking toward her desk.

"I'm doing great, actually." She stopped in front of the desk, turned around, and rested her butt on the edge.

"I'm glad to hear that." They stood staring at each other for several seconds. "Last Thursday was our wedding anniversary."

"Really." She was not about to acknowledge that she had remembered, even though it had not hit her until almost the next day. When she had remembered the significance of June 28, it had been an afterthought, like remembering the details of a dream. And the thought had left her mind just as quickly as it had appeared. She was hoping this visit from Peter would be as brief and have just as little significance.

"I guess that's why I've been thinking about you . . . remembering our marriage."

He had a look on his face that she remembered all too well: he was trying to charm her. But she was not the same person he once knew, and she had no intention of letting him manipulate her like he used to.

"Peter, that's a lovely sentiment, but why don't you just get to the point of your visit," she stated.

"C'mon Jade, don't be like that." He took another couple of steps toward her. "Is it so hard to believe that I just wanted to say 'hi' and see how you're doing? Are you saying that you haven't thought about me at all?"

Jade did not do anything but roll her eyes at his melodrama.

"You don't believe me. That's okay. It has been a long time." At her blank stare, he turned away and walked toward the window. "You've done well; the studio looks great."

"Thank you," Jade replied, starting to feel a little less defensive. "How are you?"

"I'm doing okay," he answered, as he turned to look at her again. "Things are pretty much the same. Still working at Ford." He was an automotive technician.

Jade nodded, then stared at a spot on the floor. What else was there to say? While Peter had been talking, she thought she had heard the street-level door open again, but had gotten distracted by his next statement.

"Do you remember Andrea? You know: Tyrone's ex? I ran into her about a week ago. She mentioned that she saw you at an art show recently."

Jade waited for him to get to the point.

"The truth is Jade, I really haven't been able to stop thinking about you."

"Why? Why now?"

Peter shook his head. "I don't know. I guess I realized a long time ago that our marriage was the best thing that ever happened to me. I know I made it difficult, and I know I didn't always act right. But, I miss you. I miss us."

The statement hung in the air between them. Peter had said it without arrogance or practiced charm. His stance with his head bowed seemed to indicate embarrassment and humility.

"Peter, I—"

He cut her off. "No, I'm not saying that I expect anything from you." Peter stepped forward to stand in front of her and spoke very softly. "I just wanted to let you know how I felt."

"I guess I'm just a little confused and surprised."

"I know. Look, do you want to go and get something to eat? Maybe do some catching up?"

Jade just stared at him. There was a time when she would have been so happy to hear those words come out of Peter's mouth. Back then, despite everything he had done to her, she had still wanted him to love her. That need had always been the hardest thing for her pride to accept.

"Unfortunately I can't, Peter."

Standing up from her seat on the edge of the desk, she walked toward the office door. Peter followed her and grabbed her arm before they reached the doorway. She snatched it back on reflex.

"I meant what I said, Jade. About our marriage, I mean. It might be a little late, but I think it would be great if we could spend some time together to celebrate our anniversary. How about later this evening?"

"Peter, I don't think that's such a good idea." Again, Jade thought she heard a sound, this time in the hallway outside her office. She paused to listen, but when no one appeared after a few seconds, she continued.

"It was nice of you to stop by, and I appreciate everything that you've said. But I think it's better if we just leave things as they are."

"Are you saying that we can't be friends?"

"What I'm saying is that we can't just pretend that things did not happen the way they did."

"I'm not suggesting that we do. I'm just saying that we can still salvage something."

"Why?" She was getting impatient. "Why, Peter? You treated me like garbage, Peter. I moved out of our apartment, and you didn't even bother to ask me why. I'm not sure what 'friendship' you want to salvage."

Though her tone was very biting, her expression was calm and her voice barely above a whisper. She watched Peter nod his head while looking at the floor.

"I know," he said. "Look, why don't I leave you my number, and you can give me a call when you're available to get together."

"I don't—"

"Don't say anything, just take the number. Please." He took a card out of his wallet. "I just want to talk, maybe explain some things."

She took the card, then stepped away from him.

"Good-bye, Peter."

He took the cue and nodded to her before he walked out the door. Jade listened to his footsteps as he went down the steps and out the street-level doors.

Slowly, she turned her back to her office door and stared at her desk. Her notes about the open house were scattered around as she had left them. Everything looked the same as it did a half hour before, yet everything was very different.

* * *

Noel didn't notice the blinking light on his phone until he was ready to leave his house. He was already running about ten minutes late to get to Jade's place, but he stopped to retrieve the message in case it was important.

"Noel, it's Nicki. Um . . . I need to speak with you. Please give me a call when you get this message. I'll be at home. 'Bye."

Noel checked the time of the message, and the automated voice told him it was left at 3:17 that afternoon.

What more did she have to say to him? Whatever it was, he was not in the mood. Decisively, he erased the message, then left the house and put Nicki out of his mind.

Chapter 16

The doorbell rang just after six o'clock. Jade checked the wall clock to confirm that she had not lost track of time. Noel was early. She was not dressed yet and had been working on her hair, wearing only her bra and panties. Quickly, she grabbed her robe from behind the bathroom door and hurried to the front hall.

"Coming!" Without thinking, Jade assumed that Noel was the person at the door, since she was not expecting anyone else. She opened it with a big smile, underwear revealed provocatively through her cover-up. "Hey, babe . . . Oh!"

Instead of a tall handsome man, she found George, the gaunt, red-faced maintenance assistant. As quickly as she could, Jade tied the ends of her robe together and positioned herself behind the door.

"Hello, George," she said while he stared at her as though he could see her flesh through the solid wood. "George!" she repeated a little more sharply when he still did not say anything.

Finally he lifted his oversized head until his flat fish eyes met hers. A prominent Adam's apple bobbed sharply under the pale skin of his thin neck.

"Hi, Ms. Winters," he finally said. "Sorry to disturb you."

"That's okay, George. I was just expecting someone else," Jade responded kindly. Somehow, he always made her feel compassion and repulsion at the same time. George was not obviously disabled in any way, but his behavior and mannerisms were so strange most people thought that he was mentally challenged. "How can I help you?"

"Well, Mr. Stein upstairs was complaining about water pressure problems, so I thought I would check and see if you were, too."

George took a step forward as though he intended to enter the apartment. If he was planning to inspect her plumbing at that moment, Jade did not have the time, nor was she dressed appropriately. On reflex, she closed the door slightly while still hiding her body behind it.

"You know what, George? I haven't had any problems at all," she explained. "Why don't I just keep an eye on it, and I'll call Cliff right away if anything weird happens." Cliff was the head maintenance man for the building complex.

Jade continued to smile sweetly even though she thought she detected a flicker of anger pass through George's eyes, bringing faint light to their dead gray depth. When his thin lips stretched into a thin smile, revealing small uneven teeth, she assumed it had been her imagination.

"It'll only take a minute," he assured her with a confidence that was out of character for him.

His hand was now flat on the door indicating that he was about to push it open, but Jade was too pressured by the passage of time to let that happen. She still needed to do her hair and makeup, and Noel would be there in less than fifteen minutes.

"I'm sorry, George," she explained as she started closing the door. "I'm in a bit of a rush. Just tell Cliff I'll give him a call. See ya later," she finished as she shut the door and turned the deadbolt.

Jade shivered lightly as she stared at the door. She felt very uneasy. It might have been her imagination, but she had the distinct feeling that George had meant to push the door open and enter the apartment despite her protests. She then shook her head and laughed softly to herself as she walked back to the bathroom. She was obviously still feeling the effects of the visit from Peter.

Since he left the studio that afternoon, she had been unable to keep her mind on anything of importance. She had given up on working on the open house after staring out the window for over twenty minutes. Peter's visit itself had not been all that disturbing; it was how she felt afterward that had thrown her off. Somehow, alone in her office, she got the sensation of being exposed.

It was as though a spotlight had been shining on her, and there was nowhere to hide. Standing in that bright light, many memories had flooded her brain, none of which were particularly pleasant. She saw herself overweight and frumpy; saw Peter's arrogant smirk as he ridiculed her; felt the anger that had come when he ignored her while they were out with friends; saw him flirting with other women; felt the shame of wanting his love while knowing he did not deserve hers.

She suddenly saw and felt all of those things at the same time, and was left naked and stripped of the defenses she had built up over the years. The shadows had been removed and all the pain was in the light.

Within a few minutes, while staring out the window into the bright summer sun, Jade saw the person she had been. It made her sad and angry: sad that she had suffered so much and angry that that person might still be inside her.

Surprisingly, she was no longer angry with Peter. She did want some answers from him, though. Jade had resisted the urge to throw away his business card and left it on her desk next to her computer. No matter how much she tried to dismiss his suggestion that they talk, she knew it was inevitable. It was just a matter of when.

When the doorbell rang for the second time twenty-five minutes later, Jade was dressed in a dark blue denim skirt and a white cotton top. This time, she answered the door with more caution and was pleased to find Noel standing in front of her when she opened it.

They both smiled at each other, then leaned into a tender embrace that ended with a playful kiss.

"Ready?" he asked when they parted.

"Yeah, I'm just going to put some lipstick on." She stepped out of his arms and went back to the bathroom. "Where are we going?"

"I hope you're hungry," Noel replied, avoiding her question.

"I'm starving. Where are we going to eat?" By then, her attention was on sliding her feet into black strappy heels.

She looked up at Noel when he did not answer her and found him watching her with a teasing smile. "Well?" she prompted.

"You look beautiful," he stated simply.

Jade felt her body flood with a warm sensation.

"Maybe we should just eat here," he suggested, while his eyes rested on the peaks of her breast that had pushed through the thin fabric of her top.

"I don't think we would be eating anytime soon if we did." Though her voice had lowered, revealing the warmth of her body, her tone was teasing.

"Maybe you wouldn't, but I definitely would." Noel's tone was anything but light, though the pun brought a smile to his lips.

Jade slapped him lightly on the arm, and they both laughed at her embarrassment.

They left the apartment holding hands and chatting about their week. Jade gave Noel a brief update on the open house, and they exchanged ideas on possible venues. As Noel drove them downtown, the discussion switched to his latest advertising project. He did not often talk about his work, but Jade would not let him get away with his usual quick summary and insisted he explain some of the details of the strategy.

When Noel parked the car he switched the topic of discussion to the unique local culture of the area. The shops and restaurants offered an eclectic choice of foods and fashion, drawing patrons from all social levels. Young Bohemian students with dreadlocks might be seated at a table next to executives from the media industry; and the server might be a person with studded eyebrows and pink hair.

After walking less than a block, Noel guided her into the entrance of a small, nondescript storefront. It turned out to be an intimate restaurant in which they were escorted to a table in the back. The interior was decorated in a minimalist fashion using lots of mahogany wood and pewter accents. Tiny cable lights ran in creative patterns along the ceiling. A young black waiter brought over their menus and introduced himself as Tony. As Tony went through the specials, Jade was certain she was hearing wrong. Grilled red snapper, mango chicken, oxtail?

"What kind of place is this?" she whispered to Noel after he had ordered them a bottle of Cuban white wine.

"I read about it last week. It just opened," Noel responded. "The whole menu is Caribbean. What do you think?"

They were both flipping through the menus. Soursop juice and ginger beer. Ackee and saltfish served with green banana and fried dumplings.

"Wow!" Jade said with surprise in her voice. "This is great!"

"The review was very good," Noel added.

For the first time, Jade noticed the name of the establishment scripted at the top of the menu: *Kingston House*. "I wonder if the owner is Jamaican," she mused.

"I don't know, but they apparently stole the chef and assistant chef from two of the top restaurants in Montego Bay."

"Cool!" After their late-night dinner of a few weeks before, she was developing a taste for Caribbean flavors. If the food was as good as she anticipated, Jade would tell everyone she knew about the place.

When Tony brought their wine, he also brought them complimentary appetizers: fried overripe plantain. Jade was in heaven as she savored the sweet treat. After ordering their meals, Jade prompted Noel to continue telling her about his week. With obvious hesitation, he told her that the advertising pitch he had worked on for over two weeks had gone very well. The client, a large urban fashion company, had been working with him for about four years, and he was very comfortable with representing their style. His pitch had been for their next spring/summer campaign, and he had suggested a brand new image to suit several of their new lines. The CEO and VP of sales had appeared very impressed and excited, but they were not willing to commit to the project until next week. Noel translated that to mean that they were still fishing for ideas and probably accepting pitches from other firms. Advertising, he told Jade, was not an industry that recognized loyalty. He was used to that fact and felt prepared for the competition.

Noel continued to talk about his work while they ate. Jade enjoyed listening to him. She found it fascinating that he could continually come up with new and exciting ways to market everyday products. She also liked the sound of his voice.

When a natural pause ensued in the conversation, Jade took a few moments to enjoy the subtle details of the restaurant while Noel refilled their wineglasses. Throughout the meal, soft reggae music played in the background. Jade could not resist swaying to the contagious rhythms.

When Tony came by to clear their table, he asked if they had enjoyed their meals. Both Jade and Noel were very sincere in their praise of the food. He asked if they would like to see the dessert menu, but they both declined. Tony said he would bring their bill.

"Are you in a rush to leave?" Noel asked Jade.

"No, not really. Why?" she inquired.

"Well, there's a live performance that should start soon."

"Okay."

As they spoke, a band began to set up on the edge of the small dance floor. Jade watched as one of the artists stepped up to the microphone to do a mic check.

"Do you remember the CD that I gave you last week?" Noel asked her. "The guy at the mic is Ronnie Davis."

While at Noel's house, Jade had developed a liking for several songs on one of the discs Noel had played, so he gave it to her. He had explained that the reggae artist, Ronnie Davis, was a local up-and-comer and that his new album was doing well worldwide. Jade had played it several times in her car.

"No way," Jade replied. Now she knew why Noel had kept the evening a surprise.

"Yeah. He just came back from several gigs in England."

She was about to persist in her questioning but was interrupted by a tap on her shoulder. When she turned around, a slim, petite woman stood behind her, dressed in skin-tight capri pants and a Spandex tank top.

"Hey Jade," she said with a false smile.

"Janice, how are you?" Jade responded.

"Cool, cool. I haven't seen you around in a while. What have you been doing?" Janice asked, her eyes were clearly focused on Noel.

"Nothing much." Janice was not exactly the type of person you told your business to. "Noel, this is Janice. Janice, Noel Merson."

"Hey, Noel," Janice said after they shook hands, her

head bent to the side allowing her long false hair to hang freely. Then, she combed it back with her blue-painted nails that were studded with tiny crystals. The smile she now gave Noel was much brighter than the one she walked over with.

"So, what have you been up to, Janice?" Jade asked, to be polite.

"Girl, I've been so busy, it's crazy! I just need to get out and have some fun!" Janice was a manicurist in a downtown salon. "Where have you been, girl? I haven't seen you in forever. Probably not since you and Peter came to that party Kevin and I had. Someone told me that you and Peter split up. I was so surprised, 'cause you guys looked so happy together. But that was a while ago, I guess."

Jade had never liked Janice. She was catty, jealous, and crass. She had not changed very much in five years. Jade only smiled thinly in response to Janice's statement and avoided looking at Noel.

"You look good, though," Janice went on to say, obviously willing to have a conversation that did not include any feedback. "You musta lost, like, fifty pounds or something!" It did not sound like a compliment, so Jade just ignored it.

"Are you here with friends?" Jade asked in an effort to avoid further reminiscence.

"Yeah, me and the girls are just chilling. You know how it is," she responded. "And there are some fine brothers here tonight." Her eyes had deliberately settled on Noel after she scanned the room. He was probably the finest man in there.

"Well, it was nice to see you again, Janice," Jade said, to end the pointless conversation.

Before Janice could respond, a man approached

their table, and Noel stood up. Ronnie and Noel embraced in a street-style man-hug. Jade and Janice looked on in surprise.

"What's up, man? How you doing?" Ronnie asked, their hands still clasped.

"I'm all right, Davis. I don't have to ask how you are."

Ronnie smiled widely, then lowered his head shyly.

"The album is wicked!" Noel continued. "The rhythms are so classic. Straight from the roots."

"Seen, seen," Ronnie replied in agreement. "I just had to sing what was in my heart, you know what I'm saying? Sing for the love of the music."

Noel nodded in understanding while Jade and Janice continued to stare.

"And who are these fine ladies, Noel?" Ronnie asked, still smiling.

"Don't even bother licking your lips, man," Noel said laughing. It was obvious that Ronnie was ready to start putting on the charm. "Jade, Ronnie Davis."

"Nice to meet you Ronnie," Jade said as he grasped her hand in both of his. "Noel's right, the album is great."

"Thank you."

"You can let go of her hand now, Davis," Noel stated.

"If this guy's not treating you right, you just let me know, cool?" Ronnie said to Jade, ribbing Noel.

"Hey, Ronnie," Janice said, unable to wait for an introduction.

"This is Jade's friend . . ."

"Janice," she supplied, when it was obvious that Noel did not remember her name.

"Nice to meet you, Janice," Ronnie replied when he

finally released Jade's hand. He was briefly distracted as one of the band members motioned to him that they were ready. "You guys are going to stay for the show, right?"

"Definitely," Janice responded.

"Cool, cool." With that he was on his way to the stage as the MC recited Ronnie's bio, then presented him to the audience.

While Noel and Jade moved their chairs closer together to face the ad hoc stage, Janice shifted her weight from leg to leg. It was obvious that she wanted to ask Noel some questions about Ronnie. But once the band started up, the volume made any conversation almost impossible. Admitting defeat, she wiggled her fingers in farewell and made her way back to her table of girlfriends.

From the corner of her eye, Jade watched Janice attempt to fill them in on what had happened. Janice even stuck out her finger to point out where Noel and Jade were sitting.

Before long, Jade was so engrossed in the music that she was able to put the whole incident out of her mind.

Chapter 17

That night, Noel stayed over at Jade's apartment. After a lengthy session of intense lovemaking in the morning, she made them breakfast, then he left to play basketball.

Jade finished several chores around the house before she left to meet with Jerome. He had completed the collection of photos he had taken of her and was about to submit them for the album cover. Jade had offered to help him decide which ones should be submitted.

She didn't get to his apartment until 3:15 P.M., forty-five minutes later than their arranged time. Jerome was already annoyed by her late arrival, then become irate when Jade told him what had delayed her: Peter had called just as she was about to go out the door. He was returning her call from Saturday evening before her dinner with Noel.

"You're lying!" Jerome exclaimed, obviously hoping that he was correct. They were sitting in his living room, and he was about to pull out the finished photographs.

"No, I'm not. He wants to take me out to dinner later to talk." Jade then filled him in on yesterday's encounter at the dance studio.

"So, he just shows up after four years and thinks that you'll want to hook up with him again? I hope you told him to take a hike!"

Peter was not one of Jerome's favorite people, and Jade had not even told him the worst parts about their relationship.

"I have no idea what he wants," she responded. "But I think I should talk to him."

"You're joking! What about?"

"Well, think about it. When I moved out, I did it without confronting him. I never asked him why he was treating me the way he was. He never gave me any explanations or justifications. I mean, I suspected that he was seeing someone else, and I knew that he was pushing me away, but I never looked him in the eye and asked the question."

"But that's what I'm saying. Why would you want to let an asshole like that back into your life? It just doesn't make any sense!"

"I'm not letting him back in, but I still deserve an explanation, even after four years."

"I thought you were over him."

"I am, and I have been for a long time. But I have to admit, sometimes I still wonder what happened."

"He still has you thinking it was your fault, that's what the problem is." Jerome shook his head in disgust.

"C'mon, Jerome. Give me a break. It has nothing to do with that."

"Then what is it? Tell me why you would want to spend any time with him at all."

"I just want an explanation. I don't know why I need one, but I do." Jade stood up and walked over to the stereo system, suddenly filled with nervous energy. "I know he didn't deserve me, I know he's an asshole, and I know that leaving him was the best thing for me to do. But I had to come up with my own justification."

"Isn't that enough?" Jerome asked.

"It was, until I realized that I could get the truth."

"What makes you think you'll get it?"

"I might not. But then again, I'm not the same person." She flipped through his collection of jazz CDs. "I want to hear what he has to say, and I'll try to take the truth out of that."

"Well, what about this new guy, Ned?" he asked as he started to spread out the black-and-white photos on the coffee table. His concern had clearly subsided.

"His name is Noel, Jerome."

"Ned, Noel . . . whatever. How does he feel about all this?"

Jade chose a disc with a saxophone player on the front jacket and popped it into the player. Her silence was very telling.

"He doesn't know anything about Peter, does he?" Jerome guessed.

"Well, it's never come up."

"So you guys aren't very serious, then." It was a statement, not a question.

"I don't know," Jade said very softly. That was a whole other issue that she was not prepared to analyze at that time. Once the music came on, she walked over to the couch and used that opportunity to change the subject. "Guess what we did last night?"

Jade told him about the restaurant, the reggae concert, and Noel's Jamaican heritage. Jerome did not seem to be too impressed, even though she knew that he was a major Bob Marley fan. Clearly, it was going to take more than that for him to relax about the new guy in her life.

"What do you think of this one?" He held up an 8" x 10" of her wearing a long black wig, a black bolero jacket, and a full black-and-red ankle-length skirt. Character shoes completed the outfit, and she stood in a traditional tango pose. It was very striking. The contact sheets she had reviewed weeks ago had not done justice to the finished shots.

"Wow!" was all that she could say. It was hard to believe she was looking at a picture of herself. "You made me look so Spanish!"

"I'm thinking of showing those last four to Carlos Rodriguez and his manager."

"That's the guitarist, right?"

"Yeah. I have a meeting with them on Tuesday." He was clearly very excited.

"Wow. Well, they're amazing." She still could not believe the images. She had never liked pictures of herself, always seeing her faults magnified in them. But these were wonderful. Jade picked up a couple of the shots that had been done at the beginning of the photo shoot. At that point, she had been wearing only a long black unitard and *pointe* shoes. Her hair was pulled back in a classic bun. By using a special filter and a slower shutter speed, Jerome had softened the image and created a blur behind her movement as she did various kicks *sur les pointes*.

"Jerome, could I use some of these for the open house?"

"Sure, as long as they're not the ones I plan on selling."

"Okay."

They spent another half hour flipping through his

portfolio and talking about his plans. When it was time to go, it was obvious that Jerome wanted to say something more about her dinner plans. Jade just gave him a kiss and a hug, then promised to give him a call later that evening.

Jade hoped that Peter did not know where she lived, and she had insisted that they meet at a restaurant. She did not want to give him any impression that she was going to get cozy with him. An emotionally detached discussion in a busy public place was the best solution.

When she pulled into the parking lot of a popular steak house several miles north of her apartment, Jade looked around to see if he was already there. It was 7:10 P.M. and though she was a few minutes late, she was in no rush to go inside. She shut off the car and sat staring out the windshield for several minutes. The keys jingled noisily in her hands as she toyed with them. Was this a bad idea? Was Jerome right about her motives? Why had she not told Noel about Peter at all? Before she could further second-guess herself, Jade stepped out of the car and strode into the restaurant with her head high and shoulders back.

Peter had a beer in his hand as he stood at the bar waiting for her. He paused with the drink halfway to his mouth when she walked in. Jade's presence had always had a strong impact on him, and today was no different. She was dressed causally in loose khaki pants and a black camisole top. The straps of her top were so thin that the lacy straps of her black bra were also clearly visible. Peter lowered his beer again, forgetting to take the drink.

When Jade caught him staring at her, she did not walk over to him. Instead, she planted her feet and waited for him to join her. He was the one who had requested this meeting, and she was not going to do any additional work to facilitate it. She knew it was petty, but so be it.

As he walked toward her, she deliberately did not wave or smile in welcome. Instead, she watched him approach with an impassive expression on her face.

"Hello, Jade." He was prevented from saying more by the hostess, who approached them and led them to their table. "I'm glad you came," he finished when they were both seated.

Jade did not say anything in response.

"Would you like something to drink?" he asked.

"Perrier water would be nice," she said before she picked up her menu. Trying to appear calm and collected, Jade chose a meal while Peter placed their drink order with their waiter.

"For a moment, I wondered if you were going to show up," Peter continued.

"Why?" Jade responded, her face still covered by the large menu.

"Well, you made it pretty clear that you were reluctant to come."

Jade lowered the menu to respond, looking him straight in the eyes. "To be quite honest, I'm not sure what your motives are, that's all."

"What are your motives?" Peter asked, with a provocative smile on his thin lips.

Jade saw right through it and was not interested in his games.

"Why don't we just get to the point?" she suggested without returning his smile. "Why are we here?"

"Okay, it's obvious that you're suspicious, but I swear, I just want to talk."

"What about?"

"Well, for starters, how are you?"

"Peter, cut the crap. What do you want?"

"I just told you. I want to know how you're doing. You look great, by the way."

"Thank you, and I'm doing great." Her sarcasm was obvious.

"Is it so suspicious that I would want to see how you're doing?"

"Very suspicious, actually, considering it's been so long since I left."

They were interrupted again by the waiter, who brought their drinks and took their meal orders.

"Well, that doesn't mean I haven't wanted to call," Peter responded. He then did this thing he always did when he knew she had every right to be angry with him: he lowered his head to one side and looked up at her with sheepish eyes. Had he always been this transparent?

"None of this explains why you would want to talk to me now." Jade was surprised at how easy it was to resist being pulled into his false charm. It was becoming very clear that he no longer had an effect on her, and she was very relieved. This whole discussion might be kind of fun. He had no clue how much she had changed, and he was in for a rude awakening!

"I guess I've just been thinking about you a lot lately, you know? Wondering what's been going on with you, what's going on in your life."

"Why?" Jade sipped her drink, completely unaffected by his claim of concern.

"Jade, we used to be very close. I mean, there was a time when we were inseparable."

"You didn't find it that difficult to 'separate' when

I packed up all my things and moved out of our place. You certainly didn't try to stop me." She deliberately kept all traces of emotion out of her voice.

"I know, and I recognize that my behavior at that time was unacceptable. I'm very sorry about that."

Jade could not believe it when he actually reached out to hold her hand in consolation! He must be on crack! She looked down at his outstretched palm, then back at his face, and pulled her hand farther away. Peter took a drink from his second beer.

"Look, it's obvious that you're still angry with me," he said. "And I know you have every right to be. But I swear, my intentions are just to talk, to explain what happened."

"So, explain."

Peter took a deep breath. "Okay, okay." Another breath. "After you left, I moved in with Fiona."

"Fiona?" Jade repeated, with a wrinkled brow.

"From the shop." He looked at her to see her reaction, but Jade stayed perfectly still. She remembered Fiona, an administrative assistant at the manufacturing plant, as a ghetto-girl with bad teeth and a huge behind.

Peter continued. "I swear that I wasn't seeing her or anything while you and I were together, but shortly before you moved out, she told me she was pregnant."

Jade burst out laughing. There was not much humor in what he was saying, but she couldn't help it.

"Let me get this straight," she said when she calmed down. "You weren't seeing her, but she got pregnant? I think you need to explain that one a little more."

"What I mean is that we only slept together one time, I swear it! It wasn't like I was in love with her, you know?" he explained.

"Yet you moved in with her."

"Look, it was clear that you weren't going to change your mind and come back, and she was pregnant. I knew that I had created a bad situation, so I did what I thought was best."

Jade did not respond.

"I wasn't planning to stay with her. I just moved in to get my situation together. Like I said, I wasn't in love with her or anything."

"Why didn't you tell me this? Why did you start to treat me like dirt?"

"I don't know. At the time, I didn't know how to deal with the situation. Plus, things weren't right between us."

"Really? What gave you that idea?" She could not hold back her sarcasm. "Could it have been the fact that you were cheating on me? Or perhaps it was because you raped me?" Jade had not meant to bring up that awful final night, but the words could not stay lodged in her throat.

Peter did not say anything, nor did he look up from the label of his beer.

"What exactly was right about our marriage?" she asked.

"I didn't rape you."

"What did you say?"

"I didn't rape you." He said it louder and stronger the second time. "Maybe I was a little rough, but I didn't rape you."

Jade shook her head in disbelief. *Did he really believe this crap?*

"I was angry and under a lot of stress, okay? I didn't know what I was going to do about my situation, but I didn't rape you! We were married for God's sake!"

"So the bruising on my body and the bleeding and soreness I had for days afterward were from rough sex?" It took every ounce of control for Jade to keep her voice even and unemotional. "But that's right, I left the next day, so you would hardly know any of that. It's not like you even called to see how I was doing, or perhaps to apologize."

"Come on, Jade. I'm sure it wasn't that bad, but I'm sorry if I hurt you."

"If," she repeated.

"Look, I know I was an ass at times. But things just got out of hand. I didn't know how to tell you about Fiona or her pregnancy. At the time, I just thought it would be better for you if I was out of your life."

"When did she tell you that she was pregnant?" Jade asked.

"I don't know, sometime in the summer."

"When, exactly?"

Peter paused and Jade waited with false patience. "In April."

Jade had moved out in August of that year.

"And how pregnant was she at that time?"

"About four months."

Jade did some quick math. "So, she was about eight months pregnant when I left." It was a statement of fact that Peter did not dispute. "So you lived with me for four months while another woman was pregnant with your child."

"How was I going to tell you that? It was the worst time of my life," Peter explained, shaking his head.

"You don't really expect me to feel sympathy for you, do you?" Jade asked incredulously.

"I'm not saying that, I'm just trying to explain what happened."

"So you moved in with her. When was the child born?"

"September 17th. It was a girl, and we named her Camille. She's going to be five years old soon."

Jade just nodded. She had to admit she was a bit in shock. How come no one had known about this? Or maybe people did and just didn't tell her.

"So, you're still with her?"

"You mean Fiona? No, we were never really together."

Their meal arrived at that point, filling the uncomfortable pause in the discussion. Jade ate a forkful of her chicken salad, but it might as well have been grass. Her mouth was dry and her taste buds numb. The more she thought about the whole thing, the more it made sense. Even the timing clicked. Though Peter was often mean and insulting when he was in a bad mood, it had gotten much worse over the last six months they were together. For some reason, her very presence had been something for him to mock and ridicule. She was now coming to realize that his treatment of her was a result of his infidelity and the situation that he found himself in.

"What are you thinking?" Peter asked after the silence continued until they were halfway through their meals.

"Why are you telling me this now?" she asked.

"I don't know. When Andrea told me about seeing you at that art show, it got me thinking that I should clear things up between us."

Jade did not know what she was thinking, though her mind was filled with a million images. The thing that stood out the most was her clear understanding that none of this had anything to do with her. The way

Peter had changed near the end of their marriage was clearly due to the pressures of an extramarital affair. Even his brutality on that final night was clearly because Fiona was going to give birth within a few weeks. None of it was because she was too fat, or too ugly, or too ambitious, or too needy.

"I had always wondered if you cheated on me. Why did you do it?" Jade asked finally.

"I don't know, Jade. It was just one of those things, you know? I ran into her at a party one night when I was out with the boys," he explained. "She got drunk and I had a few beers. One thing led to another, and the rest is history."

Jade did not mention the fact that he obviously had not used protection. But he was right about one thing: the rest was definitely history. She had heard enough to finally understand that part of her life.

"Can I ask you something?" Peter said. They were both finished with dinner.

"It depends on what it is," she responded. Her voice was still surprising calm, her demeanor very collected. Later, she would marvel at her strength and composure.

"Why didn't you ever file for divorce?"

It could have been her imagination, but Jade sensed some hope in his voice.

"Actually, I did."

"What do you mean? I've never received anything."

"I know. About a year after I left, I went to a lawyer and had everything drawn up. I just didn't finalize it."

"Why?" he asked.

"Well, to be honest with you, I didn't want to have to seek you out. I didn't want to speak to you or have any contact with you at all."

"I understand."

"Do you?" Again, her sarcasm was obvious.

Peter ignored it. "So where do we go from here?" he asked.

"What do you mean?"

"Well, we're still married."

He definitely was on crack, Jade thought.

"Peter, just in case you're confused, we have not been married for over four years. The rest is just a technicality."

"Look, Jade, you have every right to be angry with me. But I've thought about it over and over, and I'm convinced that if you really wanted us to be through, you would have served me those divorce papers a long time ago."

He was clearly working his way up to some sort of declaration. Jade just could not believe the direction he was heading in.

"Let me understand what you're trying to say," she cut in. Her composure was not going to last much longer. The anger was building slowly but surely. "You thought you could just show up on my doorstep after over four years without a word, take me to a cheap dinner, and because I haven't sent you divorce papers, we could begin again like nothing happened? Are you crazy?"

The last sentence was much louder than acceptable for normal conversation in a restaurant. The couple at the table beside them looked over to check out the action.

"That's not what I meant, and you know it. I'm just saying that if you were honest with yourself, you would admit that you still have feelings for me. Otherwise, I'm sure the divorce would be finalized by now." His voice had taken on a smug confidence that made her want to smack him. "Why else would you still be single after all this time? I mean, it was you who called me last night."

"What makes you think I'm single?" Jade demanded. She could not believe his gall!

"You are, aren't you?" he asked as though he had inside information and was sure of the answer. "I'm just saying that there is no reason for us not to see if we can work this out."

"Peter, if you must know, I'm not single at all. I'm involved with someone who is very special to me." It was clear by his expression that he did not believe her. "Your source is either very unreliable or very outdated," she responded, her disgust obvious in her tone.

"Does he know you're still married?" His smugness had faded slightly.

"I told you, we haven't been married for several years. The legal technicality can be corrected at any time," Jade stated, suddenly wanting to go home and take a shower. The conversation was no longer of interest to her. "In fact, why don't you give me your address, and you'll get your papers real soon."

"Come on, Jade. Don't be like that," Peter cajoled when he saw her begin to collect her purse and prepare to leave.

"In addition to your papers, you will also get documents listing everything that belonged to us," she continued, deliberately ignoring his words. The only remaining evidence of her fury was the rapid rise and fall of her chest.

"What are you talking about?"

"At the advice of my lawyer, I listed everything that

was owned by both of us that I left behind. I expect to be reimbursed for half the value." She stood up to say good-bye.

"Come on, Jade. None of that is important to me." Peter also stood up and reached out and grabbed her arm. "Let's just take some time to think about all this and discuss it later. I still care about you."

"Peter, trust me, there is nothing else to discuss." With obvious distaste for his touch, she pulled her arm away from his grasp and stepped out of his reach. "Thank you for dinner. Good-bye, Peter." With her head held high, she walked away and did not look back.

Chapter 18

It was after eight o'clock Sunday evening when Noel remembered Nicki's voice mail message from the day before.

He and Kyle had picked up some food and went to Kyle's place to eat and hang out after playing ball. By five o'clock, they were both fully engrossed in a military-style video game on Kyle's Xbox. Noel then refused to leave until he had beaten Kyle by killing all of his troops in the final game. It was the only game he had won all afternoon.

After he stepped into the house and dropped his gym bag by the staircase, Noel checked his phone messages. There was only one message, and it was from Debbie, not Jade. He had not made any plans to see Jade that night, but he was still disappointed at not hearing her voice checking in. Sunday night was not their regular night to get together, but sometimes they had really long phone conversations that lasted until they were both yawning or nodding off.

Noel plopped himself down onto the couch and started flipping through television stations as he listened to Debbie's voice with half an ear. It was one of her typical messages, informing him that she was in town for a couple of days on a stopover and that she would love for them to get together.

It was not until the very end of the message that Debbie referred to their last discussion about his growing relationship with Jade. And it was only to state lightly that she was sure that their silly disagreement was water under the bridge, and that she was looking forward to "kissing and making up," punctuated with a teasing giggle.

For whatever reason, it was Debbie's voice that reminded Noel of his last discussion with Nicki, and then of her ominous message that she had to speak to him. Reluctantly, he dialed Nicki's number.

Laura answered the phone.

"Hey, Uncle Noel."

"Hi, sweetheart. How are you?"

"I'm okay."

"Good. How was your dance class yesterday?"

"It was great! Jade started to give us some moves for the open house. It's sooo cool."

"Great! Well, I can't wait to see them," Noel said with sincerity. "Is your mom home?"

"Yeah, one sec." The phone crackled as Laura dropped it onto a counter, and he could hear her yelling in the background. Nicki picked up from another line.

"I got it, Laura. Hang up the phone!" Noel and Nicki both listened as the first phone rattled around, then went dead. "Hello?" Nicki asked.

"Hey Nic, it's Noel. I got your message."

"Noel! I've been trying to reach you since yesterday. Where have you been?"

Noel ignored her tone. "What about?"

"One second."

He waited patiently as he heard her close a door in the background then return to the phone.

"Okay," Nicki said. "I want you to promise to listen to what I have to say. I know you're going to get upset, but I'm only telling you this to protect you, okay?"

"What?" Noel asked, no longer lounging. Something in Nicki's voice made him sit up straight.

"Okay." She was clearly nervous. "For whatever reason, I had forgotten all about it until I heard them talking. I mean, it's been over two years since someone had mentioned it, so . . ."

"Nicki, what are you talking about?"

"Okay, I'm just going to come out and say it."

He could hear her take a deep breath.

"Has Jade told you about her husband?"

At least ten seconds of silence passed before Noel processed what he had heard. "What? What are you talking about?" He shook his head in confusion.

"Noel, I'm serious. Jade is married."

"Nicki, I was going to forget the things you said yesterday, but now you're going too far!"

"Noel, listen to me. I'm serious. Somehow, I had known about it when Laura started taking lessons at the studio."

"I don't believe this. What? Someone tells you some gossip and—"

Nicki cut him off. "Noel, listen to me. I saw them together."

Again there was silence. Nicki rushed on. "I went by the studio yesterday to drop off a check. I had forgotten to give it to Laura in the morning." When Noel still did not say anything, she continued. "The doors were still open, so I went upstairs to give it to Jade. Noel, I heard them talking."

He was staring at the television, unable to move.

"Noel, are you listening?"

"Go on," he responded. His tone was flat and life-less.

"They were in her office, so I didn't really see him, just the back of his head. Anyway, at first I could only hear mumbling, but when I walked closer, thinking it was a student or something, I heard him mention their wedding anniversary. I was so shocked that I stopped outside the office before they could see me."

"How do you know it was their anniversary he was talking about?" The edge in his voice was obvious. This was not for real, he thought. It was definitely Nicki's attempt at a sick joke. "How do you know?"

"Noel, he specifically said that it had been their wedding anniversary that had gone by and that he had missed her. She didn't deny it."

"What did she say?" Noel asked, his voice getting louder. He could feel the heat rising in his face while his hand felt damp and clammy. He wiped the palm of his free hand on the material of his jeans.

"I don't remember, I—"

"What do you mean, you don't remember? You seem to remember everything else! What did she say?"

"Stop yelling!" Nicki responded. "I couldn't really hear her. But it was clear that Jade was not happy to see him. She wasn't upset or anything, just kind of cold and uninterested."

"This doesn't make any damn sense!"

"Look, Noel, I didn't want to be the one to tell you this, but I had to be sure you knew. I was hoping that she had told you."

Noel's brain was racing, trying to come up with

some rational explanation to make sense out of non-sense. Nicki continued, clearly uncomfortable with the silence.

"When I was driving home, I remembered that someone had mentioned that she was married, but, like I said, it was about two years ago, back when Laura first started dancing. I just wish that I had remembered earlier."

"They must be divorced," Noel said, like a statement of fact. It was the only thing that made sense. "So she's divorced."

"Noel, I don't think so."

"How do you know?"

"Well, it was just the way he was talking, you know? Like she was still his wife," she tried to explain.

"Look Nicki, I appreciate your need to tell me about this, though I'm not sure I like you spying on Jade, listening to her conversations." His voice got louder again. "You made your opinion of her quite clear yesterday. If this is another attempt to tell me how much you disapprove, I'm not really interested."

"I'm only trying to stop you from making a mistake and getting hurt." Nicki said in defense.

"You know what? Stop! I don't need your opinions or your approval."

"How can you say that?"

"I have to go." He didn't want to talk about this anymore.

"Noel, this is—" The rest of her indignation was cut off by a dial tone.

One phrase kept running through his head over and over again as he stared blankly at the television: *What the hell is going on?*

Noel sat frozen for what seemed like hours but was

only about ten minutes. Then he picked up his portable phone and punched in Kyle's number.

"Yo!" Kyle said when he picked up his line. It was obvious that he had seen Noel's number on the call display. "What's up?"

"Kyle, man, you're not going to believe this. Are you sitting down?"

"What's going on?"

Noel burst out laughing without any hint of humor. "Well, how do I start?"

"What, man?" Kyle's anxiety was obvious. Noel could just see him with a hand on his head. It was the usual pose he had when he was impatient or upset.

"Basically, I just found out that Jade might be married." Saying it out loud did not make it any easier to believe.

"What? You've got to be joking. When did she tell you that?"

"She didn't, which is part of the problem." Noel stated.

"Look, Noel, just cut the drama and tell me what happened. How did you find out? Have you confronted her yet?"

Noel let out a dry, sarcastic laugh. "Believe it or not, I heard it from Nicki."

"What?"

"That's right. To make a long story short, Nicki was at the dance studio yesterday and overheard Jade talking to some guy. He made reference to their wedding anniversary, and Jade didn't dispute it," Noel explained, as he paced back and forth in front of his couch. The more he talked about the whole situation, the more his nervous energy increased.

"But you've been seeing her since before the summer. How could you not know if she's married?" Kyle asked, clearly confused.

"Well, it's obvious they're separated or something, because she definitely doesn't live with him."

"Did Nicki say they were still married? I mean, they could be divorced."

"That's what I said to Nicki, but she seemed convinced that that wasn't the case." Noel was not about to tell Kyle that Nicki might have an ulterior motive for believing the worst about Jade. "But, if she's divorced, why hasn't she ever said anything? That doesn't make any sense."

"Unless she has something to hide," Kyle finished. "Have you guys talked a lot about ex-partners?"

"What do you mean?"

"Well, have you told her about Sandra and that whole situation?"

Noel paused before responding. "No."

"Why?"

"I don't know. It never came up. Plus, it has nothing to do with anything because I haven't even seen her in over three years."

"The point is, if you haven't told her about your ex-fiancé, why would you expect her to tell you about her ex-husband? Maybe it just didn't come up?"

"Assuming he *is* an ex," Noel responded. Noel didn't acknowledge Kyle's logic, mostly because he didn't really want to analyze why he had not mentioned the whole Sandra fiasco to Jade.

"Does Jade know that Nicki overheard the conversation? Did Nicki say anything to them?" Kyle asked.

"No, she left the studio without saying anything."

They both digested the situation quietly for several seconds.

"What are you going to do?" Kyle asked.

"I . . ." Noel stopped midsentence when his phone beeped, indicating another caller. "Just a sec, Kyle. Someone's on the other line." Noel did not wait for a response before he clicked over. His agitation and impatience were very thinly veiled as he answered the second line.

"Hey, babe. You're home." The voice was silky smooth and thick with familiar intimacy.

"Hey, Debbie." She was not someone he wanted to deal with right then. "Can I give you a call back? I'm just on the other line."

"Sure."

"Okay. Give me a few minutes." Noel clicked back over to Kyle. "Yeah."

"Was that Jade?" Kyle asked.

"No."

"Noel, you're going to have to ask her what's going on."

He was thinking the same thing. "How? How do I even bring it up? How do I explain how I know? I can't exactly tell her that Nicki was spying on her."

"I don't know, man. But this is serious."

Noel scratched the back of his neck with his head bowed. "I don't know, man. Maybe I figured the whole thing all wrong."

"How's that?"

"Well . . ." Noel was hesitant to verbalize the direction of his thoughts. All he knew for sure was that he was pissed. Yes, the situation with Jade was puzzling and would have to be figured out, but it didn't really upset him. Not yet. What pissed him off was that he was scared. "I don't know. Jade and I have had a good time together. Maybe that's all it is."

"Come on, man. Don't jump to any conclusions or anything. Just talk to her." Kyle clearly heard the disillusionment in Noel's voice.

"Yeah," was all he said in response. "Anyway, I'm going to head into the shower."

"Cool," Kyle said. "I'll see you tomorrow."

After Noel ended the call, he pressed the speed-dial button programmed with Jade's number. The voice mail kicked in. For a second, he contemplated just hanging up. Instead, he left a generic message for her to give him a call when she got home, then tossed the phone onto the couch. He stood for several minutes in the living room with his head bent, staring at a spot in the carpet. When nothing appeared any more clear or sharp, he sighed and headed up the stairs and into his bathroom.

He was sitting on the edge of his bed with wet hair and a towel when the doorbell rang. His alarm clock indicated that it was a few minutes before ten o'clock. With haste, Noel pulled on a pair of soccer shorts before running downstairs. His elevated heart rate betrayed his hope that it was Jade.

But it wasn't.

Chapter 19

Noel swung open the door to find Debbie leaning casually against the wall of his porch. Her seductive smile dimmed slightly when she noticed his bare chest and wet hair.

"I hope I'm not interrupting anything?"

"Debbie," was all Noel said. He was disappointed.

"Hey, babe." If she noticed his lack of enthusiasm, she did not give any sign. "Is this a private party or can I join?"

Noel stepped back into the house and Debbie followed.

"Sorry I didn't call you back."

"That's okay. I hope you don't mind me stopping by. It's been a while." Before the summer, and before Jade, Debbie occasionally came over on Sunday nights on her way to the airport for her regular red-eye flight to Los Angeles. Noel had always given her the impression that it was a welcome way for him to end the weekend. It was clear that Debbie was testing the waters and was uncertain how welcome she would be.

"Would you like something to drink?" he asked as he headed into the kitchen to grab himself a beer.

"Anything is fine," Debbie responded as she walked into the living room. She interpreted Noel's question as an invitation to stay and get comfortable. After placing her oversized purse on the floor, she sat on the couch and crossed her long, lithe legs for display. High-heeled sandals caressed perfectly pedicured feet. Carefully, she arranged the edge of her silky skirt to hit midthigh and checked the neckline of her thin button-down shirt. Thick, erect nipples added the perfect finishing touch.

Noel took in the display when he entered the room and placed both their drinks on the coffee table. It was a familiar routine, and as usual, Debbie looked hot. Noel sat down beside her.

"It has been a while, hasn't it?" Debbie commented. Their relationship had never included subtleties. She leaned forward to pick up her iced tea and conveniently revealed the edge of a lacy white bra. "I've missed your touch."

Noel watched as she licked the rim of her glass before taking a sip. Still, he did not say anything. It was a very seductive performance.

"How are you, Noel?" she asked.

"I'm all right. How are things with you?"

"Things are good. Hectic as usual." She took a second sip from the tall glass, then set it back down before uncrossing her legs.

"Are you on your way back to L.A.?"

"Yeah, the usual trip," she replied. "From there, I think I might be able to get a run to France."

"Cool."

"Are you sure you're okay? You seem tense."

"Just the usual," Noel responded. It was his turn to pick up his beer and take a long drink. He was not surprised when Debbie slipped off the couch to kneel on the floor beside him. He watched her through hooded eyes.

"Well, I think you need to relax." She tugged on his bare knee to open the space between his legs, and gracefully placed herself between them. Noel took another drink. That was the way things had always been between them.

As Debbie unbuttoned her shirt to reveal her bra, Noel contemplated the situation. Most of Noel's brain was telling him to stop her and tell her this wasn't going to happen. Except the part that was angry. That part of his brain was telling him that it had been a mistake to stop thinking of himself as a single guy who was free to do what he wished. He had made no commitments or promises of fidelity. More important, neither had Jade. He had been acting like a punk but not anymore.

Debbie pushed the edges of her shirt aside. Her small, well-shaped breasts were spilling from the underwire push-up bra, and their dark-tipped ends were clearly visible. When she tugged at her nipples bringing them to their full swollen length, Noel smiled in appreciation before he tipped his head back and swallowed the rest of his beer. She was really hot. What single man in his right mind would not appreciate her efforts? Noel reached out and brushed the back of his hand across an engorged nipple, but could not force the image of Jade's darker, fuller breasts from his mind.

He sighed deeply as put down his beer on the coffee table then used both hands to rebutton Debbie's shirt and cover her nakedness. It took her several moments to realize his intentions. When she looked up from her position on her knees between his legs, he could see her surprise and confusion.

"Look, Debbie, I'm sorry, but this just isn't going to work," he stated.

Her face fell before she looked away. As graceful as possible, she got her feet under her and stood up. Noel stood up as well.

"Do you mind if I borrow the bathroom to freshen up?" she asked while trying to reassemble her bra and shirt. Her voice was cool.

"No problem," Noel responded as he went into the kitchen carrying her half-full glass of iced tea and his empty beer bottle. He stood in front of the sink and cursed his body for betraying him. His flesh had not responded to Debbie's blatant sexuality, something that had never happened to him before. He had let her continue to tease him in the hopes that he would get hard for her. He did not want to believe that Jade had ruined him for other women.

Noel cursed again.

When Debbie emerged from the powder room looking just as polished as when she arrived, Noel met her near the front doors. They were both silent as she double-checked her purse to ensure nothing was left behind.

"Well," Debbie said as she looked up and fixed her gaze on a spot behind his shoulder. "She must be some special woman."

"She is," he replied softly, automatically.

"You're serious, aren't you?" she asked, this time looking directly into his face. "You're in love."

Noel was too confused to respond.

"I thought you had made it up."

"Made what up?"

"That you had met someone."

"Why would I make that up?"

"I don't know. It just seemed so unlikely. You've always insisted that you have no interest in a relationship," Debbie explained. "When you said that we couldn't see each other anymore, I wondered if the real reason was that you had gotten bored with me."

"Debbie, come on," Noel said as he shook his head.

"I know, it does sound silly when I say it out loud," she acknowledged. "But that's the only reason I came over here. I guess I wasn't ready to give up what we had, and I thought I could convince you that I was worth keeping around."

"Debbie, I—"

"Noel, you don't have to say anything," she said with a bright, genuine smile. "You're really in love."

Noel said nothing as she stepped up to him for a hug. While in his embrace, she whispered into his ear, "I hope that she deserves you."

"Have a safe flight," Noel replied neutrally.

After a final squeeze, he closed the door behind her. As he walked back to the family room, his mind wandered back to a time not too long ago, when the only sex he had was the type that was forgotten once it was over. The women he had it with were just as forgettable. It was not that the sex had not been good or that the women were not beautiful. Simply put, Noel had wanted it that way. If the women wanted more, that was when he cut them loose. They all knew the way it was from the beginning, just like Debbie did. If they expected more or wanted things to be different, it was not his fault.

The irony of his current situation was not lost on him. There he sat on a Sunday evening waiting for a woman to call him, and wondering if she was as serious about their relationship as he was. She had not made any promises or declared any particular feeling for him over the past few months. But that had not stopped him from falling in love with her and hoping that she felt the same. And to add insult to injury, she could very well be married.

Yet, there he sat flipping channels on a Sunday night, waiting for her call, waiting for an explanation. It was ironic and pathetic.

Noel watched the news for several more minutes before he switched off the television and went to bed.

At the same time, in another suburb of Chicago, Jade and Trish were leaving a movie theater. They decided to see a movie at the last minute, so they had been stuck with the late show. As they stepped out of the air-conditioned comfort and into the muggy heat of the July night, Jade suggested that they grab a cup of coffee. They dodged people and cars until they reached the nearby gourmet coffee shop. There were several available tables on the patio. Trish picked out the one with the best people-watching view while Jade signaled the waiter.

"What time does your shift start tomorrow?" Jade asked Trish. She had been very surprised that Trish had agreed to go out so late, much less to stay longer for coffee. She was very greedy when it came to her sleep.

"I'm supposed to start at eleven, but I'm thinking about calling in sick," Trish responded.

"Why, what's wrong?"

"Nothing, really. I've just been feeling really tired lately."

"Have you gone to the doctor?"

"Not yet. I have an appointment on Wednesday. It's probably just my iron level. I'm supposed to be taking supplements, but I hate pills."

"Hey, ladies," their waiter interrupted them. "What can I get you tonight?"

Trish went first. "Ummm, I'll try one of those chilled coffee drinks. Medium-size and the one with caramel on top. And a slice of chocolate mousse cake."

"No problem," he promised before he turned to Jade.

"Just a latte, please," she requested.

"What size would you like?"

"A regular, please."

"Anything else?"

"No, thank you," Jade responded. For a second, the rich, smooth flavor of a cheesecake tempted her taste buds, but she didn't change her mind.

"So, where is Noel tonight?" Trish asked as they waited for their orders.

"I'm not sure. He's probably at home, or still out with his friend Kyle."

"Sooo . . . how are things going with you guys?"

"Pretty good. I think so, anyway," Jade added. "I don't know, Trish. I don't really have any complaints."

"You sound like there is something wrong with that."

Jade laughed lightly. The truth was that it did feel a little strange to be in harmony with a man.

Their beverages arrived, followed quickly by Trish's

dessert. Jade took that opportunity to introduce a new topic of discussion.

"Trish, guess who I had dinner with today?" She had deliberately not told Trish anything about Peter's reappearance.

"Who?" Trish did not even bother to guess.

Jade took a sip of her hot latte. After two, then three slow sips, it was clear that Jade was prolonging her actions for dramatic effect.

"Who?" Trish asked again, with more emphasis and anticipation.

"Peter." Jade waited for the shocked reaction, but instead saw only mild confusion.

"Peter who?" Trish went back to eating her cake. "Kashira's ex?" Kashira used to be a good friend of theirs.

"Peter Johnson."

It was a good ten seconds before Trish really processed the information. Jade continued to sip her drink to hide her secret smile. It was clear that Trish was speechless, and Jade wanted to savor the victory.

"What? You can't be serious!"

"I'm very serious."

"Whoa! Back up! How the hell did you end up eating dinner with Peter? Please tell me you're joking!" Clearly, her speechlessness was short-lived.

"Basically, he showed up at the studio yesterday."

"Just out of the blue? Why?"

"I have no idea," Jade responded. "He just walked in and casually said 'hi.' Like he was visiting an old acquaintance instead of the wife he hadn't contacted in four years."

"Why now?" Trish was clearly blown away.

"I have no idea." In the briefest way possible, Jade

told Trish about her talk with Peter at the studio, then his request that they meet for dinner. "You probably think I'm nuts, Trish, but the time had come. If I didn't accept his invitation and hear what he had to say, I knew that I would just be running from the truth."

"The truth about what?" Trish asked.

"About what happened to us. Don't get me wrong, it wasn't really going to change anything, but I still needed to hear it, you know?"

Trish nodded.

"It's funny, whenever I thought about what it would be like to see him again, I always thought it would be very emotional and painful. But it wasn't. I didn't really feel anything at all. Well, maybe I was a little annoyed and disgusted, but that's it." Jade explained her feelings with a sarcastic smirk that made Trish burst out laughing. "Maybe I just imagined the worst so that I could deal with the worst."

"Seriously, though," Trish asked between chuckles, "how did you feel when you saw him?"

"I *am* serious. I didn't really feel anything. What was weird was that it was like I was in somebody else's body. I was watching the whole thing like a fly on the wall. It was very surreal." Jade stared into her half-empty cup as she remembered the effects of Saturday afternoon.

"Now that I look back on it, it was almost like seeing a very old acquaintance, like someone from high school," Jade continued. "It's interesting to see them and you sort of recognize them, but you're not really all that interested in catching up on old times, you know what I mean?"

Again, Trish nodded.

"So, what's the story?" Trish asked, when it was clear that Jade was not about to volunteer any of the juicy information.

"Well, it's nothing all that interesting. It's not like he was dying of cancer or anything. It went something like this: Peter got another girl pregnant. He claims that he didn't know how to tell me. After I left, he moved in with the pregnant girl and has a daughter who is now four years old. He thinks it's a good idea for us to try again."

Trish's mouth dropped lower and lower as Jade told her tale.

"You can't be serious!"

"As serious as a heart attack!" Jade confirmed. "He sat there looking so pathetic and told me how rough it was, and how he hadn't wanted to hurt me, so he let me leave."

"What an ass!" Trish exclaimed.

"You're too kind."

"How can you be so calm about this? I swear to God, someone would have had to pull me off that son of a bitch!"

"Well, like I said, for whatever reason, the whole thing felt like I was listening to the life story of an old acquaintance. What really pissed me off was his insinuation that we could work it all out."

"What?"

"I'm not kidding! Peter sat there with a straight face and actually suggested that since I hadn't filed for a divorce, we should try to work things out."

"He must be crazy!" Trish determined.

"Funny, that's what I thought," Jade responded, while Trish struggled to take in all the details. "And that, my dear, was pretty much the whole story."

Jade deliberately left out the discussion about that painful and violent last night with Peter. She had been too ashamed at the time to tell anyone but Trish about the assault, and she was definitely not going to bring it up now. The fact that Peter had labeled her pain and bleeding as "rough sex" only added insult to injury.

"I just can't believe that guy. I mean, I knew he was a slime bucket, but this is just ridiculous!" Trish declared. "Is he still with the chick?"

"He claims that they were never really together, and that he moved out of her place soon after their daughter was born. Personally, I don't believe every word he says."

While they finished their coffee, Jade filled in some more details. Though neither said it out loud, they were both very aware that this day was a turning point in Jade's life. She had spent so many years in a state of suspension, and it had started months before she had moved out. She was technically married but practically single, yet not enjoying the benefits of either. It was obvious to everyone who cared about Jade that she deliberately chose complete isolation from men. Until recently, anyway. She and Trish had skirted the issue on several occasions, but neither had ever really addressed the heart of the problem.

"So, the last thing I said to him before walking out," Jade said, as she finished telling the details of her lunch, "was that he would get the divorce papers soon."

"Umm," Trish tried to respond, but the rich cake in her mouth made her words muffled. "So, what happens now?" she finished after a big swallow.

"Well, I need to book an appointment with my

lawyer. I'm sure some of the paperwork will have to be redone. Then it's just a matter of having the papers delivered to Peter," Jade speculated.

"You know what? I think Peter walking into the studio was the best thing that could have happened," Trish said, after slowly licking mousse from her fork.

Jade laughed in a short, sarcastic bark. "You know what? I think you're right. It seems bizarre to me to admit it, but I needed to see him. And I really needed to hear what he had to say. Like I said, I don't really believe everything he says, but his story replaces some of the ones I came up with on my own."

"Not only that, but soon you're going to be a divorced woman."

"Tell me about it," Jade acknowledged ruefully. "Too bad I can't just get an annulment and pretend the whole thing never happened."

"Either way, the timing is perfect." At Jade's inquiring glance, Trish continued, "I'm talking about Noel. Now there's no reason why things can't work out between you two."

"Oh, come on. There are other issues between us than my marriage," Jade stated.

"Like what?"

"Like the fact that I have no indication that he's even interested in something more serious."

"Then ask him," Trish responded simply. "Better yet, tell him what you want and see what he says."

Jade sighed loudly. That was easier said than done. First, she would have to define and acknowledge what *she* wanted.

Trish scraped the last forkful of dessert off her plate. She slowly savored the final bite before continuing her advice. "I mean, what's the worst that can happen? You keep telling me that he might just be looking for a good time, so if he clearly confirms that, at least you won't be surprised. But I don't think that's what it is. You guys have become very consistent. And he seems like a pretty sincere guy. I think you're more worried that he does want to get serious. Because then you'll have to really think about everything. And I don't just mean the divorce."

Trish's assessment came pretty close to the truth. Closer than Jade was going to reveal out loud. But it was not that simple. Before Jade could point out the complications, Trish almost jumped in her seat after checking her watch.

"Damn, I gotta go. It's almost quarter to one." The waiter had brought the check to them much earlier. Trish dug into her purse and pulled out a ten while Jade matched her rushed pace and added five dollars to the total.

When they stood up, Trish pulled Jade into an affectionate hug. "Everything's going to be just fine."

Jade nodded in agreement.

With a final squeeze, the women parted.

Chapter 20

It was after two o'clock on Monday afternoon before Jade was able to give Noel a call. She was downtown walking toward her car.

"Hey, Noel," she said with a smile in her voice after he picked up his office extension.

"Jade," Noel stated.

Jade thought she heard a slight flatness in his tone, but she dismissed it.

"How's your day going?" she asked.

"Busy," he said. "I left you a message last night."

"I know. I didn't get it until I got home after one." There was another pause, as though Noel was waiting for more information. "Trish and I went to a movie, then hung out drinking coffee for a little bit." She did not add that the topic of conversation had been Peter and his four-year-old daughter.

"Okay," was all that Noel said in response. "Are you at the studio?"

"No, I'm on my cell phone. I was checking out a few venues." Jade ignored the awkward flow of the conversation to tell him her exciting news. "Guess what? I think I found the one I want."

"What are you talking about?"

"A spot for the open house. I think I found the perfect one. It's a small theater just around the block from my apartment. I have seen a couple of plays there before and it's a really nice set up. For a while there, I thought I was going to have to arrange the whole thing in a school gym." Jade laughed lightly at her joke.

The sound became hollow, then faded away when she realized that she was laughing alone. The silence on the other end of the phone made her wonder if she still had a connection.

"Noel, are you still there?"

"Yeah. That's great. So you're all set to confirm a date."

"Yeah, I think a Saturday night is best, and the second weekend in September looks good."

"Cool. Laura said that you guys were practicing the new routines on Saturday."

"Yeah. Everyone is so pumped, especially Laura. You guys are going to be so proud of her," Jade said passionately. She had just reached her car. "Noel, I'm about to get on the road again and head for the studio. I'll speak to you later?"

"Yeah, sure."

"I hope your day gets better. 'Bye."

Noel replaced the handset on his phone after the line went dead. For two minutes, he continued to review the sales report spread out on his desk but gave up when it was clear he was not retaining the information. He threw down his pen in frustration and spun his chair around to stare out the windows at the edge of Lake Michigan.

Until he had fallen asleep the night before, all Noel could think of was what Jade was going to say when he confronted her about her marriage. He had played out many possible scenarios in his mind. In one, she explained that she had been married very young and divorced for years. In another, she told him that she was still in love with her husband and could not see Noel any more. There were about a dozen variations between the two extremes.

Right before falling asleep, he acknowledged to himself that the question of Jade's marriage was not the only thing that bothered him. What if she meant for the relationship between them to be only casual and temporary? The possibility made his stomach hurt because for the first time in a long time, Noel wanted more.

In the shower that morning, his brain took over his threatened heart and questions cluttered his mind. When was Jade going to tell him about her husband? Was their relationship so superficial that he did not deserve to know? Those questions raised other issues. When had he started thinking of her as more than a woman to date? What made him think that she wanted more? Why the hell had he stopped thinking and acting like a single guy?

He must have been crazy but not anymore. What he needed to do was to remember the rules that had served him well for so long. He needed to remind himself that all he wanted to do was to have a good time, nothing more.

By the time he had buttoned up his sky blue cotton shirt over tan chinos, he had realized that confronting Jade with what Nicki had discovered was not the best move. For one, he would have to tell her how he knew, and that would be an uncomfortable discussion at best. After all, Nicki and Laura were her clients.

Secondly, he was not about to put his feelings on the line by demanding information and explanations like an upset boyfriend. He knew better than anyone that it took more than good times and great sex to solidify a relationship. He and Jade had no such commitment to each other—a fact he had obviously ignored until yesterday. Noel had no right to expect her to reveal any private details about her life. For the same reason, he was not obligated to tell her about Debbie or Sandra.

Over and over, throughout the day, he silently repeated his resolve to keep the information to himself and to back off from Jade. The situation with Debbie had only proved how much he had lost his head. He acknowledged that he had tried to use Debbie to try to prove that Jade was no different from any other woman, that she did not have any particular hold over him. But all he did was prove the opposite. Sex with Jade had always left him completely overwhelmed and fully satisfied. It always made him want to hold her close and fall asleep with her head on his chest.

The best solution was to put some space between them.

When he had picked up the phone and heard her voice that afternoon, his first feeling was relief. She sounded so natural and normal, as though nothing had changed. Until he realized that something had, if only for him. He would not be warmed by her intimate tone or cheered by her infectious excitement. He refused to feel anything except mild interest. That was the way it was going to have to be until the situation no longer suited him.

Noel sighed heavily and then swung his chair back around to face the reports again. He picked up his pen and began to study the columns of numbers.

But, no matter how hard he tried, he couldn't focus.

His thoughts went right back to his relationship with
Jade. Maybe he should just end it now. Why was he even
bothering to make sense of this situation? He should
just tell her it wasn't working for him and move on.
That's what he would tell one of his boys to do.

There was only one problem: he still wanted to be
with her.

Jade's day was just as unproductive and frustrating
as Noel's but for very different reasons. Yes, she was
excited to finally confirm the venue for the studio's
open house, but everything else about that Monday
went from bad to worse. It may have started with a fit-
ful night sleep or the headache she woke up with.

While doing the laundry that morning, she noticed
a leak in the laundry room. It was with trepidation
that she left a message for Cliff, the maintenance
man.

She only hoped that he did not send George again
to assist her. Perhaps, in hindsight, she should have allowed George to inspect her water pressure on Friday,
but his behavior had been very strange. Maybe she
was overreacting, but she was still kind of uneasy over
the incident.

Jade left written permission for Cliff to enter her
suite and take care of the necessary repairs, then
headed to the gym. She had hoped that a vigorous
spinning class would help her headache and her
mood, but it did not. Instead, the instructor didn't
show up for the class, and Jade ended up jogging for
forty-five minutes in the wrong shoes. She just knew
she was going to pay for it later with leg and back
pains. Worst of all, when her heartbeat stabilized, her
headache returned with a vengeance.

Seven hours later, at four o'clock in the afternoon,

the pain in her head had finally been reduced to a dull pressure behind her eyes, with the help of Advil. However, the relief lasted only as long as it took for her to check her home voice mail from her office at the studio. As she listened to Peter's voice asking her to call him back so that they could talk some more, she could feel the effects of the painkiller dissipate and the throbbing pressure return.

She had always known that she would run into him again some day and be forced to resolve their issues. Now that the time had arrived, part of her wished she could have avoided it. Maybe it had been a mistake not to have contacted him years ago. They would have already been divorced by now.

Jade had to be honest with herself. She had not been very strong emotionally after she had left Peter. There was no way to know how the news of his infidelity and new child would have affected her.

She was aware that Jerome and Trish questioned her motives for meeting with Peter now, just as they had questioned her motives for avoiding him four years ago. They were worried that she still loved him. They had nothing to worry about, however. The one thing Jade was certain of was that the only strong and lasting emotion she felt for Peter was disgust.

She slumped into her office chair and pressed the button on her phone that deleted Peter's voice mail message. Now that she knew everything, she was certain that she would no longer be haunted by shadows of the past. And after she met with her lawyer on Wednesday, she would have no need to communicate with Peter ever again.

The only class scheduled at the studio on Mondays was an intermediate-level ballet class that started at five o'clock. Knowing that she had some extra time, Jade closed her eyes and tried to relax. The only bright spot in her overall crappy day had been her call to Noel earlier that afternoon. Just thinking about him made her smile. Things were going so well between them that it was a little scary. No matter how much she tried to tell herself to keep things light and casual, she could not prevent her feelings for him from growing.

Noel had been very kind and considerate to her from the very beginning. They had great conversations and rarely argued about anything of importance. All in all, everything was pretty amazing, especially sex. But her own cynicism and experience (mostly other people's) told her that it didn't neccessarily mean she and Noel were heading toward something more permanent.

Was she even ready for something more permanent? Furthermore, did she want something more permanent with Noel? Now that she was on the way to putting closure on her marriage, Jade needed to ask herself those questions and not just push them away because they seemed irrelevant to her situation.

Her meeting with Peter made her self-examination easier. For many painful months after her separation, it had been so easy to blame herself, her body, and her perceived inadequacies. At that time, and from early in her teens, her self-image had been very damaged and negative. Peter had often used those insecurities against her. He had played on her weaknesses to get her to do what he wanted and act the way he wanted her to act. Looking back, she could see the manipulation so clearly. Well, that was the power and clarity of hindsight.

It was one thing to get involved with Noel physically

and perhaps even emotionally to a certain extent. It would be a completely different thing to give in to the lure of love. Was she ready to expose herself to that kind of vulnerability again? She was very aware of the kind of damage a man could do when he used a woman's emotions against her for his own gain.

At quarter to five, the footsteps and chatter of students pulled her out of her relaxed introspection. She shook her head lightly to test the resulting pain level. When the only response was slight pressure behind her eyes, Jade sighed in relief, then walked into her bathroom to change into her dance clothes. Less than ten minutes later, she was stretching and warming up in the studio with Jamiroquoi playing in the background. Once the room was full, she switched the music to a Mozart compilation CD, then began the class.

The rest of the evening went much more smoothly. When she arrived home after a quick stop at the grocery store, she found a note from Cliff explaining that he had replaced a leaking water hose and that her washing machine was usable again. With a lighter step, Jade put away her fruits and vegetables, then got to work on her weekly laundry.

Between loads of whites and colors, she whipped up a salad and watched sitcoms. Before she knew it, it was after ten o'clock and she was dozing off on the couch. Her intention had been to call Noel before she put away her folded laundry, but once she entered the bedroom, the temptation to dive into the softness of her sheets proved too much to resist. She fell asleep almost as soon as her head hit the pillow, her folded laundry left abandoned beside her footboard.

* * *

Sometime in the middle of the night, Jade woke with a start. Her heart was beating so fast that it vibrated in her chest.

"Who's there?" she shouted. "Who's there?"

After several seconds, she switched on the lamp next to her bed. The light revealed an empty room with shadowy edges.

Jade sat still for several minutes trying to understand why she woke with a feeling that someone had been in her room. In the blankness of her sleep, she had felt the presence of a man standing over her, watching her. She had even felt the air above her as his fingers swept over the shape of her cheek. It had felt so real!

But her room was empty.

Jade kicked her comforter off her legs and sat up on the edge of the bed. Slowly, her heart rate returned to normal. She was starting to feel a little silly. Of course it had just been a dream. The idea that someone had been in her locked apartment watching her sleep was just stupid.

On impulse, Jade jumped off the bed and headed toward her front door, switching on all the lights in her path. A quick tug confirmed that the door was double-bolted and secure. She slumped against the wall feeling even more foolish.

Though she still felt creepy, Jade made her way back to her bedroom determined to get some sleep. The only concession she made was to leave on the hall light.

Chapter 21

The rest of the week sped by for Jade. So many things had happened so quickly in the course of a few days and she was swept up in the momentum. On Tuesday, she confirmed the location for the open house, and started looking at the cost and options for advertising. Wednesday morning started with a visit to her divorce lawyer and ended with dinner at Trish's house to update her and Ian on all the details. Thursday and Friday were packed with numerous mundane but necessary errands ranging from banking to dry cleaning.

It was almost 8:30 on Friday night before she realized that she had no plans to see Noel that evening or for the weekend. They had spoken several times in the last few days, but all conversations had taken the same tone as the one on Monday: brief and somewhat one-sided. Instead of being alarmed or disturbed by the unusual distance between them, however, Jade was relieved.

Ever since Peter showed up, she had become very aware of the fact that she was a married woman in an intimate relationship with another man. It was an uncomfortable feeling of guilt. Worse, the "other man" had no idea that she was legally tied to someone else. The feeling was irrational, considering the circumstances of her separation, but it had intensified as the week went by.

The reality was that she was going to have to tell Noel everything very soon. Should she make an issue about it and plan a specific moment to tell him or just bring it up in normal conversation? Should it be the sob story of a victimized wife or just an outline of the facts? Either way, she was dreading it.

It would be easier if she knew how Noel normally reacted to shocking and unexpected news. What if he freaked out and reacted with extreme anger, maybe even violence? Or just told her that he could not trust her and walked out of her life? She may be overreacting, but there was no way to predict how a man would react to that sort of information.

Jade had also seriously considered not saying anything at all. She could quietly get her divorce, then someday explain to Noel about her marriage at a young age as though it was a bad memory. But there were so many things that could go wrong with that plan. For one, Peter was being very persistent in his attempts to talk to her. She could easily see him showing up at her apartment or the studio at just the wrong moment and creating an embarrassing scene.

The worst consequence would be guilt. She would know that she had chosen to be dishonest rather than risk losing Noel. If their relationship did grow into something more permanent, what else would she keep from him out of fear? That was not the type of relationship she wanted to have.

So, she was going to tell Noel all the details of her current situation, and whatever was meant to be, would be. She had already delayed it for too long.

With hardened resolve, Jade sat on the couch,

picked up the phone, and dialed Noel's home number. When she got his voice mail, she hung up and dialed his cell phone.

"Hello," he answered after the first ring.

"Noel, it's Jade," she replied.

"Hey, what's up?"

"Nothing. How are you?"

"Okay. Are you at home?" he asked.

"Yeah."

"I'll call you back."

The line went dead before she could respond.

Now she was anxious. Something was very wrong. It was not that he was unable to talk, it was more his tone. It was completely void of warmth and tenderness.

Jade spent a few seconds chewing on the side of her mouth before she stood up and headed into the bathroom to take a shower. She took the portable phone with her just in case Noel called back right away. As she washed her hair and shaved all the usual parts, she could not get rid of her anxiety.

Over an hour later, Jade started to wonder if he was really going to phone her back, and she contemplated calling his cell again. With her shiny hair blow-dried and hanging straight, she went into the bedroom with a towel wrapped snugly around her body. As soon as she opened her closet to pull out a T-shirt, the phone rang from the bathroom. She ran to pick it up before the third ring.

"Hello," she said trying very hard not to sound rushed and out of breath.

"Hey," Noel responded.

"Hey." There was an awkward pause. "What's up?"

"Nothing. What are you doing?" he asked.

"Nothing, just relaxing. What are you up to?" Jade

wanted to ask him if he wanted to come over, but for some reason the words were stuck in her throat.

"Nothing, really. Do you feel like company?" he asked.

"Sure. Where are you?"

"Just coming up the highway. I'll be there in about ten minutes."

"Okay." Jade smiled in relief. She had obviously overreacted. "Are you hungry?"

"No. I ate a little while ago. Do you want me to bring you anything?"

"No, I'm okay."

"Okay. So I'll see you in a bit."

"Okay."

As soon as she put down the phone, her heart started beating fast. This was it. It was going to have to be tonight. She rushed back into the bedroom while unwrapping herself from the damp towel. She needed to look good; sexy, but in a natural way. She swept by her stack of old faded T-shirts and opened her underwear drawer. She had the perfect lacy set that Noel had not seen yet. It consisted of the most delicate lilac French-cut briefs with a matching push-up bra that was pretty much see-through. Jade had washed them a few days before in anticipation of wearing them for the first time.

She stepped into the panties, then looked at herself in the mirror. She liked what she saw. The narrow cut in the back stretched over her firm flesh, showing her buns to perfection. The sheer lace left very little to the imagination from all angles. It was perfect. Now she just needed to add the bra.

It took a full two minutes of searching before Jade realized that it wasn't in her drawer. When she stopped looking, she realized that she did not remember putting it away, either. Yet it had definitely been washed, and she even remembered removing it from the dryer. It was so bizarre, and it reminded her of the other two pairs of underwear that she also could not find. With a curse, Jade looked at herself in the mirror again. What should she do? The underwear she had selected was so perfect, and she was running out of time.

Without any further thought, she reached into her closet and pulled out a white cotton/Lycra slip-dress. It looked innocent enough on the hanger, but when she pulled it over her naked breasts, it turned into an enticing, sexy piece of lingerie that wrapped her curves and revealed the shadows of her nipples. It was perfect.

Jade was applying lip gloss when she heard a knock at the door. With a secret smile, she teased her nipples to budded fullness before heading to the door. She checked the peephole before she opened it.

Silently, they looked at each other as Noel stepped into the apartment. His eyes took in her body with obvious pleasure. It had been almost a week since they last saw each other and the sexual interest was immediately obvious. While Noel took off his shoes, Jade walked toward the living room and gave him another angle to appreciate.

She was standing in front of the television flipping through the channels when he approached her and cupped her breasts from behind. Jade stood immobilized as he stroked and tweaked her nipples with aggressive fingers. The only sound in the room was the drone of the television, until Noel began to suck and bite the sensitive tendons of her neck. Her response was loud and explosive as tremendous sensations shot through her body.

Noel fed on her moans and moved his assault from the fullness of her breasts to the folds between her legs. Instinctively, he must have known that the lace of her panties would create unbearable pleasure when rubbed against her sensitive flesh. She could not squelch the groans that clogged her throat nor the pleas for him to stop. He didn't, and she didn't really want him to.

Instead, he continued the rough manipulation of her body until her wetness coated his fingers.

On and on it went until Jade felt overwhelmed. When she tried to pull away, Noel applied more pressure and speed to his manipulation of her fragile flesh. Pleasure began to turn into irritation, and his teasing started to feel more like punishment.

Noel must have sensed the change in her groans and suddenly let her go by turning him around to face him. With relief, Jade parted her lips in anticipation of an intimate kiss that would recapture the delicate arousal that she had lost. Instead, Noel pressed down on her shoulder to indicate what he wanted. He then confirmed it as he casually unzipped his pants. It was with a wrinkled brow that Jade lowered herself to her knees and took hold of his hot flesh at its base.

For the most part, she was filled with the feeling of heady anticipation and power. She deeply wanted to pleasure Noel this way and had been looking forward to the opportunity. Yet, as she ran her hands up and down his thick pulsing penis, there was a needle of trepidation poking her shoulder. This was not happening the way she had anticipated. There was definitely a coldness and lack of intimacy that she had never experienced with Noel before, and she did not know how to explain it.

Jade tried to put her uneasiness out of her mind to give Noel what he wanted. She looked up into his eyes as she held him firm and ran a wet tongue along the tip of his hardness. Arousal returned to her as she witnessed the strength of his response. Noel closed his eyes in obvious rapture while his finger ran over the hair on the top of her head.

"Oh, yeah," he groaned when she slowly sucked him into the heat of her mouth. "Oh, yeah, that's it."

Her excitement blossomed with his urging. She started with playful brushing and licks designed to make him beg for more. When the pressure of his fingers in her hair increased in urgency, Jade switched to slow and titillating sucking. Deliberately, she bathed his flesh with her saliva. It was not something that Jade had ever particularly enjoyed in the past, but she wanted to please Noel and give him the ultimate pleasure. She let his response drive her and instinct guide her.

She knew he was losing control. His body moved with uncontrollable urgency.

"Oh yeah, oh yeah . . ." he groaned deeply as he held himself in her mouth. "Oh, oh . . . ."

After a couple of shudders it was over, and Noel stepped away from her. She sat down on the floor to relieve the pressure on her knees while Noel turned away from her and walked into her kitchen.

Jade was very confused. Why did she feel so uncomfortable about what had just happened? Why did she feel violated and discarded? Where was the intimacy and affection that she had come to relish when they were together? While she sat on the carpet, she wondered why he did not return to her, kiss her, and tell her how good she had made him feel.

Jade slowly got up and went to the bathroom. She closed the door and quickly rinsed out her mouth. With her palms resting on the counter, she stared at her face in the mirror.

She had been here before. She had felt this kind of detachment in the past. Sex tonight felt like it always had with Peter: strictly physical and lacking in tenderness and emotion. This was all she had known until she had met Noel. Yet here she was again, wanting to cover her body in shame.

Jade closed her eyes to prevent the tears that clogged her throat from seeping from her lids. She took a deep breath, then rinsed her face with cold water. Maybe she was just overreacting. Noel was probably just feeling really excited, that's all. She would go back to him and resist the urge to change her clothes. Everything was going to be fine.

Noel was in the living room sitting on her couch with a glass of water in his hand. The light from the evening news flickered on the walls of the room. Jade smiled and sat beside him. Noel smiled back. She felt reassured and took a deep breath, ready to start discussing the strange details of her marital status.

The telephone rang and interrupted her. Quickly, she jumped up and went to the wall phone near the kitchen.

It was Peter.

"Finally, I can speak to you live," he stated.

Jade looked at Noel, who looked back at her. She stepped into the kitchen and out of his line of vision.

"I was beginning to think that me and your answering machine had something going on, we talked so much."

She ignored his attempt to be cute. "Peter, what do you want?"

"I just wanted you to know that I got the package from your lawyer today. You weren't kidding."

"So why are you calling me, then?" She was in no mood to be nice to him. "Just read the papers and sign them. There's nothing there that you can object to."

"I know, I know. I'm just saying that we should sit down and go over the details together, that's all."

"Why?"

"I might have some questions, you know?"

"Look, if you have any questions, get your lawyer to call my lawyer and they can talk." She wanted to say something more, but Noel chose that moment to enter the kitchen to put his glass in the dishwasher.

"Why do you have to be like that, Jade? I'm not trying to stop anything, I just want to talk about it."

Jade didn't respond because Noel was looking at her while he slouched against the kitchen counter. She cleared her throat and covered the phone.

"I'll be out in a sec," she said to Noel with a tight smile and then clenched her jaws when he walked away. *Damn!*

"Jade, are you there?"

"Peter, I really have nothing else to say. Read the papers. I have to go." She hung up before he could protest, then prayed he would not call again. The evening was not going well so far, and deep down, she knew it was going to get worse.

Chapter 22

"I have to **get** going."

"What do you mean?" Jade asked as she stepped out of the kitchen. Noel deliberately avoided eye contact as he turned around and headed for the front hall. "Where are you going?"

"I'm going home to take a shower, then I'm going out." He did not turn around but instead began to put on his shoes.

"But, Noel, you just got here," Jade reminded him. She could not believe what was happening. "I thought we were going to spend the evening together."

"Well, I can't stay. And I don't remember us agreeing on that plan."

"Noel, what's going on? Is something wrong?" Jade asked. She hated the anxiety in her tone but could not prevent it.

"Look, what's the big deal? I have other plans," he stated. He really was supposed to meet up with his boys at a nightclub. He just hadn't bothered to tell her about it.

"I don't understand. Then why did you bother coming over at all?" The volume of her voice was elevated, reflecting her increasing anger. She could not believe that Noel was acting that way. She had never heard him talk to her in such a nonchalant, arrogant tone. Couple that with his earlier behavior while they made love—or had sex—and she was getting really pissed off.

"Come on, Jade. It wasn't a total waste of time." His reference to their intimacy was meant to be obvious and insulting. "Plus, I'm sure you can make other plans for the night."

"What is wrong with you? What are you talking about?" Jade demanded as she stepped in front of him and blocked his path to her door. "Noel, this is ridiculous. I need to talk to you about something."

"What?" he snapped. Instantly Jade knew that he was angry with her. It was in his tone and his eyes. It was evident in the clench of his fists. Yet, he wanted to hide it. He would rather act as though their intimacy had been deliberately casual than tell her what was wrong. He had wanted her to think that the night had been a booty call. He wanted to hurt her.

Her own anger faded and was replaced by concern. Deliberately, she continued to stare into his eyes while she reached for his hand. When he tried to pull away, she persisted, then walked back into the living room with him in tow.

"Tell me what's wrong," she said softly after taking a seat. When he stubbornly stood in front of her, she tugged lightly on his hand still clasped in her own. "Sit."

Reluctantly, he complied but shook his hand free in rebellion.

"Noel," Jade persisted, "what's going on?"

"Look, now that you've kept me here by force," he replied sarcastically, "why don't you just say what you want to tell me." He ended his statement with a patronizing stare.

"Well, it's not easy to talk to you while you're being so snappy. Why don't you go first? Why are you angry with me?"

"I don't know what you're talking about. Just get to the point!" He checked his watch to add insult to injury.

Strangely, Jade found his anger slightly amusing. She was pretty sure that he would tell her the cause eventually, and she would wait patiently until he did.

Peter would have laughed in her face, said something truly cruel then walked away. That is what she had been afraid would happen, but clearly Noel was different. He was angry, but he still sat down to hear her out. It made her less worried about telling him her story.

"Well, like I said, I have something to tell you. The truth is, I should have told you weeks ago, but it just didn't seem relevant." She paused to search for succinct words to describe her murky circumstances. With her eyes focused on her hands clasped between her legs, she cut right to the chase. "When I was twenty-three years old, I got married."

After several seconds with silence swelling between them, Jade risked a glance at Noel to judge his immediate reaction. He was staring forward, his face blank.

"Well, it's obvious that things didn't work out well," she stated with a shaky, dry laugh. "Over four years ago, I packed my clothes and left. I never heard from him again. Well, not until recently, anyway."

"What do you mean, 'packed up and left'?" Noel asked. He appeared very reluctant to ask the question, but he could not resist.

"I mean, when he got home from work, I was gone."

"Why?"

"What do you mean 'why'?"

"Why did you leave? Like that?"

"I don't know. At the time, it was the only thing I could do. He had gotten progressively cruel and abusive, and I didn't know how to face him. So I just left," Jade explained. "We were having a lot of problems almost from the start, so it wasn't surprising that we didn't make it. For a long time, I was completely wrapped up in what I did wrong. Like an idiot, I thought it was all my fault. In the end, I just moved on and put the marriage behind me."

Noel didn't appear to have any more questions, so she continued the story. "I guess it was inevitable, but last week, Peter showed up at the studio. I don't know why he chose now, but he gave me some flimsy excuse about it being our anniversary recently. Anyway, it turns out that several months before I left, he had gotten some woman pregnant. He has a daughter almost five years old."

Noel continued to watch her but still did not say anything.

"So, the long and the short of it is that as of Wednesday, my husband has been served divorce papers." Finally, she looked into Noel's eyes in an attempt to gauge his thoughts and reaction. "Let me guess: you want to know why I didn't get a divorce years ago? Well, the truth is, I don't know. It was so much easier not to think about it."

"Do you still love him?" Noel asked instead.

Jade laughed. "I find it hard to believe that I had a real love for Peter. I think it was more of a need for him to love me. Whatever it was, it didn't last long. Now, it's like a distant memory."

Noel nodded but looked away again. "So, you're married," he confirmed.

"Separated. I'll be divorced soon." Carefully, Jade shifted in her seat to be closer to him. "Look, Noel, I'm sorry I didn't say anything sooner. It's just that I haven't thought of him, or my marriage, for a long time. In my heart and mind, it was over the day I left."

Jade leaned in closer to Noel. He did not pull away, but he did not exactly pull her into an embrace either. She chose to take it as a good sign.

"Are there any more deep, dark secrets that you haven't told me?" Noel asked as she put her head on his shoulder. On impulse, he wrapped his arm around her shoulder. "No children away at boarding school or untreatable psychotic conditions?"

Jade laughed lightly. "No, nothing. Everything else about my life is pretty normal and boring."

"Good," he said, before he pulled her into his lap until her legs were draped over his. A light peck on her forehead preceded the deep, penetrating kiss on her lips.

Vaguely, Jade realized that it was their first real kiss in over a week. She would have spent some additional thought on Noel's odd display of anger but was distracted by the thumb that brushed her nipple.

The warm, delicious feeling of arousal was returning and she welcomed it. His touch was so gentle that it left her intoxicated. The feeling was familiar and comforting, reminding her of the unique physical and emotional bond they had shared from the moment they met. It was a feeling that could never be compared to how things had been with Peter, despite her earlier apprehension.

Neither of them had any interest in the inconvenience of moving their lovemaking to her bedroom. Instead, they engrossed themselves in the erotic potential of her couch as Jade settled herself in Noel's lap. Though their movements appeared slow and leisurely, the harshness of their breath revealed a deep urgency.

Very soon, their need to be joined by flesh could no longer be postponed. Jade's dress was scrunched at her waist while Noel's pants and boxers created a pool at his feet. Jade gracefully placed a knee on either side of his hips and took control. Her eyes held his as she moved slowly and sensuously to an instinctual rhythm. Her fingers gripped his shoulders to maintain her balance as she stroked his full length within the wetness of her body.

Noel let her work at her own maddening pace until he could not stand it any longer. Wordlessly, he gripped her hips and changed the pace. When the final moment gripped him, Jade savored the intense feel of his throbbing deep within the center of her being. They remained joined until several moments after the last shudder rippled through his body.

Eventually, they did retreat to the cushioned comfort of her bed but not to sleep. After they both got naked, Noel spooned himself against Jade's back. With infinite care and patience, he touched and stroked her flesh. Her moans of frustrated pleasure only fueled the intensity of his manipulations. When she could not resist it any longer, the waves of convulsions ripped thorough her body with overwhelming strength. As Jade experienced the ultimate pleasure with complete abandon, Noel held her close to share the experience.

They snuggled closely under her comforter while the fine sheen of perspiration cooled on their flesh.

With lazy voices, they discussed the everyday things about the past week. Jade told him about all of her accomplishments with the open house and bemoaned the million things she still had to decide on. Noel vented about his difficult clients and made her laugh with outrageous examples of their fickleness. It was time spent attempting to recapture the effortless companionship that they had both missed over the last few days. They really wanted to put the awkwardness of secrets and mistrust behind them.

The moment was broken when Noel unwrapped himself from her arms and swung his legs over the edge of the bed. Jade sat up as well.

"I have to get going," Noel informed her. His reluctance was obvious as he checked his watch but did not make a move to stand up. It was almost three o'clock in the morning.

"Okay," Jade said. The air conditioning made her shiver without the heat of his flesh beside her. She quickly pulled the comforter up to cover her nakedness.

"Believe it or not, I have to wake up at six o'clock to tee-off at 7:30," he explained.

"You mean 7:30 in the morning? That's crazy!" Jade said.

"I know."

"I didn't even know that you played golf."

"I don't. I mean, I play but not very well," he explained ruefully. "My friend Jason is a golf-freak. I think he plays every Saturday."

"Who's Jason?" Jade asked as she watched Noel finally get up and search for his discarded clothes.

He did not respond to her until he located his underwear within the folds of the comforter. His focus was then on finding his pants and shirt. "He's a really good friend of mine from college. One of his regular golf buddies canceled at the last minute to play instead at some exclusive club up north. So Jason talked me into the round—in a moment of weakness. Apparently, there is nothing better than playing golf first thing in the morning."

Jade smiled but did not say anything. When Noel was fully dressed in his wrinkled clothes, she scurried out of the bed and put on her robe to follow him to the front door.

"What are you doing tomorrow?" he asked.

"Nothing much. I have to do some shopping after my classes."

"Okay." He had slipped on his shoes. "I should be home by about one o'clock. Give me a call, okay?"

"Okay," Jade confirmed before he pulled her into a deep kiss.

When they broke apart, Noël hesitated, then rested his forehead lightly on hers and entwined her fingers in his. "I'm glad that we talked earlier."

"Me, too," Jade said. They stood still for several seconds suspended by shared emotions. "I love you, Noel."

Time appeared to stop. The words had slipped out and could not be taken back. Jade was on the verge of stammering out some excuse or apology or joke to cover up her shocking utterance, when Noel pulled her so close she could barely breathe.

"I love you, too," he declared with his face buried into her neck. "See you tomorrow, okay?" With one last lingering kiss, he left.

While Jade collapsed against the closed door in stunned disbelief, Noel walked slowly toward the ele-

vator. Within the space of several hours, his world had
turned 180 degrees. Everything he had been feeling
and trying to resolve for the last week had resolved
itself. Acknowledging his feelings for Jade out loud
made everything make sense. The cause of his anger,
disappointment, disillusionment, and fear became
very clear the second the words formed on his lips.

When he reached the elevators, Noel paused before
pressing the down button to smile to himself. He remembered Jade's shocked reaction to her own
declaration. It was clear from the tension that straightened her back that the words had probably surprised
her more than they had him. It was clear that the outburst had not been intentional or planned in
advance. Perhaps that was why it had moved him so
deeply. Perhaps it explained why he had revealed his
own feelings with very little hesitation.

The elevator arrived and the doors opened. Noel
stepped into the empty cube with his thoughts still on
Jade and the revelations of the evening. He let out a
deep breath with a loud sigh. He had been living with
heaviness in his heart and pressure on his shoulders
since his momentous telephone discussion with Nicki.

Out of self-preservation, Noel had forced himself to
accept a variety of outcomes to the possibility that
Jade was indeed married. He had fed himself with
anger and indifference to stave off anything deeper
or more painful. Yet, not once did he conceive of a result like tonight. Not consciously anyway. Yet there he
was one week later, unable to dim his smile after sat-
isfying his body and his soul.

Noel walked through the lobby of Jade's building
toward the visitors' parking lot. Except for three piti-
ful and lonely street lamps nearby, it was very dark

when he stepped outside. His car was parked along the back wall of the paved lot, and Noel cut a clear path through the few cars that remained. His thoughts were scattered in several directions, resulting in a limited awareness of the details around him. As he stepped past a large dark utility jeep, his head snapped to the right when an unexpected shadow fell across his path. He could have sworn he was alone in the darkness.

The crippling heat of pain that spread from his abdomen outward to every limb prevented further speculation. Noel dropped like a stone, the air frozen in his lungs. It seemed like hours of suspended time before his brain could grasp what had happened, but it was actually only a few seconds: someone had slammed something thick and heavy into the center of his torso, and that person was standing over his fallen body watching the results.

Through the desperate sounds of his own gasps for air, Noel could hear harsh breathing caused by rushed adrenaline. He could also hear the words uttered with surprising calmness: "Stay away from Jade, she's mine. Do you hear me? Stay away . . ."

The rest of the warning escaped Noel as he lost the battle with conscious thought.

Chapter 23

Saturday crawled by at a snail's pace for Jade. Though she had tried not to focus on the events of the night before, it was nearly impossible. As a diversion, she had increased the complexity of the footwork in the new jazz routine. Then, she increased the intensity and duration of the intermediate ballet class. Other than frustrate her students and exhaust her body, she did not accomplish much. The new development in her relationship with Noel was never really far from her mind.

When three o'clock finally rolled around, Jade had already been at home for almost twenty-five minutes. For whatever reason, she had decided that she should wait until that precise moment to call Noel. Any second earlier would have made her seem too anxious or needy or dependent.

Jade was not sure if she really expected him to be at home, but that was the number she tried first. During the first and second rings, she took a deep breath to calm herself. By the third ring, it was obvious that she was incredibly nervous. It had been many years since she spoke with a man she knew loved her. Would his voice be different? Would it change the content of their everyday conversation? She did not know how different things would now be between them, and she certainly could not remember what it had been like with Peter.

The anticipation was really making her anxious. What if nothing had changed, and his voice and words were the same as usual? Would that be a good thing, or would it mean that he regretted telling her his feelings? Why was she forcing herself to analyze it all so deeply? There were no available answers.

When Noel did not answer, she left a brief message on his voice mail saying that she was at home and would try him on his cell phone. Jade did not leave a message on his cell phone when he did not answer. Instead, she dialed Trish's number. It was an effective, temporary diversion.

Trish was very happy to hear from her and launched into a description of her latest woes.

"Jade, I feel like I'm being sucked into a deep, dark hole!"

"What do you mean?" Jade asked.

"I don't know, I just can't stand my life anymore," Trish tried to explain. "I can't even wake up anymore."

"Trish, you're worrying me. Are you sure you're not experiencing depression? I mean, serious depression?"

"I don't know," Trish replied with a sigh.

"I'm serious. Maybe you should see a doctor, or a therapist, or something."

"Honestly, Jade, I don't know what to do."

Trish went on to tell her about a recent incident with Ian in which he changed their plans and instead went to a club alone. She felt that they were spending less and less time together. Whenever she brought it up, Ian would change the subject or become defensive. Trish didn't know if she was imagining things or if her relationship was in serious trouble. In either case, she didn't know what to do.

Jade didn't know what to tell her. It was possible that Trish was being overly sensitive. Ian always seemed very devoted to Trish and their relationship. However, there was no denying the building sense of panic that Trish was experiencing. When it came to a man, a woman's intuition was usually accurate.

Though Jade was very concerned, she could not stop herself from wishing that their discussion would be interrupted. She waited impatiently for Noel's call.

Unfortunately, it didn't come.

At that exact moment, in the middle of Saturday afternoon, Noel was on his couch snoring and occasionally wincing in pain. The painkillers in his system were making the world a warm and fuzzy place where phones did not ring. After hours of severe discomfort and shortness of breath, he had finally found relative peace. He also finally stopped wondering how the hell he had wound up in this situation.

"She's mine!" Those were the exact words that the asshole had spit into his ear before Noel nearly puked. Those were the words that later played in his mind before drug-induced numbness took over.

When the blackness had ebbed from his vision on Friday night, Noel had found his face pressed to the cold pavement of the parking lot. Over his desperate gasps for air, Noel heard the rapidly retreating footsteps of his assailant echo into the emptiness of night as he ran away from the scene. Noel had lost consciousness for only a few seconds, but it had been enough for him to miss the shout of a passerby who had witnessed the assault on the way to his own car. When the concerned stranger leaned over to give his assistance, Noel recoiled reflexively.

"Hey, it's okay," the guy had assured him in a gentle but urgent voice. "He's gone."

Noel could not respond because of the knot that had twisted his intestines. The most he could muster was a raw groan.

"Are you okay? Can you get up?" Without waiting for an answer, the guy had managed to get Noel to his feet.

The pain was something that Noel was not likely to forget for the rest of his life. He had been convinced that he was going to pass out again, except that numbing unconsciousness did not arrive. Instead, sharp needles had wormed their way up his spine and into the nerve endings behind his eyes.

"Should I call an ambulance?" the guy had asked.

Noel had shaken his head, then took a moment to rest with his hands on his knees. The guy had put his arms under Noel in case he was falling.

"I'm okay," Noel had managed to gasp.

"I don't know, man. You're in bad shape."

Noel had cut him off with a voice that was stronger. "I'm gonna be fine."

He even attempted to straighten up but stopped when more sharp pain shot through his spine.

"Did you see the guy?" Noel asked.

"No, man. It was too dark. Listen, I think you should go to the hospital."

Even in his haze, Noel had been able to see that the stranger was in a situation he did not want to be in. He was trying to be helpful but was clearly not interested in the drama that had become Noel's life. Noel took pity on him and pulled himself together.

"No, no. I'm fine. I just have to get my breath back," he had assured the stranger, trying to imitate a normal voice. "Thanks, man. God knows what would have happened if you hadn't come along."

"No problem."

Noel had watched the guy drive away, then sat in his vehicle for almost thirty minutes before attempting to drive. The reality of what had happened to him finally sunk in. After a week of uncertainty and anger, he had finally cleared the air with Jade and discussed her marriage. He didn't like the fact that she was someone's wife, but he would accept the situation. It was better than losing her.

Then, just fifteen minutes after declaring his love for Jade, her husband proved her to be a liar. Wasn't that a bitch?

Finally, Noel had started up the Jeep and cautiously maneuvered his way onto the dark streets. He moved at a snail's pace all the way home and was surprised that he had not been stopped for driving under the speed limit. Once he was inside his home, he could only crash on the sofa.

The real pain didn't hit him until around 8:30 the next morning, when he had attempted to get up and go to the bathroom. With tears threatening to spill from his eyes, he practically crawled to the toilet. He didn't even attempt a trip back to the couch until he had swallowed codeine pills. They were the expired remnants of dental surgery two years before, but they were his only option.

The drug-induced, comatose state helped Noel to pass the day. He did not wake up until almost ten o'clock that night. The first thing he did was to flex his stomach to test its tenderness. It may have been his imagination, but his abdomen seemed a bit less knotted. And if he held his breath and remained completely motionless, he practically didn't feel any pain at all. Unfortunately, he could only maintain that position for about thirty seconds at a time.

The fact that the day was almost over did not occur to him until he thought of Jade. The events of the night before hit him all over again. When he had looked into her eyes, made love to her, and told her that he loved her, he had firmly believed her version of the situation. Her husband and Noel's bruised body told another version. The only question that remained was what Noel was going to do about it. More precisely, what was he going to say to Jade?

Strangely, the anger Noel had felt when he had originally found out about Jade's marriage was missing. He could not quite define exactly how he felt. Numb? Hurt? Stunned? No word seemed quite right. Before yesterday, and before Jade, a situation like this would have made him shake his head and throw out the woman's number. He just did not get involved in this type of situation. There were too many available women in the city. Yet now, his first impulse was to call Jade and hope there was a perfectly good explanation for the whole thing.

Noel closed his eyes and gingerly reclined back on his couch. This time, he welcomed the throbbing. It was better than focusing on the increasing pain in his heart.

Life was so strange. It had taken so long for him to

finally be honest about his feelings. Jade had invaded his soul to a depth that no other woman had. Last night, he had allowed himself to be wrapped up in his feelings for her.

Then, with the snap of fingers and the swing of a bat, she was exposed as a liar and a cheating bitch. The situation with Sandra seemed like a walk in the park in comparison. If it weren't so pathetic, it would have been comical.

He slowly **exhal**ed and closed his eyes, concluding that he could **n**ot go back to the way things were. He was not capable of walking away from the situation with a shrug and an eye for the next sexual adventure. He was not going to be able to think clearly until he spoke to Jade.

Noel rested for another minute, then looked around for the cordless phone. Mercifully, it was on the coffee table and within arm's reach. As he pressed it to his ear, a series of beeps indicated that he had messages in his voice mail. His curiosity got the better of him and he called the message center. There were four messages waiting.

The first was from Kyle. They were to have hooked up last night to check out the new club that Dave had recommended. Kyle also hinted, like he had yesterday after work, that there was something he wanted to talk about. Noel had no clue what it was or why it was so secretive.

The second call was from Jason at 7:40 that morning, wondering where he was and telling him that the group was going to tee off without him.

The third message was from Jade. Noel was so intent on deciphering any meaning in the tone of her voice that he barely heard her words. He played it again. She sounded so normal, though maybe a little nervous. He could hear the shy smile on her face and feel her anticipation to talk to him. Or maybe that was what he wanted to believe. He could not really be sure of anything in her message other than her words.

The fourth message was just a hang up. When he checked to hear the caller's number and time of call, it was from Jade's cell phone at 8:30 that evening. Either she was still expecting to meet with him that night, or she had found out what her husband had done and was checking on Noel's condition.

Noel hung up the phone and was about to call her at home when the buttons lit up, indicating a caller.

"Hello?" he said, attempting to sound as normal as possible.

"Where have you been? I've been trying you all day!"

"Hey, Kyle," Noel began. "Listen, sorry about last night, but—"

Kyle cut him off: "What the hell happened?" he shouted. It was clear that he was in a very noisy public place. "I thought you were going to meet me outside the club?"

"Kyle, man, you're not going to believe what happened."

"What?" he shouted above the noise. "I can't hear you!"

"Where are you?" Noel shouted back, though it probably was not necessary.

"What? I'm at The Players' Club. It's too loud in here. I'll have to call you back later!"

"Cool, call me tomorrow," Noel advised.

"What? Did you hear me?"

Noel did not bother to reply.

"I'll call you later!" Kyle repeated before he hung up his phone.

When he first heard Kyle's voice, Noel had felt relief. First, because although he was prepared to dial Jade's number, he was not really ready to hear her voice. Secondly, Kyle presented an opportunity for Noel to verbalize the situation and bounce it off a relatively uninvolved, and therefore objective, person. In theory, anyway. In reality Kyle would tell him to dump Jade and move on. Noel knew that because it was the same thing he would tell Kyle or any of his friends to do. It was the same thing he would normally tell himself. Which is probably why it was better that he and Kyle had not been able to discuss it now. Deep down, Noel knew that he was going to call Jade that night, regardless of what was rational or smart.

It was not a good evening for Jade. When she did not get a call from Noel, she decided to go to sleep early. But for the past hour and a half, she could not find a comfortable position. Her pillows were too flat, her comforter was too stifling, and the mattress felt lumpy. Jade knew that it was her imagination. Everything on her bed was the same as it had been the night before. Yet, for whatever reason, it was almost 11:30 in the evening and sleep eluded her.

When she took a break from counting sheep, her thoughts went back to Noel and the fact that he had not returned her call. Now that she thought about it further, their conversation and interactions over that last week had all been a little sour. With everything going on with Peter and the divorce, she had been so distracted and self-involved that she had not noticed it at the time.

Jade also remembered Noel's anger and attitude the night before, prior to her big revelation. She had never discovered what that had been about. They had become very close by the end of the night, but Jade sensed that there had been something wrong. She could not put her finger on it. What had happened since last weekend? Why didn't he call her like he said he would?

The longer she spent blinking in the dark, the clearer it became. It was so clear now that it was almost pathetic. Jade could not avoid the most obvious answer: she had scared him away with her declaration of love. Noel had just repeated her words out of a sense of obligation and to avoid embarrassing her. He did not feel the same way that she did. She was so stupid and naive. After going through a divorce on which the ink was barely dry, she still clung to a belief in "happily-ever-after."

Jade tried to swallow despite the lump in her throat, but it was not possible. The sound that erupted was part gulp and part sob. Stubbornly, she clamped her lips together and closed her eyes tightly. She would not add insult to injury by sobbing in the middle of the night about a man. She was going to be stronger than that.

So what if Noel was not in love with her? If her honesty scared him, then it was his loss. She had nothing to feel ashamed about. If it turned out that they broke up over this, then it was not meant to be.

Her little silent pep talk staved off the tears for a solid ninety seconds. Despite her wishes, the moisture that escaped her eyes turned into salty rivulets. She gave in to the luxury of feeling sorry for herself and hoped that the lump in her throat would dissipate. It did not. Instead, it grew to the point where the sob it contained had to burst forward or choke her. Jade buried her face in her pillow to muffle the ragged and pathetic wails until none were left in her.

When her eyes finally dried up, she gave a frustrated sigh and sat up in her bed. It was clear that she was definitely not going to fall asleep anytime soon, so there was no point in continuing the effort. She should probably just go into the living room and watch television until she dozed off. Anything would be better than lying in the dark lamenting the consequences of words and actions already said and done.

Before she made a move to throw off her comforter and swing her legs off the bed, Jade was determined to calm her erratic heart. She sat straight against her headboard and took a deep breath. The result was a moment of complete silence and stillness.

It was in those six seconds in which she held her breath that she heard movement: the sound of warm air shifting through still space. Rationally, it could be dismissed as the wind against the window or as just someone moving in an adjacent apartment. But it made the hair on Jade's body stand on end. She knew with absolute certainty that someone else was in her apartment. It was the whisper of someone very close to her bedroom door.

Jade sat frozen in her bed. One instinct told her to hide under the sheets, while another told her to pick up something heavy and launch herself into the bedroom doorway. The shrill ringing of the phone shocked her into movement. Her head whipped around to find the portable unit. The moonlight shining through her window revealed the phone resting on her dresser in front of the bed. When the second ring again broke the silence, Jade leaped forward to grab it.

"Hello?" she answered, unable to hide the anxiety in her voice. With desperate eyes, she searched the inky space around her bedroom door, hoping she was just imagining things.

"Jade, it's Noel," he stated, careful to keep his voice neutral.

"Noel," she said, then paused. "Where are you?"

"At home," he replied briefly.

"I've been waiting for your call. I thought we were going to get together," she said, clearly confused if not upset.

"Yeah, I know. I got your message." Noel knew that he was waiting for a sign or some evidence of what she knew about the events of night before.

"Noel, are you okay? You sound funny."

"Yeah, well, it's a long story."

"What do you mean? What's wrong?" She sounded so concerned and sincere that Noel was tempted to rethink everything. Maybe there was an explanation. It was so tempting to believe.

"Nothing really, I'm just in a little pain," he explained vaguely.

Jade had waited for his call for so many hours that when she picked up the phone, it had been hard to hide her annoyance. But the idea that Noel was hurt caused her annoyance to be quickly replaced with concern. "Why, what happened?"

"I got hit in the stomach," was all he said.

"How? Was it during the golf game?" she asked. "Do you want me to come over?"

"No." Noel was having the hardest time getting to

the point. "Listen, Jade . . . we need to talk. Well, at least I need to talk to you," Noel stated ominously.

"Okay," was all that Jade could manage to get out.

"I met your husband last night."

"What?"

"I said, I met your husband last night." Each syllable was overenunciated to convey his exasperation. "And he wanted me to know that I should stay away from you."

"Noel, what are you talking about?"

"Apparently, your husband is not aware that your marriage has been over for years. He was quite clear that he did not appreciate me spending time with his wife," Noel explained sarcastically.

"That doesn't make any sense. Peter doesn't even know who you are."

"Well, he was pretty clear about who I was when he attacked me in your parking lot last night!"

"What!" Jade demanded. "That's impossible."

"You know what, Jade? I'm not interested in being a part of this game," Noel stated with a tone that chilled her to the bone. "Forgive me if I don't believe a word you're saying. I learned firsthand that you're a liar."

Jade could not even begin to think of a response while her mouth hung open in shock.

"We both know that you only told me about your marriage after he called you while I was there."

"That's not true!"

"Oh, really?" Noel countered. "Are you saying that it wasn't him that you were whispering to last night in the kitchen?"

She couldn't answer. What could she say?

"I thought so."

"Noel," Jade pleaded quietly, "everything I told you last night is true. I don't know what happened to you last night, but I did not lie to you."

"It doesn't even matter, Jade. I have more than enough experience with women like you."

"Women like me?" she demanded. His sarcastic and condescending tone was starting to piss her off. "What the hell is that supposed to mean? Where the hell do you think I've been hiding a husband over the last few months?"

"Like I said, it doesn't even matter anymore."

"Noel, I know I should have told you about my marriage and Peter. I know that," Jade emphasized. "But everyone has a past. We just never discussed ours. Are you saying that you've never had any significant relationships?"

"Yeah, I have. And that's how I know how far a woman will go to get a little action on the side. I'm just not interested in being a part of it."

Before she could reply, the phone clicked and the dial tone rang in her ear.

Chapter 24

Jade felt numb for the next twenty-four hours.

After Noel hung up on her, tears from shock poured down her face. She finally fell asleep from exhaustion only to wake up on Sunday morning with swollen eyes and a massive headache. When she finally rolled out of bed, she dragged her blanket with her to the living room couch. She remained there for the rest of the day with the television humming in the background. Tears continually seeped out of her eyes no matter how hard she tried to suppress them.

The reality of Noel's accusations did not occur to her until later that evening.

Was it possible that Peter had attacked Noel on Friday night? She knew firsthand that Peter could be violent when he was angry or frustrated. Yet, she could not imagine him creeping around in the middle of the night like a psycho.

As far as she knew, Peter didn't even know where she lived. If Noel was correct, it would mean that Peter had been spying on her.

Jade shivered under the warmth of her blanket as she remembered the feeling of being watched in her sleep. Was Peter capable of something like that? Then she recalled the distinct sensation that someone else had been in her apartment last night. Was she crazy, or was it for real?

Noel better have made a mistake because she was not going to let Peter ruin her life again. If he was playing games, dangerous games, he was going to find out that he was dealing with a different woman from the one he married. And if Peter had hurt Noel, she would make sure he lived to regret it.

Jade displayed the first sign of energy as she dug up Peter's phone number from her purse and pressed the digits.

"Hello?" he answered.

"Peter," she stated, "it's Jade."

"Hey." It was very clear that he was surprised to hear from her. "What's up?"

"Where were you Friday night?" She didn't see any point in beating around the bush.

"What?"

"Friday night. Where were you?"

"Why?" Peter replied.

"Just answer the question," Jade demanded.

"All right, all right. I was at home until eleven o'clock, then I went to a club," Peter responded. "What's going on, Jade?"

She ignored his question. "What time did you leave the club?"

"I don't know," he replied, clearly getting annoyed. "Sometime after four, maybe."

"Do you know where I live?" she asked quietly.

"What?"

"Where do I live, Peter?"

"How would I know?" Peter answered. She could

tell that he thought she was acting crazy. "What the hell is going on?"

Jade sighed deeply. She believed him. He didn't have anything to do with Noel getting hurt.

"Nothing," she said. "Sorry to bother you."

"Seriously, Jade, what's going on?"

"'Bye, Peter," she said softly before she hung up the phone.

The discussion had resolved one issue: Peter had not turned into a crazy, possessive stalker. However, it did raise other questions: What had happened on Friday night? Had someone really attacked Noel on purpose, or had he mistaken a random act of violence for something personal?

The burst of energy Jade had felt moments before was suddenly gone. She felt defeated and deflated by a situation she could not understand. A muffled sob escaped her throat and she folded herself back onto the couch. The lump in her throat threatened to choke her. She couldn't even muster the energy to make it back to her bed for the night, and she wondered how she would go back to everyday life without Noel in it.

Eventually, Jade's life did go back to normal but not the normal that existed prior to meeting Noel Merson. Though she was single again, it was not the same as before. This time, she was divorced and ready to move on to the next chapter of her life. She still felt pain in her heart, but it was from lost love, not from lost dreams.

Jade made other changes in her life as well. The first was to book a vacation for the first time in five years. On impulse, she walked into a travel agency near the studio and booked a two-week stay at a spa resort in the Bahamas for mid-August, four weeks before the open house. The travel agent had suggested Jamaica, but Jade vehemently declined. She could not go to Noel's native island without him beside her.

The second big change was to hire another dance instructor for the studio. Karen Jackson was a dancer who had taken classes from Jade at the studio for over three years. Before the summer, Karen had expressed an interest in teaching. When Jade returned to her office after confirming her vacation, her first thought was of her scheduled classes. Immediately, she called Karen to discuss her potential employment.

One month later, while Jade soaked up the sun on a Caribbean beach, her new employee taught her classes and maintained the rehearsal schedule for the open house.

During those weeks of the summer, Jade waited for the anger toward Noel to arrive. She had been ready to welcome it, but it never appeared. She was honest enough with herself to acknowledge that their breakup was her fault. She should have told him about Peter from the beginning. She could not fault him for not trusting her.

His words had been very painful to hear and his assumptions had been insulting. She had tried very hard to conjure up some negativity toward him. How could he think that she had lied to him? Did he really think that she would proclaim her love one day, then be with her husband the next?

Jade recounted the injustices to herself as often as possible, particularly late at night. Yet when sleep came, all she could dream about was how good Noel had made her feel. He was no longer in her life, but he had left something good behind: the knowledge that she was beautiful, desirable, and self-confident. She was living, not just existing. Those were the feelings she woke up with every morning. It felt much better than anger and resentment.

Noel stood inside his office with his back to the door. The upcoming weekend would mark three weeks since he had broken up with Jade, and he was still not himself. His temper was short and he had little interest in his normal activities. He had even missed basketball for the past two Sundays. He simply didn't feel like doing anything.

Kyle's opinion was that he just needed a new woman in his life, and, of course, Kyle volunteered his matchmaking services. Coincidentally, Kyle and Monica had broken up a few days before Noel and Jade. Now, Kyle was looking for a partner to prowl for women with. After three failed attempts to gain Noel's interest, Kyle had kicked it up a notch. The final candidate was proposed several minutes earlier as they stood in the hall outside Noel's office. Kyle described her as a 5'10" model who was an exotic mix of black and Japanese. Noel's response was to stare at him with cold eyes, then walk into his office. The slam of Noel's office door punctuated his lack of interest.

He knew that Kyle was just trying to help, and he also knew that a new woman was probably the best thing. But he couldn't bring himself to consider it. Not yet, anyway. Going out with a woman, regardless of how beautiful, was not going to change his feelings for Jade. Plus, Kyle did not know all the details.

With a sign of regret over his short temper, Noel walked over to his desk and sat down in his chair. Automatically, he reached into the top drawer of his desk and pulled out the glossy flyer that rested above his knickknacks. Carefully, he placed it on his desk, then leaned back to stare at it. It was an advertisement for the First Annual Winters School of Dance Open House in September, with bold blue lettering outlining the "where" and "when." With a routine he had followed for the past five days, Noel scanned the words printed on the paper, then looked past them to focus on the background picture. The camera had captured a female dancer poised on the tips of her toes with arms stretched out high like the wings of a bird. Though the face was not visible, and the picture had been modified to a misty, blurry image, Noel knew that it was Jade.

Laura had given him the flyer on Sunday when he had stopped by the house at Nicki's request. He had not spoken to his sister in more than a month, and it was clear that she was extending an olive branch.

When Laura ran down the stairs ten minutes after Noel arrived, she was babbling so fast that he paid little attention to her words. Then she shoved the paper in his face.

"So, are you gonna come?" she asked, practically skipping with excitement.

Nicki shook her head and went to the kitchen to get Noel a glass of water.

"Come where?" he queried before he could read the details.

"To the open house! Weren't you listening? Didn't Jade tell you about it?" Laura asked innocently.

Noel could only nod faintly. He had forgotten all about it.

". . . but she seems to be doing a little better. Karen's okay, but everyone will miss Jade so much. Is she okay? 'Cause sometimes she seems so sad . . ."

"Wait, wait . . . what?" Noel asked, when Laura's words finally registered in his brain.

"Jade," Laura repeated with impatience. "Is she okay?"

"What do you mean? What was wrong with her?"

Laura stared at him, clearly confused. "Uncle Noel, where have you been? Aren't you guys still dating? Did you break up . . . ?"

"Laura," Noel demanded loudly, effectively stopping her incessant questions. "What's wrong with Jade?" The words came out clipped.

Nicki reentered the hallway at that point. "Noel, what's wrong?" Clearly, she had heard him raise his voice. "What's going on?"

"Nothing, nothing," he had replied, trying hard to contain himself. He started to feel as though he had overreacted. "Laura mentioned something about Jade, and I was just asking her to repeat herself."

"Do you mean her trip?" Nicki asked as she handed him a tall glass of ice water.

"What trip?" Noel asked. After a quick exchange of looks between mother and daughter, Nicki finally answered his questions.

"Jade's going away for two weeks." Nicki made the

last statement to emphasize a point: *Why didn't Noel know about it?* He chose to ignore it.

"Lisa told me she heard Karen on the phone one day," Laura added, "and she heard her say that Jade was going away because she was sick!"

Both adults just looked at her.

"What?" Noel shouted.

"Who's Lisa?" Nicki asked at the same time.

"Mom, you know Lisa. She's the one with the black hair that you said should—"

"Laura! What do you mean she's sick? With what?" Noel had started to feel as though his head was going to explode.

"Laura, don't spread rumors," Nicki chastised.

"Mom, I'm not making it up. Someone else told me that Jade . . ."

The discussion had gone in too many directions for Noel to recall, but it did reveal one fact: Jade was going away on a trip and was leaving someone else in charge of her studio. He could not stop the questions that popped into his head: Was she really ill? Where was she going? Who was she going with?

After escaping the questioning eyes of his sister and niece, Noel sat in his car and used his cell phone to dial Jade's number. When there was no answer, he did not hesitate to leave a message. It was very general and made no mention of the obvious issues between them. He requested that she call him back.

On Friday, he was still waiting to hear from Jade.

Noel stared at the photo for another few minutes before he put the flyer back in his drawer. Eventually, he was going to stop expecting to hear Jade's voice on the other end of the phone. And he was going to come to terms with the fact that she had no interest in clearing up the events of that fateful weekend. Eventually, he would stop hearing the denials and shock in her voice the last time he heard it.

One month later, he was still waiting.

Chapter 25

Jade retied the laces of her *pointe* shoes for the third time. They fit fine, but her nervousness made her fidgety. After months of preparation and practice, the open house was almost at its finale. The show had started at 6:00 P.M., right on schedule. Ninety minutes later, things were still going fairly smoothly. Some of the younger children had gotten scared and had forgotten some of their steps. April, a very shy seven year old, actually broke out in tears when she missed the first cue to the junior ballet performance. But those things were to be expected and were all part of what made the night special. For many of her students, it was their first performance on a stage with lights and an audience. It was a night that they would never forget.

There was one more performance before Jade's solo to complete the show. While Jade changed into her costume, Karen helped shuffle the students to and from backstage. She had become invaluable to Jade and had done an excellent job while Jade went on vacation. Without Karen, she would have had to temporarily close the studio. Other than canceling a couple of daytime stretch classes, things had run like clockwork.

"Jade, are you okay?" Karen asked as she stepped in front of her. Concern was visible in her blue eyes. Jade jumped, clearly startled that someone had approached her unnoticed. She had been sitting alone in an office in the back of the theater. The music from the stage was loud but muffled.

"Yeah . . . yeah, I'm fine," Jade replied, smiling warmly at her employee. "Is everything okay?"

"Wonderful, actually. The senior jazz routine just started, and we're only running fifteen minutes behind schedule," Karen said, all smiles. Karen was the stage manager for the night, and her size-four body was dressed in a classic black suit. Brilliant blond hair cascaded over her shoulders in soft waves.

"Karen, what would I do without you? You're a godsend."

"What about you?" Karen asked, brushing off the compliment. "You have about four minutes. Are you ready?"

"As ready as I'll ever be, I guess."

"Well, the students have already begun to sit in the aisles in front of the stage. They can't wait to see you perform. I'm not sure the fire department is going to like it, but I didn't have the heart to say no," Karen informed her with a giggle. "You've created quite a suspense."

Jade smiled back and stood up. During the six weeks she had spent preparing for the open house, she had not performed her solo for anyone at the studio. The choreography was done while the studio was closed, and with the help of a professional dancer, a cast member of *Chicago* who was an old friend from school. Jade seemed very secretive, and the students thought that she was deliberately trying to surprise everyone. It was not true. The reason was a lot less interesting and dramatic. It boiled down to simple insecurity.

Jade knew that she was a good teacher. She understood how to work with people and how to provide them with solid, fundamental technical skills. She also knew that she was meant to own her own business. But performing was something totally different. She had never had the confidence and presence to get up on stage and display herself to an audience. That was the power of performance to her. It was not just about doing dance steps and smiling charmingly. It was about baring your soul under a spotlight, and it required freedom and no inhibitions. These were the qualities of a truly talented dancer. Jade was fairly certain that she did not have what it took.

Yet here she was, ready to perform for over 250 people. There was no way that she could have put on this open house as a showcase for the talent and potential at Winters School of Dance without doing a performance herself. Jade had already contemplated that. Would parents trust her to teach their children to dance if she had no real talent herself? It was a gamble she was not willing to take. The only option was to put herself into performance-shape.

The exercise had turned out to be very therapeutic. It had been years since she had spent that much time just dancing by herself, for herself. With the studio doors locked, she was able to immerse herself into the beauty and purity of movement and music. She was able to relearn the limits to which she could push her endurance and body. It had felt wonderful.

Best of all, somewhere along the line, Jade realized that she was just fine the way she was. It was okay that she was better at teaching than at performing, and that she was never going to be a professional dancer. It was okay that she was divorced and single. She was a strong, successful black woman. No man, husband, or boyfriend was going to bring her down. It took a while, but eventually she believed the message that her inner power revealed to her.

Now the moment was here.

"Okay, they have about one minute left," Karen advised her.

Jade could hear the excitement in Karen's voice.

"You better head backstage."

Together they approached stage left. The lights went black and the curtains closed on twelve panting young adults frozen in place. As the audience began to applaud, the dancers took their cue and ran into the wings, some brushing by Jade in their haste. Karen left Jade's side to assist those who seemed confused about what to do next. Jade took a deep breath, brushed her hand down the side of her skirt, and stepped into the dark center of the stage.

Once the applause ended, the music started. There was no introduction. The show's program said it all.

Smooth versus filled the auditorium as En Vogue sang the a capella introduction of their hit song, "*Hold On.*" Heavy black curtains parted to reveal Jade's silhouette.

Jade took her first step in her *pointe* shoes, her body poised gracefully on the tips of her toes. Her arms rose slowly, curved in a perfect oval, then parted to fourth position—one arm reaching to the ceiling, the other extended to her side. She wore a black bodysuit cut with a halter top and an open back. Her thighs flirted with a transparent black wrap skirt. Silky sheer tights covered her legs.

When she stepped forward, it was to extend a straight kick, displaying perfect balance and control. Then she stepped into a double *pirouette*. Each move was slow and smooth to matching the lonely words of the song. The turn ended with a dramatic lunge.

Everything paused . . . then the soulful beat of the song's instrumental music kicked in. The audience sat forward as Jade leaped up, stepped forward dramatically, then rotated her body to stride upstage. She moved with feline grace and allure. With her back toward the audience, the real performance started. Energy and power radiated from her body. The choreography demonstrated a fusion of classical ballet technique, jazz dance, and street vibes that was fresh and unique. Everyone was spellbound.

For Noel, the feeling was very familiar. As she moved under the spotlight with such strength and flexibility, it was very much like it had been the first time he saw her. She took his breath away. He had hoped the effect would be gone. If he felt nothing, he would have been able to go home and move on. Clearly, he was not going anywhere until he spoke to her.

How many times had Noel heard the words sung by one of his favorite groups back in the day? The lyrics were about mistakes and lost love. Had Jade deliberately used that song? Of course not. She would have had to know how miserable he had been over the past weeks, and she would have had to know that he would be here tonight to see her dance. Most of all, she would have had to be thinking about him. Noel was not going to kid himself. She had not returned his phone call. He had no reason to think that he was anything but a memory to her.

He was temporarily distracted by Laura, who was bobbing her head while she stood in the aisle beside their seats. She was back in her street clothes, since the junior jazz class had done their performance midway through the show. When Noel caught her eye, she waved at him, flashing a big smile. He waved back, and beside him, Nicki looked over and waved at Laura as well.

With Laura participating in the open house, Noel had the perfect excuse to be there. She would never have forgiven him if he had missed it, and Nicki didn't question his presence. Only he knew that it was just an excuse to see Jade.

About two weeks prior, Nicki had attempted to bring up the subject of Jade. At that time, there were too many open wounds for Noel, and he told her point-blank that he would not discuss it with her. He was still upset and concerned about Nicki's involvement in the situation. It was not the information that she gave him that bothered him, it was her motives. Nicki had revealed a side of herself that made him uncomfortable. They were on speaking terms, but he was not going to forget her snobbish attitude any time soon. He was not going to bring it up, either.

Noel's attention was pulled back to the stage as Jade extended her body into an *arabesque* to emphasize the final lyrics of the song. Then she stepped into four sequential *pirouettes*, traveling across the front of the stage. With a *chassé* to prepare, she leaped into a *grand jeté*, her legs almost completing a perfect split in midair. When she landed, Jade slid into a jazz split, her torso and arms arched back in a perfect bow.

There she remained as the music faded away. The stage went pitch black.

The audience and the students exploded into thunderous applause. Several cheers and shouts of approval could be heard. Noel felt his chest expand with pride. He had watched her teach and rehearse classes many times, but he had never imagined that her dancing could give him goose bumps.

The noise died down when the stage lights and house lights came back on. Jade walked from backstage with a microphone. The applause started again. Jade smiled shyly, occasionally bowing her head in thanks until the thunder faded out again. Her skin was slick with perspiration, her breath slightly labored.

"I just wanted to take a moment to thank everyone for coming to the First Annual Open House for Winters School of Dance," she began in a soft voice. "Your support has meant so much to your children and friends. I would also like to thank my students for their hard work and tremendous performances. Everyone, please give them a round of applause!"

The crowd did as instructed and the students beamed with delight.

"Finally, I would like to thank Karen Jackson for doing an amazing job tonight, making sure that everything went according to schedule. Karen, please come out!" Jade instructed. Again, everyone clapped on cue.

Karen was clearly surprised by the attention. When she stepped on stage, her ivory complexion was flushed. She waved with a flutter of her fingers but stayed in the light for only a couple of seconds.

"I hope you enjoyed what we had to show. Refreshments will be served in the foyer. I look forward to seeing you all next year!" With a bow, Jade ran backstage.

Karen immediately accosted her. "I can't believe you did that!" she said in mock anger.

"You didn't really think you were going to leave tonight without getting on stage, did you?" Jade replied. "Plus, you deserve the applause just as much as the rest of us."

"Well, some warning would have been nice." It was clear that Karen was touched by Jade's consideration. "Okay, I'm going to organize everyone in the dressing rooms. You need to get to the foyer as soon as possible. The caterer told me that everything is all set."

Jade nodded at the instructions. "Give me fifteen minutes and I'll be out there," she promised.

It actually took her longer than she had expected to quickly shower and get dressed. She took extra time to recurl her hair and perfect her makeup.

Along with performing solo, mixing and mingling made her extremely nervous. She could never think of the right pleasantries to exchange with strangers. But as owner of the studio, it was another duty she couldn't avoid.

When she walked through the theater toward the foyer, there were several people still milling around. One by one, they complimented her on the show and her performance. They all seemed to have really enjoyed themselves. In the foyer, the responses were very similar.

After checking with the caterers on the status of the food, Jade began the obligatory rounds among the parents and friends of the students. Within the first twenty minutes, her cheeks were tired from smiling.

She was extremely relieved when she spotted Trish and Ian. Since Jerome could not make it, they were her only guests. Jade was still pissed at Jerome.

"Oh Jade! You were amazing!" Trish said as they hugged tightly. "Ian, wasn't she amazing?"

"I have to agree, Jade. I'm so impressed." He hugged her as well, then gave her a peck on her cheek. "Do you think you could teach Trish how to do that split thing?" Ian grunted when he was elbowed in the stomach by his new fiancée of one week. They all laughed.

"Do you want us to wait for you?" Trish asked.

"No, you guys go on home," Jade replied. As she looked around the crowded space, it was hard to predict how long people were going to hang around. Most of the students were dressed and mingling with their families. "I might have to stay for a while."

As Trish and Ian walked away holding hands, Jade smiled to herself. She was so happy to see two of the most special people in her life so happy. When Jade heard about Ian's proposal on the fourth anniversary of their first date, she had been moved to tears. It turned out that he was just as unfilled and unsatisfied by their current situation as Trish was. He was also ready to have children, but he wanted to get married first. Jade was thrilled for them.

It took another twenty-five minutes for the crowd to thin out. It was a good thing because Jade was hitting her endurance threshold. She had experienced a rush of adrenaline after the excitement of the show, but now she just wanted to go home and sleep. When almost everyone had left except the caterers, she went into the theater to find Karen.

Noel watched her from a nook near the door.

He had spent most of the time outside after the show. Laura, Nicki, and Vince had stayed for only a short time so that Laura could say good night to a few of her friends. As the four of them made their way to the parking lot, Noel gave the excuse that he needed to use the bathroom. Since they had come in separate cars, there was no need for them to wait for him.

Left alone, he stayed out of sight while occasionally checking the foyer to monitor Jade's movements. He felt a bit like a stalker, but he had no choice. The alternative was to approach her in the middle of a crowded room. Since he didn't know how she would react, he didn't want to take the chance of being embarrassed by her rejection.

When Jade returned to the foyer with the girl she had introduced as Karen, Noel took a moment to watch her. All signs of her exertion had been replaced with polished elegance. She wore a slinky, fitted wrap dress in deep wine red. When both women stopped to talk, Jade's back was toward him. He could not help admiring her bare legs as she stood in sexy black heels.

Noel knew that he had run out of time. It was now or never. Nervously, he ran a hand over his cropped hair, then quickly looked down to check on his blue cotton sweater over blue jeans. Then he stepped forward.

Chapter 26

Karen saw him first, since she was facing his direction. They had never met, so she showed only mild interest in his presence. Noticing Karen's distraction, Jade turned around. Her surprise was evident as her eyes opened wide. As Noel got closer, she turned away momentarily. When she faced his direction again, her face showed only polite blankness. He stopped directly in front of her.

"Hello Jade," he stated with a warm smile.

"Noel," she said simply. "How are you?"

"I'm fine," he replied. He wanted to say that he was fine now that he was standing in front of her, but he knew that wouldn't be appropriate.

"Karen, this is Laura Thompson's uncle, Noel Merson."

"Nice to meet you, Karen," Noel stated, but his eyes remained fixed on Jade. Jade stared at the floor while Karen looked back and forth between them.

"Well," Karen said a little louder than necessary. "I'm going to straighten up backstage a bit. Nice to meet you, Noel."

Jade looked up when they were alone. He sensed her discomfort.

"So, did you enjoy the show? You must be so proud

of Laura. I know she did a great job. She—" Her words were cut off.

"Jade, I'm not here because of Laura. I came to see you," he stated plainly.

"Oh . . . okay." She was looking at the floor again.

"How are you?" The concern in his voice was very evident. "Laura told me that you weren't well." When Jade finally looked in his face, she noticed the shadows beneath his eyes. They were new, and they made him seem tired and stressed.

"I'm fine, Noel," she replied with a light smile.

Noel nodded, then looked away. He took a deep breath before he turned back.

"Jade, I'm sorry." Against his will, his throat closed up, preventing him from speaking.

"Noel, it's okay—" Jade began.

He cut her off. "No, it's not okay. I'm not okay and I haven't been for a long time." When Jade made a move to speak, he rushed forward. "Please, Jade, just let me say a few things, then I swear I'll leave you alone."

A member of the catering team walked by at that moment. With a touch at her elbow, Noel guided her into a secluded corner. When he faced her again, he realized that he didn't want to see the look in her eyes. He stared at a spot over her left ear instead.

"The truth is, Jade, I was miserable long before Laura told me about your trip. That night, when I hung up, I was so frustrated that I just reacted without thinking. My stomach was killing me and I . . ." He paused as he struggled to rationalize his feelings at that time. "I was afraid that you . . . anyway, when I woke up the next morning, I already knew that I had made a big mistake. But I guess I just had too much pride to call you and take back my words."

Noel closed his eyes for a second before he risked a glance into hers. They were unreadable, so he continued. "Look, I know that if you wanted to see me, you would have called me back. And I know that I have no right to force you to talk to me. But I just needed to tell you how I feel."

Noel just couldn't seem to get the words he wanted to say to form on his lips. He searched her face for some sign of what she was thinking. He was hoping for some indication of her feelings, but she just avoided his eyes. Eventually, the silence between them grew uncomfortably long.

"You don't have to apologize, Noel. It wasn't your fault," Jade finally stated in a soft voice. She smiled calmly as if to reassure him of her words.

Noel blinked rapidly to force back the moisture that threatened to seep from his eyes. It was clear that she thought he was there just to soothe his conscience about the way he ended things. He shook his head sadly.

"No, you don't understand." He could no longer resist touching her, and he reached out a hand to brush her cheek with his thumb. When she did not pull back, he summoned his courage.

"I can't sleep at night, Jade. I miss you so much." The final sentence came out as a rough whisper. Noel cleared his throat before he moved on. "Anyway, all I really wanted to say was that . . . I still love you, and I'm sorry. I should have trusted you more."

Noel used his thumb to brush away the tear that fell from one of her eyes as she shut them tightly. He held his breath and waited for her response. When she remained silent, he felt his heart tighten in his chest. After several seconds, he let his hand fall from her face. It was done.

"Good-bye, Jade."

As Noel walked away, he felt as though the world was moving in slow motion. His heavy steps echoed loudly in the empty foyer. With his head bent low in defeat, he pushed through the front doors of the building and out into the cool night air. He made it down the front steps before he stopped, his hands clasped in tight fists.

He was in that spot, struggling for control, when Jade burst through the doors. Noel turned around just as she began to run down the steps as delicately as possible. His heart accelerated to a thunderous rate. When she stopped in front of him, her eyes were shiny with unshed tears.

"Noel," was all she said, but it said everything. Noel pulled her to him and covered her lips with his in rough abandon. The kiss lasted forever since neither of them wanted it to end.

When they did pull their lips apart, Noel held her in a tight embrace that allowed him to feel every inch of her against him. He felt warmth for the first time in weeks.

"Guess what?" Jade demanded into his ear.

Noel pulled back to look into her face questioningly.

"I'm a divorced woman," she stated.

He closed his eyes, then rested his forehead against hers.

"Can we go somewhere? Are you almost done here?" he asked.

"I just have to check on the cleanup, but I should

be free in about fifteen minutes," she replied. They were still in an embrace.

"Okay. Are you hungry? Can we get something to eat?"

"Okay," Jade answered with a shy smile.

Before they separated, they agreed to meet at her apartment in thirty minutes, since it was only a couple of blocks away. Noel would pick up their meal from a local burger joint.

When Jade returned to the theater, she had a smile on her face and a dazed look in her eyes. She ran into Karen backstage and discovered that there wasn't much left to do. While they worked as a team to put together all the personal items left behind, it was clear that Karen was dying of curiosity. Though Jade could not hide the glow on her face, she didn't want to talk about it and successfully dodged Karen's teasing questions and innuendos. When the women parted, Jade promised to fill Karen in later on the whole story.

Jade had walked to the theater earlier that morning, carrying her clothes in a travel bag. Though Karen offered to drive her home, she declined, preferring to spend some time outside in the fresh evening air. It was a dark night, but the city streets were well lit and busy with other pedestrians. She entered her complex several minutes before she was due to meet Noel.

Two men were standing outside the main entrance doors smoking cigarettes.

"Hey, Jade," George said as she approached them.

"Hi George, Cliff," Jade replied while giving both men a radiant smile. "How are things going?"

"Okay," George replied.

Cliff only nodded to her. He watched her with eyes

squinted to see through the thin haze of smoke that surrounded them. As Jade walked by to open the glass doors to the building, the smell of musky male sweat mixed with tobacco assaulted her nose.

Inside the lobby, she paused to decide if she should wait for Noel there. She was about to head up to her apartment when an arm snaked around her waist, causing her to jump and scream softly. She swung around quickly to confront her assailant.

"Sorry," Noel offered. "I didn't mean to scare you." He pulled her into a quick, reassuring hug.

"It's okay. I didn't see you pull up," Jade said with a giggle to hide her embarrassment. It didn't help that George and Cliff were watching them from outside. "What did you get us to eat?" she asked, as she pulled out of his arms and they started walking toward the elevators.

"The biggest, juiciest burgers on this side of Chicago."

Jade giggled again, feeling giddy with happiness. She transferred her radiant smile to Stuart as they walked by the concierge desk.

"Hi Jade," Stuart said as he returned her smile. His eyes shifted speculatively from Noel to Jade and rested momentarily on their joined hands.

"Hi Stuart, how are you?"

"I'm doing fantastic," he replied warmly. "How did the open house go?"

She had told him about it over the last couple of weeks.

"Absolutely amazing," Jade replied.

"Congratulations!" he said.

"Thank you, Stuart. See you later."

When they entered the elevator, Noel pulled her

into his arms again and into a deep, hungry kiss. They struggled to get closer while juggling her gym bag and his burden of take-out food containers.

"I missed you so much," Noel whispered into her ear while nibbling on the sensitive tendons of her neck.

"I missed you, too," Jade replied breathlessly.

When they got into her apartment, they both recognized that they had a lot to talk about and resisted reigniting the sexual sparks. They worked together to get the meal on the table before it got too cold to enjoy.

"You were fantastic tonight," Noel commented. They were sitting on her couch eating their messy burgers.

"You enjoyed the show?"

"It was really good. Very well organized," he stated solemnly. "I was so proud of you."

"Thank you," Jade replied. "It was a lot of work, but it turned out better than I expected."

"Laura had mentioned that you went away a few weeks ago."

"Yeah," she replied. "I went to the Bahamas for the most relaxing two weeks of my life."

"For a vacation?"

"Yeah. Everyone thought I was nuts, considering the open house was just around the corner, but I really needed to get away, and I didn't want to wait until after the show," she explained. "Plus, I had Karen working for me by that time. I know I couldn't have done this whole thing without her."

"Who did you go with?" Noel asked. If he was trying to sound nonchalant, it didn't work. Jade thought it was cute and there was a twinkle in her eyes when she replied.

"I went alone."

He nodded and was silent for several moments. Then, Noel picked up one of Jade's hands and held it tenderly in his.

"You said something to me that night that I've thought about over and over again," he stated as he stared at the spot where their hands joined. "You said that we hadn't talked about our past relationships, and you were right."

Jade looked expectantly at his bent head.

"The more I thought about it, the more I realized that I really had no right to judge you for not telling me about your marriage," Noel continued. "I was engaged once, and I never told you about it. Why would I? It had ended years ago. I caught her cheating on me while she thought I was out of town. Deep down, Jade, I knew that you were telling me the truth about your separation. But I was afraid that my feelings for you were clouding my judgment. It took me a while to admit that my anger toward you had more to do with my own issues than anything else."

"Oh, Noel." Jade moved closer to him and he pulled her into his lap. "One of the reasons I didn't tell you about Peter was that I didn't know where our relationship was going. I tried not to have any expectations beyond our immediate situation. I guess I didn't want to reveal too much about myself. My marriage is not a bright spot in my life, and I wasn't ready to share the details with someone who was just passing by."

"Sweetheart, I'm not going anywhere," Noel whispered as he sprinkled loving kisses along the line of her cheek. "You can share anything with me."

"You promise?" she teased.

"I promise."

For the moment they were content to cuddle and kiss, reveling in their renewed commitment to each other.

"I hope your ex hasn't been bothering you, Jade," Noel stated. "I mean, he's obviously crazy, and I've been so worried about you."

"Noel, I haven't spoken to Peter for weeks," Jade replied.

"Thank God. The way he attacked me that night was bizarre. I kept having nightmares that he was going to hurt you and I wouldn't be there to help you."

"Noel, I don't know what happened in the parking lot, but it wasn't Peter that attacked you," Jade stated softly.

"Come on, Jade, who else could it have been?" he disputed.

"I don't know. Maybe it was a random attack. Maybe they were after your money," she offered, while Noel shook his head to dismiss the suggestions. "How do you know it was him? Did he say he was my husband?"

"He told me to stay away from you, and he said your name. Who else could it be?"

"I don't know, Noel, but I'm almost positive that it wasn't Peter. Like I said, we hadn't even spoken for over four years. When I confronted him about it, he really didn't know what I was talking about."

"Well, it hardly matters now. I just want to make sure that he's not bothering you or anything," he insisted.

"Nope," Jade replied. "I'm all yours."

She slowly leaned forward until their lips brushed softly, then brushed again. With a groan, Noel pulled her tightly against him and kissed her with abandon. His tongue delved into her mouth with teasing strokes, his fingers became entangled in her hair. On and on he kissed her, savoring her sweetness. Jade lost the ability to think as overwhelming arousal swept through her, leaving her body limp.

"Ah, sweetheart," Noel groaned into her ear, causing shivers to travel down her back. "You feel so good. I don't want to let you go."

She responded by brushing her tongue over the whorls of his ears.

"Baby, you have to stop. You're going to drive me crazy," he pleaded breathlessly.

"Would that be so bad?" Jade asked huskily while she continued her teasing by gently biting his lobe.

"Yes, because I can't finish what I've started." Noel gave a painful laugh. "I'm serious, Jade. If I stay now, I'll be here all night."

Jade pulled away from him slowly, clearly disappointed by his statement. Noel read the disappointment on her face.

"Sweetheart, I don't want to rush us. I want to spend hours doing the things that I've dreamed about for the past two months." He paused to brush his tongue over the plump flesh of her swollen lips. "But, I promised one of my clients that I would stop by a commercial shoot tonight. If I leave now, I'll catch the end of it."

"Okay," Jade replied. Slowly, she swung herself off his lap and stood up.

"Can I come back later?" Noel asked as he stood up as well.

"If you want to."

"I definitely want to."

"Okay," Jade said. She took his hand and walked with him to the door.

"Okay," he echoed. It was clear that he didn't want to leave. He pulled her into his arms again, holding her tightly against his heart. "I love you."

Jade pulled back to look into his eyes while hers filled with moisture. "I love you, too."

"I'll call you when I'm on my way back, okay?"

"Okay," Jade agreed.

They reluctantly parted and Jade closed the door behind him. She spent several minutes with her back pressed against the door while tears of deep joy and happiness raced down her cheeks and splashed on the front of her dress.

Eventually, she wiped her face with her fingers and went into the bathroom to take a shower. She was pulling on an oversized T-shirt when the phone rang. She raced into her bedroom to answer it. The room was dark, but she found the handset on the night table on the right side of the bed near the window. It was Noel calling from his cell phone.

"Hey," he said. She could hear the smile on his face.

"Hey," she answered.

"I just wanted to say that I can't wait to get back, and I really wish I didn't have to leave."

"I know, me too," Jade replied. She sat on the edge of the bed and looked out the window at the lights of the city night.

"I also wanted to say that I want to be with you. I

mean, I want to be with you for as long as you want me," he clarified.

"Oh, Noel. I—"

Her words were cut off when she heard a harsh whisper in her ear as steel fingers gripped her left forearm.

"Hang up the phone, now!" the intruder said into the side of her face while his stale, smoky breath surrounded her like a cloak.

A shocked scream ripped from her throat. Her fingers went numb and the phone tumbled to the ground to rest at the foot of the dresser. The red-lit talk button indicated that the line was still open. Jade instinctively pulled her arm back and tried to stand up. The man had her arm locked in his grasp like a vice and she barely moved an inch.

"What—? What are you doing? What are you doing in here?" she sputtered in disbelief. Off in the distance, she could hear Noel's voice calling her name, but he was so far away. "Let me go!"

As she watched, a hairy hand reached down and picked up the phone. Fear entered her veins, then pure panic began when she watched the red light on the phone go out. Frantically, uncontrollably, she began to struggle against his grip, her voice getting louder and louder. He turned off the ringer and threw the phone onto the bed near the headboard.

"Let me go! Let me go! What do you want?" When she finally realized that her right arm was still unimpeded, she attacked his grip with her nails. It did little good.

"Be quiet, Jade. Just sit still and be quiet. I don't want to hurt you." His voice was whisper-soft but sounded deadly to her ears. She started to scream every bad word she could think of.

She was quieted by a palm brutally clamped over her mouth. Immediately, Jade switched her attack to the pressure that was blocking her air and clawed at his hairy hand. Suddenly, her arm was freed from the vise grip. For one second, Jade thought she had actually won the fight and had done some damage. In another second, both her wrists were clasped in front of her body from the power and size of one of his. Under the pressure of his hands, she could barely move. She began to whimper uncontrollably.

"Shhhhhhhhh . . . it's okay," he told her in a soothing voice. Her shiny, bulging eyes stared into his, silently begging for an answer to what was going on. "Just be quiet and everything's going to be fine."

Jade closed her eyes after seeing the glassy insanity of his. There was no mistake; he was there to do something horrible. It was not going to be okay because there was a madman in her bedroom. He was definitely not there to make everything okay. He was going to hurt her and they both knew it.

Noel shouted Jade's name into the headset of his cell phone for several seconds before he realized that the line had gone dead.

"What the hell . . . ?" He was driving down the highway, on his way to the nightclub where his client's commercial was being filmed. After checking his mirrors, he pulled over to the right shoulder.

Noel looked down at the phone still clutched in his hand. He pressed the redial button and listened while the phone rang four times. He closed his eyes and clenched his lips as Jade's voice mail announced her unavailability.

"Jade, it's Noel. What's going on? Call me back."

After leaving his message, Noel pulled back on to the road as quickly as possible and took the first exit off the highway. He could not control his panic as he remembered the shock in Jade's voice before they got disconnected.

Chapter 27

Jade was suffocating. After the attacker had shifted her body around to secure his grip, the hand over her mouth was suddenly also blocking her nose and cutting off her air supply. She began to hyperventilate and struggled frantically within his grip.

"Keep still!" he demanded roughly. His fingers gripped hers tighter.

Blackness started to invade the edges of her vision as fear and frustration partnered with lack of oxygen. Finally, she managed to wiggle one arm free and gripped the hand over her mouth. It took all of her remaining energy to slip his index finger a fraction of an inch lower; it took her two seconds to realize that she could breathe. Suddenly, Jade collapsed against his body, her eyes closed, her body spent and exhausted. She just wanted to take a minute to enjoy the air in her lungs.

Then, she felt cold steel pressed against her vulnerable skin. He had a knife pressed to her neck.

"That's right," he said in the same patronizing tone. "I'm the one in control now. I need you to keep quiet and behave. Otherwise, I'm going to have to hurt you. You don't want me to do that, do you?"

Jade shook her head on cue, unable to look away from his feverish eyes. He was crazy!

"I don't want to hurt you, either. I want to enjoy you." He brushed the knife's silver blade lightly against the silky skin of her throat. "But I will if I have to. You understand that, don't you Jade?"

Again, she responded with a nod on cue. He was crazy and he thought this was a game. In that moment, she knew with absolute certainty that he would slit her throat without a blink.

"If I remove my hand, will you keep quiet?" he asked in his patronizing, falsetto voice.

She nodded.

"You know that if you don't, I'll slice your pretty skin, don't you, Jade?"

This time, she didn't bother to respond. Instead, she tried to keep as still as possible. After watching her for several seconds, Cliff seemed to be convinced that she understood the consequences. He peeled his fingers off her lips with slow deliberation. Then, with great display, he trailed his hand along the line of her neck, over her cotton-covered shoulder, and stopped playfully where her flesh emerged from the short sleeve of her T-shirt. Jade sat rigidly as he flirted with her skin, perhaps testing her silent promise not to start screaming like a lunatic. He was really enjoying himself and his intense pleasure was palpable.

Though her mouth was finally uncovered and she had the urge to gulp fresh air in great waves, Jade forced herself to remain perfectly still. She was petrified to move. It was becoming clearer to her that she may not live through the night. Her only chance was to buy time, which meant she had to play along with

him. For now. Until the right time came. It was her
only chance until Noel got there.

The only way that Jade could manage to seem pli-
ant and subdued was to mentally remove herself from
the situation. She knew that Cliff was touching her
skin, but she refused to acknowledge his touch. With
a fixed stare, she watched the scene through the reflection of her bedroom window. One of his hands
caressed her like a tender lover; the other held a
sparkling blade to her neck. The more she stared, the
more she could believe that she was watching a scene
from a badly written script.

Only in a sick movie could she accept that a man
she had known for over four years was holding her
captive in her bedroom. A man she had invited into
her home on countless occasions was now pressing a
knife against her neck.

They remained like that for what could have been
minutes or maybe close to an hour: Jade was no
longer able to judge time. She did know that he was
not going to let things stay like that. His touch gradu-
ally got more aggressive and his breathing became
escalated. He was clearly ready for the next level of his
game. Jade became cold with the knowledge.

With frantic eyes, she began to search the room.
Her only hope was to injure him in some way, maybe
even knock him out. But with what? Eyes darting
wildly, Jade started to consider the size, shape, and
weight of everything in the room that she could see in
the mirror. Her clock radio? Maybe the metal candle-
holder on the dresser? What?

"Stand up!" Cliff's command. His voice was void of
the soft persuasive tone he had used up to that point.

Jade's heart began to beat frantically while her breathing became harsh and erratic.

"I want to look at you. I want to see you the way you let *him* see you."

He was talking about Noel! He was angry about Noel!

"Look, Cliff," she whispered before she realized what she was doing. "You don't want to do this." Jade clenched her lips together to swallow a sob.

"Shut up!" The blade was pressed deeper into her skin. She was sure she felt the sting of a cut.

"Please—"

"I said, shut up! You don't get to talk! You just do what I tell you. I'm the one in control here, not you." He cruelly gripped her left arm and propelled her to her feet to stand in front of him, her back to the window. His breathing had become so loud that she could hear it clearly over her own harsh respiration.

Think! She told herself. *Think fast!*

"Take it off," he demanded, his eyes fixed on the bare spot just below her collarbone. It was clear that he was referring to her T-shirt, but Jade pretended not to understand. He was still holding her arm in his right hand, but it was almost as though he had forgotten the weapon in his left hand. Jade could not take her eyes off the silver blade. "I want to see what *he's* seen."

She had to move, had to pretend that she was willing and compliant before he remembered the knife. It was her only chance. With a smooth tentative step, Jade moved her body to the right side of his and stepped back. Cliff did not stop her, but neither did he break his hold. She was conscious of the side of her knee brushing the edge of her mattress. And she was conscious of his eyes, glazed with excitement, as they focused on the outline of her breast, barely visible through the thin cotton.

Jade held her breath and began to toy with the bottom edge of her T-shirt with her left hand. His eyes shifted to follow her fingers. Encouraged, she played with it some more; lifted it slightly to reveal more of her satin-smooth thigh. Her right arm, hidden from view, reached behind her back.

It was so hard for her to move slowly. She knew that at any moment, he was going to grab her, but she could not rush. Timing was everything. The idea of him tearing at her clothes, touching her skin, or putting his mouth on her was enough to make her want to scream. But she kept it inside because she was only going to have one chance. If she blew it now by showing him her revulsion, her fate was sealed. Though she was certain that Noel was on his way, he might be too late to help her.

When Jade was sure that Cliff was not going to remain motionless for much longer, she slipped her hand under her shirt to lift it all the way to the top of her thigh. The bulging of his eyes told her that he actually thought that she was going to remove her clothing. The hand holding the knife dropped a notch lower. On cue, Jade committed herself to a course of action and wrapped her fingers around the face of her digital clock radio resting on the night table.

Using all of her strength and weight, she whipped the weapon across the front of her body. She watched with fascination as a sharp edge of the radio connected with the back of his head. But she did not wait around to see the result. As his upper body pitched forward, caught off guard, Jade threw the radio in his general direction and ran past him to around the edge of the bed.

Cliff cursed and shouted in pain. "You bitch!"

She almost reached the bedroom door when he grabbed her T-shirt, tearing it at the neck and stopping her in her tracks. Jade started screaming.

"Help! Somebody help me!" she sobbed. "Please!"

Though he was able to wrap a confining arm around her stomach, Jade kept on fighting. With fear, anger, and desperation as her energy, she struggled against his hold. Where was the knife?

"Cliff, you don't want to do this. You don't want to hurt me," Jade cried, panting from her exertion. "Please . . . why are you doing this?"

"Shut up!"

Despite her desperate efforts, his grip remained strong and he began to drag her back toward the bed. Where was the knife?

"This is all your fault. It's time for you to pay for your games. I'm in charge now!"

The cold metal reappeared, its tip pressed to the vulnerable space above her right breast.

"No . . . no! Please, don't do this! I don't know what you're talking about . . . Nooooooo!" Jade could not allow him to get her on the bed.

Frantically, she grabbed at the collection of perfumes and creams on her dresser. Tears seeped through her eyes as the awkward items slipped through her fingers and scattered across the wooden surface. Just before he dragged her off her feet and onto the bed, she managed to secure a hold on one glass bottle with her left hand.

Their struggles resulted in Jade lying facedown on

her comforter with Cliff leaning over her with one knee on the mattress and one arm pressed against the center of her back. The perfume bottle was trapped under her body. They were both frozen in a tableau, each trying to catch a breath, planning the next move.

Cliff moved first by gripping her left shoulder to turn her over. Jade responded by smashing the perfume bottle into his forehead as he rolled her onto her back. She followed it with a second hit to the side of his head. Caught off guard, Cliff recoiled from her, almost falling on the bed as well. Jade used that moment to slam her foot into his crotch.

While he crumbled onto the floor near the foot of the bed, gasping animal-like growls, Jade leaped off the bed and finally made it out of the bedroom. She did not stop running until she reached her front door. Frantically, she attempted to unlock the dead bolt and turn the door handle, but the fingers of her right hand would not work!

Jade could hear Cliff lumbering out of the bedroom. His dark shape paused in the doorway to her living room. Then he started running toward her, slowly but with determination! Jade began to sob in frustration, trying over and over to turn the simple doorknob. He was in the center of the room not seven feet from her when she impulsively switched to her left hand. The lock released and the knob turned with ease.

Before she could swing it open, Cliff again got a hold of the back of her T-shirt and pulled her toward him. Despite all her efforts, she tumbled backward until his right arm wrapped around her waist. His stale breath came out in great gasps and blasted the side of her face.

"You women," he spat venomously. "You play your whore games, then expect to walk away."

"Cliff, what—"

"Shut up! Just shut up." It was clear that he was trying to think of what he would do next. "Look what you made me do. You made me hurt you. I didn't want to hurt you, Jade. Look what you made me do."

It was clear that panic was starting to overtake Cliff. His voice was shaking with urgency and frustration. They both looked down at her right arm as blood dripped from a knife cut just above her elbow. Jade almost fainted at the sight. She stopped struggling and held her body tight and still.

"Cliff, listen to me. You have to let me go. I promise I—"

She was cut off by forceful banging on her door. Cliff's arm tightened around her as though he sensed she was about to scream.

"Jade!" Noel's voice came clearly thorough the metal door. Jade felt so relieved that her knees nearly buckled. Fear came back full force when she felt the reappearance of the knife against her neck.

Noel gave another round of banging that made the door rattle in its frame.

"Jade, if you don't answer, I'm going to break down this door!" he demanded. "Jade!"

"Tell him to go away," Cliff whispered harshly in her ear.

Jade didn't know what to do. If she called out to Noel for help, Cliff could easily slice her neck in a second. If she told Noel to go away, she was stuck with a madman.

Noel made the decision for her when he finally tried the door handle and it swung open with tremendous force. Both Jade and Cliff jumped at the thunderous sound and stared wide-eyed at Noel as he advanced into the apartment. The tableau appeared to unfold in slow motion as Noel caught the glint of the knife that was still clutched in Cliff's hand.

"Jade," he breathed, clearly shocked by the scene he had walked into. She stared back at him, terrified and desperate, yet relieved to see him. The reality of the situation was far worse than anything he had imagined on his frantic drive back to her apartment.

Noel's first instinct was to lunge at the piece of scum who had his slimy arm around Jade, holding her captive. He wanted to smash the guy's face in. His second thought was of the weapon held to her neck and the fresh wound on her arm. Noel wasn't going to put Jade in any further danger. Sweat broke out on his back as he struggled with what to do.

"Look," Noel stated in an even, controlled voice as he looked Cliff directly in the eye, "I don't know who you are or what you want, but you have to let her go."

The knife tightened against Jade's soft skin. The sweat ran down Noel's back.

"You should have listened," Cliff advised in an urgent voice. Spit sprayed out of his mouth.

"What?" Noel demanded.

"You should have stayed away from her."

Suddenly, Noel recognized the voice of the man who had attacked him two months before. He saw red. This was the cowardly bastard who had waited in a dark parking lot and beat Noel without showing his face! Caution flew out the window.

It took them all by surprise when Noel leapt

forward, his arm swinging to deliver a right hook aimed at the side of Cliff's face. Jade had the good sense to duck while Cliff froze in his shoes. He didn't stand a chance and went down like a stone.

Chapter 28

After more than four hours of questions and discussion, the group of medical and police personnel finally left Jade's apartment. Noel closed the door behind the last two police detectives around 4:30 in the morning. He slowly walked back to the living room to join Jade.

Instead of resting like she had been told, Jade stood in front of the window looking out at the building grounds. She was absently rubbing the thick white bandage wrapped around her arm. A blush of red stained the cotton.

"Are you okay?" Noel asked, as he stepped behind her and wrapped his arms around her protectively.

"Yeah, I guess so," Jade whispered. "Except . . . did you know that this sort of thing happens all of the time? I mean, how often have you read in the paper about some woman getting attacked in a park, or raped in her own house? Do you know how many times it's done by someone they know or are acquainted with?"

Noel did not respond. She laughed softly without humor. He hugged her closer to him.

"It's all so unreal to me. That box they found in his apartment was full of women's underwear, not just

mine," Jade stated, mulling over the information revealed during the quick police investigation. "He has
no prior arrests, so either he attacked other women
and they didn't report him, or I'm the first that he's
gone this far with."

It was clear that she was struggling not to cry. Noel
turned her around to pull her fully into his arms and
rested his cheek on the top of her head.

"Jade, he was crazy."

"But I liked him," she lamented. "How could I not
know that he was crazy? Am I really that naive?"

"Sweetheart, no one else in the building knew there
was anything wrong. How could you? Poor George
will probably need therapy to get over it."

"See! I actually thought that George was weirder
than Cliff. I remember one time, when George
showed up to check on something, I kept wishing
Cliff had come himself. And look who attacks me!"
Jade broke out of Noel's embrace to stand alone and
stare out the window. "You know what? I know that
Cliff has been in here before tonight. Sometimes I
would wake up in the middle of the night without
knowing why. I think it was him."

The idea of that psycho spying on Jade while she
slept just made Noel sick.

"You don't know that for sure, Jade."

"I think I do," she said quietly. "And I still can't believe what he did to you in the summer. He could
have really hurt you if that stranger hadn't been
there."

"I will regret that weekend for the rest of my life,"
Noel stated solemnly. "If I had listened to you instead
of focusing on my bruised ego, none of this would

have happened. Not only did I almost lose you, but I put you in danger. I will never forgive myself for that."

Jade heard the emotional catch in his voice and turned to face him. Gently, she brushed her fingers against the side of his face then used her thumb to wipe away the drop of moisture escaping one of his eyes. He pressed his lips into the center of her palm.

"What I'm trying to say, Jade, is that I just want to be with you," he continued after he cleared his throat. "I want to be there in the morning, in the evening, and on the weekends. I want to protect you from anyone or anything that could hurt you. I want you in my life for as long as you'll have me."

"Oh, Noel," Jade replied, "I want that more than anything."

When their lips met, it was different than any kiss they had shared before. It had the same level of intensity and desire, but it held something more. It contained a sense of commitment and contentment that they had not shared before. They were both ready to move past the issues and shadows of their past. They were ready to trust again and move forward together.

ABOUT THE AUTHOR

Sophia Shaw is an avid reader and began writing in 1993. She has written several articles for independent magazines. *Shades and Shadows* is her first novel. Sophia has a bachelors degree in psychology and sociology from the University of Toronto. She lives in Brampton, Canada, with her family.